Page One: Whiteout

A Robin Hamilton Mystery

by

Nancy Barr

Arbutus Press, Traverse City, MI

Other titles by Nancy Barr in the Robin Hamilton mystery series

Page One: Hit and Run

Page One: Vanished

ISBN 10: 1-933926-17-1
ISBN 13: 978-1-933926-17-9

Manufactured in the United States of America
First Edition/First Printing

www.arbutuspress.com
info@arbutuspress.com

To Peggy Bryson, Kevin Morter, Brian Rowell and Rick Rudden,

for nurturing the seeds of inquiry.

I still hear your voices when I write.

Author's Note

No author ever writes a book by herself, especially a mystery novel. This book would not have been possible without the assistance of Det./Lt. Jeff Racine of the Michigan State Police and director of the Upper Peninsula Substance Enforcement Team. The law enforcement officers who make up this team are a unique breed and have been amazingly successful despite a severe lack of resources over the nearly two decades they've been operating. They put themselves in dangerous, undercover situations on a regular basis, guarding their real identities to protect not only themselves but their families. They rarely get recognized with plaques and medals but without them, Michigan's Upper Peninsula would have a much worse drug problem than it does. Over the last ten years, the problems of urban areas have gradually spread north to the remote reaches of the Midwest. For this cancer to be reversed, all citizens must work together to make sure dealers don't get footholds in our communities and strangleholds on our children. If you suspect something is amiss in your neighborhood, tell law enforcement. It may turn out to be nothing, but it may also be the key they need to bring down a major dealer.

I also owe a debt of gratitude to Susan Bays and her staff at Arbutus Press for all their hard work and to my family and friends, who provide encouragement when things look bleak and share in my joy when the dice roll my way.

One side note about locations: While Miami, Florida, and all the towns located in Michigan's Upper Peninsula are real, the city of Crescent, Illinois, is the creation of my imagination and is in no way meant to resemble an existing Chicago suburb. Also, those familiar with the Hiawatha National Forest will notice that, in the interest of privacy, I've taken the liberty of changing the names and geography of some of the many lakes and recreation trails that populate this extraordinary region of the U.P.

Prologue

April 20, 2006 :~ Crescent, Illinois

*A*nother bolt of lightning flashed across the sky but the rain fell so hard that Sgt. Mitch Montgomery barely blinked as he maneuvered his patrol car around myriad pools of water and fallen tree limbs. An early spring storm had raged across the Great Plains and now unleashed its fury on northeastern Illinois. Nearly every police officer and firefighter in the city of Crescent was either on call or in uniform in preparation for dealing with the inevitable mess the storm would leave behind.

"I hope we don't get a tornado," Mitch said aloud, his voice barely audible in the dark interior of the cruiser. He pushed his glasses up on his slim nose and squinted between wipers slapping across the windshield, ineffective against the torrents that pummeled the car.

He had driven these streets for ten years but he wasn't sure where he was at this point. Suddenly a stop sign loomed and he saw he was approaching the edge of town. He glanced at the dashboard digital clock—11:45 p.m. He decided to make one pass down this road to the city limit and then turn around and head back toward the station for something to eat.

As he drove, he mulled over his afternoon conversation with his contact who was worried that Mitch's identity had been compromised. Mitch tried not to think about the possibilities, but like a toddler with a new toy, his mind just wouldn't let it go. What if the chief found out what was really going on? Would he blow the whole deal? Would they try to eliminate him now that they knew who he was? What would happen to Robin? Would she understand why he'd become involved with these people? He hated lying, especially to her, but he had to protect her. He believed he was building a better future for them. Everyone just had to give him time to

1

make this work.

Ahead in the gloom he saw blinking amber lights. Flashers. "Aw, crap," he murmured and picked up the handset and radioed into dispatch that he had a vehicle in trouble and gave them his location. Pulling the cruiser behind the car, he saw that the late model dark-colored Cadillac had no license plate. He told the dispatcher he was going to check the vehicle. His hand was on the door handle when he saw movement in the side mirror. Before he could turn his head, a blast shattered the window and his world went black.

Chapter One

*M*itch Montgomery had been dead for nearly nine months.

Those well-meaning souls who'd offered advice after the murder of my fiancé had said that, in time, I would move on with my life. Right now, all I could fathom for my future was joining him.

I glared at my computer screen, willing the words to magically appear for an article updating *Daily Press* readers on the Escanaba City Council's latest plans for drawing shoppers to the aging downtown. I certainly didn't have anything intelligent to say on the subject and neither had the city council. These types of stories were the reason I'd left my hometown almost seven years before for the challenge of the *Chicago Tribune*. Sure, starting as a researcher I wasn't exactly rooting out mob kingpins but at least I wasn't writing articles about debates over which way the cars should park on the main street.

The cursor blinked mockingly at my discontent while the stench of cheap perfume that vaguely resembled lilacs past their prime enveloped me. I forced myself not to groan aloud at the approach of Bonnie Traven, our advertising director, a.k.a. "The Lavender Lush" for her after-hours drinking prowess and penchant for purple. It was just my luck that she would decide to take advantage of the holiday quiet and come in to the office. She clicked long lavender-lacquered fingernails on the edge of my desk. The sound made me think of spiders skittering across a mirror.

"Yoo-hoo, Robin," she sing-songed. "What a surprise to see you here on a holiday. That's what I love about you— you're just as dedicated as me."

I pasted on a smile and swiveled around to face her.

"Just passin' time before the walls of my apartment closed in on me. What can I do for you?"

She peered at me through half-glasses that hung on a purple-tinted chain around her neck. "You are so deep. I'm so sorry to interrupt your thoughts. I'm sure whatever you're working on will be another prize-winner."

Leave me alone, now. Go, before I'm forced to join your head with my computer screen.

"No problem," I said, trying not to grit my teeth. "You're not interrupting at all. How may I help you?"

She was still tapping those fingernails as she said, "Well, late Friday Bob volunteered you to oversee the End-of-Life special section. Isn't that great? I'm sure you'll bring a fresh perspective to it." She waved her arms at "Isn't that great", flapping the bell-shaped sleeves of her purple satin tunic and resembling a very large, ugly bird. From somewhere in that voluminous tunic she produced a piece of paper. "Now, here's a list of our regular customers that might be inclined to advertise in this section. If you could make sure to include them in your stories, that would be great. We'd like to see three to four reporter-written stories. Local content sells, not that canned stuff, if you know what I mean. People love to read about people they know."

While she continued to blather on about publication deadlines and other trivialities I wondered what I had done in some past life to deserve the hell in which I was now burning. When she finally left, I let my head plummet to my desk with a thud.

It was nearing five o'clock, darkness was descending upon the city like a wet blanket, so I forced myself to pound out a three-hundred word story, filed it on the network and turned off my computer. I shivered when I stepped into the cold, damp evening air and began to walk the six blocks to my apartment on Lake Shore Drive. Wind-battered Christmas decorations still clung to eaves, railings and small trees like toilet paper to the heel of a shoe. The ground was barren of the snow that normally added a serene beauty to Escanaba, making the Victorian-era homes and churches that populated the oldest section of town near Little Bay de Noc look like something out of a Currier & Ives painting. Not this year. Instead, it seemed that Mother Nature was intent on turning the Great White North into the Great Brown Blah. Two blocks from my apartment it started to rain. Beautiful, I thought, the perfect end to a perfectly lousy day.

The two-story (three if you counted the attic) home I occupied across from Ludington Park was dark as I approached from the alley. My landlady, Mrs. Rose Easton, the retired school teacher who lived downstairs, had finally buckled to her sister's urging to flock with her to Arizona and become like the Canada geese that called the park home in the summer—a snowbird. Belle, my basset hound companion, greeted me with a quick bark as I trudged up the stairs. At least someone was happy to see me. After taking her for a short walk around the neighborhood and feeding her a bowl of kibble, I popped a Lean Cuisine in the microwave and prepared a cup of orange spice tea. One of my New Year's resolutions had been to eat more nutritious, home-cooked food. The first day of 2007 and that resolution was already shot to hell. I poured myself a glass of cheap merlot while the water boiled, thereby trashing another resolution to drink less booze.

Belle gave me a sad-eyed look of admonishment from where she sat near my feet. "What? I thought dogs were supposed to show unconditional love and not be so judgmental."

Her ears twitched. She turned and trotted to the door, tail wagging. We had company. I set the glass on the counter and followed Belle to the door as the clip-clop of boots ascending the stairs became more audible. It sounded like a Clydesdale. It probably wasn't my detective friend Charlie because he usually called before he visited. Besides, lately he'd been spending most of his free time with the new pediatrician in town. ("I got tired of waiting for you," he'd said shortly before Christmas when we'd had lunch at the local micro-brewery steakhouse. I'd told him I didn't understand what that meant. He'd rolled his eyes and shaken his head. Whatever, I'd thought. I still didn't get it.) My dad was on a Mediterranean cruise with a new lady friend who'd moved across the street from him in November. Everyone had someone except me.

Whoever was coming up the stairs now was friendly because Bell wasn't concerned. A meaty fist connected with the door. I jumped. Whoever it was meant business. I peered through the peep hole and then laughed. Throwing open the door, I squealed, "Nick Granati! What are you doing here?"

He set down a small black suitcase and smothered me in a bear hug, his black wool coat transferring its wetness to my clothes as his chin rested on my head.

"Happy New Year! It's great to see you, Robin," he said and then stepped back and frowned as Belle sniffed his black pant legs tucked inside black galoshes. "You sure haven't gained any weight. If anything, you're even skinnier." The microwave chose that moment to ding.

"Still eatin' at the Microwave Bar & Grill? You're gonna kill yourself eatin' that junk. Now, look at me." He thumped his flat, firm stomach. "Solid. That's from eating real food."

"Yeah, yeah, yeah. I hope you didn't come all the way up here to lecture me on my eating habits. I get enough of that from my dad and my aunt. Seriously, what brings you here? You should have called. I would have had a better meal ready," I said.

He stuffed his hands in his pockets and rocked back on his heels. "I've got some leads into who might have killed Mitch. I need your help to go get 'em. I've taken a four-week leave of absence from the Chicago P.D. so I'm free to work on this. My lieutenant wasn't thrilled but I figure Homicide can survive without me for a month."

My guts quaked. I sat down hard on the arm of a nearby easy chair. To finally have some resolution to who had ambushed my fiancé while he was on patrol that stormy night back in April on a deserted road in Crescent, Illinois, seemed inconceivable. The killer had come from behind, used a shotgun to fire through the driver side window and left no tracks in his escape. Everyone assumed it had something to do with Mitch's work as a sergeant with the Crescent police, but no one inside the department could find a link. Mitch had never talked much with me about his work, not surprising since I was a newspaper reporter and he took seriously his responsibility to keep his cases confidential.

"What have you found out?" I asked in a quavering voice.

"Let's get to that later. Right now, I'm tired and hungry and a microwave meal in a cardboard box just ain't gonna cut it. What's the best restaurant in town?" he asked.

I mentioned the first one that came to mind, a place at the main intersection in town that was known for great steaks and fish.

"Fine, let's go. We'll take my rental since it's already warmed up. By the way, do you have any idea how hard it is to get a flight here? It would have been quicker and cheaper to drive from Chicago. I had a three-hour layover in Minneapolis of all places."

I just grinned and said, "Welcome to the U.P."

After tossing my Lean Cuisine in the trash, I followed Nick down the stairs and around to the front of the house where he'd parked the rented

Chevy Malibu. I felt like I was trailing Rocky Balboa in a suit. Despite being a snazzy dresser, his tall, muscled figure, lumbering gait and thick Chicago accent gave away his urban, tough-guy roots. He and Mitch had been opposites in so many ways, but the bond they'd formed in college had been unbreakable. Nick had just returned from serving four years in the Army including the Gulf War. Mitch was just out of high school and enamored with the ideals of justice for all. He'd helped Nick get through the academics of four years in the criminal justice program at Northeastern Illinois University, and Nick had helped Mitch hone his intuition and develop the physical discipline to be a good cop. At graduation, Nick joined his hometown police department and was now stationed in a precinct just eight blocks from where he was raised. Mitch waffled between joining the DEA or a suburban police department, but when his father suffered a mild stroke the choice was made for him and he settled for Crescent, within easy driving distance of his parents in Oak Park. The pair had remained close friends until Mitch's murder last year and Nick had vowed to keep pushing until the justice Mitch had fought for in life was achieved after his death.

Once settled at a table in the corner of the main dining room of the restaurant, Nick seemed to relax and looked around the room. "Not bad for the sticks."

"I'll ignore the 'sticks' comment. You're stalling. Tell me what the hell's going on," A Robin Hamilton Mystery I said.

"You've always been a get-down-to-business kinda gal. I like that, no bullshit. Alright, here's the story," he said and straightened his shirt cuffs so that each one showed an equal amount of material beyond the sleeves of his suit jacket. "I'm not positive, but I may have a line on the shooter —a former MI6 agent named Joey Leeds."

"What on earth would British Secret Service want with Mitch?" I asked.

"No, no. You're not listening. I said former MI6 agent. He got fired about a decade ago for inappropriate behavior."

The waitress arrived to take our order and then quickly brought us our drinks. Nick took a sip of Chianti before continuing.

"It seems Joey is a bit of a sadist. Anyway, he's been freelancing for various criminal elements around the world since he was shit-canned by the Brits. I found out about Joey by working backwards from how Mitch was killed. It had all the signs of a contract hit so I asked myself who would hire a hit on a small-town patrol sergeant. I didn't get squat in terms of information from most of the Crescent cops, not even off-the-record, as you reporters like to say. It's odd because Mitch seemed to have been well-liked, but when I questioned some of his co-workers, I got the feeling a few of them thought he might be dirty, that he had it coming," Nick said and stopped to take another drink.

"That's ridiculous! I can't tell you how many times we talked about the problem of dirty cops, especially around Chicago, and how mad he would get when another one came to light," I said.

"Calm down. I know it's bull, but we can't discount their insinuations completely. There might be an important clue there," he said and checked his watch. "I'm expecting a phone call from a snitch any minute. How's the cell phone service up here?"

"Same as the air service."

"It stinks," he replied.

I nodded.

"Great. Well, it can't be helped now," he said and straightened the cuff over his watch again. "Where was I? Oh yeah, backtracking. I started looking into all the Chicago area criminals with the resources and the balls to hire a hit on a cop. I figured it wasn't the mob because those guys usually steer clear of killing cops, attracts too much unwanted attention. Besides, my connections never even heard of Mitch Montgomery and had never even been to Crescent. That left me with three possibilities—an old Russian immigrant who lives in Crescent and made his fortune smuggling weapons to Third Word armies; a first-generation Vietnamese American guy who manipulates much of the cocaine and heroin trade around Chicago; and a rich bank VP that Mitch had busted for possession and soliciting a prostitute in March. The guy was ruined."

Nick was interrupted by the waitress delivering his sirloin steak and my whitefish. I hadn't realized how hungry I was until I dug into the lightly seasoned fish and twice-baked potato. I hadn't had a descent meal since my aunt had roasted a turkey at Christmas. When I was finally sated enough to ask more questions, I asked, "So where does this Leeds guy fit into the picture? You think someone on your list of suspects hired him to kill Mitch? Why?"

"I was getting to that." He started to explain when a ring emanated from his suit coat. He pulled a flip phone out of his pocket and answered it.

"Yeah? ... You're sure? ... Okay. Thanks. I'll remember this," he said and stashed phone back into his pocket. "That was my snitch. He said we can forget about the Vietnamese guy. His crowd never heard of Mitch either and, like The Outfit, they don't bother with cops. They just work around them."

"Work around them? I guess the thin blue line is getting thinner by the minute," I said.

Nick nodded. "Budget cuts, my dear. As usual, politicians talk a good game about funding law enforcement but when it comes time to hit a homerun, they strike out.

"As for Leeds, my sources tell me he's done some work for a variety of Chicago area people with too much money and too little scruples— everything from being a courier of money to sabotage. It wouldn't surprise me at all if he turned out to be the trigger man carrying out Ben Maplethorpe's vengeance on Mitch," Nick said.

"Maplethorpe, that the bank guy? I remember that story. I had no idea Mitch was the arresting officer. He never said a thing about it," I said, feeling hurt at his lack of confidence in my ability to keep a secret.

Nick sensed my discomfort and patted my hand. "Don't take it personally. He was just doing his job. Actually, Mitch's name isn't on the police report. I found out he was the one making the bust through a friend of mine in the DEA. He clued me in that Mitch was doing some undercover work and happened to be working a lead on a pot dealer when he snared Maplethorpe at that upscale bar in Crescent."

"Wait a minute," I said, waving my hand at him. "Undercover work? When did he start doing that?"

"Robin, that's a routine part of being a cop, no matter if you're a patrol sergeant or a detective. If you fit the part of a character needed in the investigation and you're smart, you get picked for undercover assignments. Mitch excelled at playing the part of the clean-cut young executive on the hunt for a good time. It's no big deal," Nick said.

"Alright, what about this Russian?" I asked, looking down at an empty plate and considering dessert. The hope that maybe, just maybe, Mitch's murder might be solved seemed to have given me an appetite.

Nick cleared his plate as well and tapped his mouth with his napkin.

"Fabulous, especially for up here in the sticks," he said with a wink. "The Russian is a guy named Dmitri Karastova. I'm a little less inclined to believe he's behind it because of his advanced age. He had three kids, one of whom was his presumed successor in the smuggling business.

Unfortunately, that guy died in a boating accident in the late eighties. The other two have vanished. I'm still working that angle, though, just in case it turns up something worthwhile."

The waitress came to clear our empty plates and tempt us with sinful sugary delights. I ordered Tiramisu, in honor of Nick's presence, but he passed on dessert.

"How do I play into all of this? You said you needed my help."

Nick flashed me a devious smile and said, "I have a plan to determine whether Leeds was involved. I've been keeping an eye on him with the help of some friends. He usually hides out in South Beach in the winter. By the way, he has a house six blocks from Maplethorpe and about ten blocks from Karastova. Apparently, he's too much of a puss—er, wimp, to handle Chicago winters. That, or he's doing some work down there.

"I had my Uncle Rudy—he lives on a boat docked at Miami Beach—and some associates put some feelers out for a hitter. Word is that Joey's interested."

"Who's he supposed to kill?" I asked.

Nick hooked a thumb at his chest.

"Excuse me?"

He laughed. "You're going to hire Leeds to kill your philandering husband and make it look like a mugging. You've got a million dollar life insurance policy and you'll give Leeds a third."

I shook my head in disbelief. "You want me to hire a hit man to kill you? This is your plan? No offense, but I can see a pretty big hole in your plan, actually, two holes. You could die, and I could go to prison."

Nick smiled as though I were a four-year-old who'd just said something precious.

"Haven't you ever heard of a set-up?"

"Haven't you ever heard of entrapment?" I shot back. "It'll never hold up in court."

Nick chuckled. "We're not going to involve the cops. My uncle will have all the bases covered. We'll only involve the police if we can make a solid connection between Mitch and Leeds. Unfortunately, anything less than a full confession will be inadequate. You have to lure him into bragging about his past exploits." He paused and toyed with the salt shaker for a moment. "This will require a lot of finesse on your part. How good a liar are you?"

I tried to picture myself sitting across from the man who may have murdered the love of my life, playing the part of the femme fatale. "I don't know, Nick. I'm not much of an actress. I never bothered trying to lie to my dad when I was kid because I knew I'd be as transparent as plastic wrap."

He put the salt shaker back in its holder and looked me over. "Don't worry. My uncle's wife will transform you into the perfect black widow woman."

"Why are your uncle and his wife willing to stick their necks out like this? I mean, this has the whiff of being a tad outside the boundaries of the law."

His face grew serous and he said in a low voice, "My uncle's always been there for me and I do what I can to help him when he needs me. Mitch was my best friend, one of the few friends I had that I knew I could trust with anything. Uncle Rudy knows how much I want the bastards behind his murder taken out of action. So, are you with me?"

What the hell, I thought. I'd always heard Miami was beautiful in January.

Before I could leave for Miami though, I had to work out something with my boss at the *Daily Press*. Nick had spent the night on the couch, risen an hour before me, gone grocery shopping and had a trucker's breakfast on the table by the time I got out of the shower. I was ready to marry him on the spot. We made plans to head for Miami while we ate. He'd bought a one-way plane ticket to Escanaba on the assumption that we would either drive back to Chicago and fly from there or fly from here. Since I wanted to visit Mitch's grave, see his parents and stop by the Crescent police station, we agreed that I would drive us to Chicago that afternoon. In the meantime, I had to get Belle to my Aunt Gina for safekeeping and I would have to talk my over-extended, very understanding editor into letting me have even more unpaid time off on top of the weeks I'd spent healing from a broken ankle in the summer and a pretty severe mental shock in the fall.

"Robin, you're pushing the limit here," Bob Hunter said with a scowl and a shake of his head when I made my request that morning after deadline. We were sitting in his office with its huge window overlooking Ludington Street. The rain of the night before had turned to ice and was now falling as heavy wet snow. The sound of vehicles splashing through the slush on the main street filtered into the small room as I smiled sheepishly at my editor. I started to plead my case again when he held up his hands. "You aren't even eligible for vacation time for another five months. What am I going to tell the publisher?"

"I understand that but …" My voice trailed off as I was suddenly at a loss for words. Should I tell him what I was really thinking? It was about time I was honest with myself and my mentor. "Bob, first of all, I'm talking about helping find out who was behind my fiancé's murder, not a holiday in Hawaii. Second, the truth is that I'm not happy here. In the last month I've been repeatedly reminded of why I left this area in the first place. I don't want to write articles about small-town politics and coordinate end-of-life special sections."

He nodded as the beginnings of a grin pulled at the corners of his mouth. "Good, good. I'm glad to hear you say that, because it makes what I have to say next all the more advantageous for you."

I felt my eyebrows narrow in a scowl. What was he up to? Didn't I just tell him, in a very polite way, that I hated my job and wanted to quit? He leaned forward on his elbows, his shifting weight eliciting a loud squeak from his ancient chair, the kind of chair one could imagine the likes of Edward R. Murrow sitting in while he wrote the copy for his radio broadcasts from London during the Blitz.

"Robin, I'm retiring at the end of April. My wife's been retired from teaching for two years and, since I'll be sixty-five in a few months, it seems like a good time for me to join her," Bob said.

"Sixty-five?! I had no idea you were that old," I blurted.

Bob laughed and rubbed a hand over his gray scraggly beard. "I suppose that would sound old to you. Anyway, Carol will probably take my job. The publisher and I were hoping you would take over Carol's position as news editor. You wouldn't have to write any more articles on small town politics, just edit them. Of course, there's more to the job than that, but we can talk about it later. You go do what you have to do. Drop me an e-mail or phone message every day to let me know what's happening," he said. Rising from his chair, he stuck out his hand. "You're a great reporter. I'd hate to lose you again."

Too many thoughts were tumbling through my head to respond intelligently so I just shook his hand and agreed to keep in contact daily. I was expecting to get fired and he was offering me a promotion. "Bob, you're the most tolerant boss on the planet," I said.

"Yes, I am. Now get out of here." He opened the door to the newsroom and stepped aside to let me pass.

Before I even made it to my desk, Amy was telling me my aunt had called three times and that the cell phone stashed in my purse had been ringing "incessantly." All I could imagine was that something had happened to my dad on his cruise. I scanned the pink slip Amy had placed on my desk with my aunt's office number at Bay College. The only message was to call her ASAP. My fingers felt cold as I entered the number.

"What's wrong? Is my dad okay?" I asked before she could finish saying hello.

"Robin? Oh, I'm so glad you called. I'm sure your dad's fine. It's me who has the problem," she said, her normally cheery voice sounding strained. "I need your help with something. Actually, it's one of my students. I think he's in trouble."

I glanced at my watch—ten forty-five. I was supposed to meet Nick for an early lunch so we could finalize our plans to head south.

"What's the problem?" I asked.

She cleared her throat. "It's kind of a long story. See, I had this student in my Intro to Sociology class last semester, a really bright young man, if a bit troubled. We got to talking after class one day and I discovered that his dad and I graduated from high school together—Rapid River Class of '69," she said, her voice trailing off to nothing.

"Aunt Gina?"

"Sorry, yes, well anyway, Kyle—that's his name—has been struggling with some personal problems lately. I've been trying to help him since his parents are divorced and he doesn't really have a good adult confidante," she said.

"You're rambling. You always ramble when you're upset, so what's the problem?"

She let out a hefty sigh. "I can't reach him. I've tried calling him several times over the last few days. He hasn't reported to work at the hardware store in a week, and he hasn't been at his apartment for days. I'm afraid something bad might have happened," she finally admitted.

"Call the police."

"I don't want to do that yet. I'd rather find him first and talk to him before I involve the cops. It could be that he just needed some time away, but I'd feel much better if I knew for certain that he was okay," she said.

"How do you know he hasn't been at his apartment? Did you go inside? Did you talk to his neighbors?" I asked.

"Both," she said.

"How did you get inside?" I asked, dreading the answer.

"Credit card. Cheap lock," she said.

"You lived in Manhattan way too long," I said in exasperation. I could see why my dad had been afraid his late wife's baby sister might be a bad influence on me. We were obviously related. "So what would you like me to do?"

"I want to check his family's camp in the Hiawatha National Forest, but I don't know that area very well and I don't remember exactly where it's located. I was only there once right after Kyle's grandparents bought the place in the late sixties. The cottage is on the northeast side of Boone Lake. Didn't you hang out around there when you were in high school and college? I seem to remember something to that effect in your letters," Aunt Gina said.

"Sure, my best friend Michaela O'Bryan's family owns a place on Boone Lake. It's huge with dozens of houses around it. I practically lived out there during vacations when I was in high school. What's Kyle's last name?" I asked, suddenly nostalgic for the seemingly endless days of simply being outside having fun. I hadn't spent a day like that since before Mitch had died.

"Sullivan. Kyle Sullivan. His father is Wayne Sullivan. He's an MD at Marquette General Hospital," she said. I could hear her opening and closing filing cabinets in quick succession.

"What are you doing?"

She slammed a drawer and cursed. "I've only been in this office a year and a half and I already can't find a damn thing."

"What are you looking for?"

"My old address book. I know I had it here when I unpacked. I'm pretty sure the address for the cottage is in there," she said, sounding almost desperate.

"Calm down. I know where it is. The Sullivans are just a few houses down from the O'Bryans. I remember they had a son, blonde and athletic. I tell you what, I have someone I want you to meet," I said and told her about Nick and why he was here. "I'll pick you up at your office in about twenty minutes and we'll drive out there."

After I rang off with Aunt Gina, I dialed Nick's cell phone and prayed that Kyle Sullivan would be safe and sound, looking for a little peace and quiet. Unfortunately, troubled young men had a nasty way of making trouble for lots of other people. I told Nick the new development. He wasn't happy with the delay but understood. His curiosity was raised when I briefly described my rather eccentric aunt who could read auras and believed in reincarnation.

I was pulling on my down parka, eyeing the snow falling outside the newspaper office when Bob Hunter came up behind me.

"Robin?"

I turned to look at his face, his steely eyes crinkled at the corners.

"Be careful. Leave the rough stuff to the pros this time."

"Sure. I'll see you in a week or so," I said and walked out of the *Daily Press* for the last time as an employee.

Chapter Two

*N*ick was waiting in front of my house on the porch steps with Belle seated next to him. They plowed through four inches of fresh wet snow and met me at the curb. He opened the back door and hooked Belle into her seat belt harness like I had instructed on the phone when I'd called him about Aunt Gina and our delayed lunch.

"This goddamned dog is more trouble than my two-year-old nephew," he grumbled as he slid into the front seat and slammed the door shut. Belle snuffled in response. He ignored her and peered through the slop being cleared by the wiper blades and asked, "This thing four-wheel drive?"

"All-wheel drive. We'll be fine," I said as I put the Outback in gear and pulled away from the curb. "One thing you learn living up here is how to drive in all kinds of weather."

I briefed him on what Aunt Gina had told me about her ersatz student while I drove toward Bay de Noc Community College on the far north side of town. The school, now in its fifth decade, was a far cry from NYU, where she had spent the last twenty-five years teaching Women's Studies, but she had grown tired of the noise, the constant fear of another terrorist attack and the pretentiousness of the faculty in the upper echelons of higher education. Like me, she had returned to her hometown, now sharing a small house just outside of Rapid River with two Yorkshire terriers, a colorful collection of exotic furniture and a few thousand books. Estranged for years thanks to my very conservative ex-Marine father, my aunt and I had become fast confidantes in the four months since I'd landed on her doorstep wet, tired and cold after searching the nearby woods for a missing girl the previous fall. I knew how much she cared about young people and the problems they faced in a culture that expected too much too soon with too few people to point them in the right direction. I didn't know Kyle Sullivan or his family, but for my aunt to take notice of him, I figured he must be special.

She must have been watching for my car from inside the entryway of the Science and Arts building where her office was located because she darted down the sidewalk and jumped into the backseat before I was barely able to roll to a stop. She settled her voluptuous frame into the middle of the seat, patted Belle on the head and then fastened her seat belt with some difficulty.

"I ate way too much over the holidays. Whew!" she mumbled as she adjusted the strap. When she was satisfied, she took off her gloves and stuck out her hand to Nick who just watched in amazement at the whirlwind of energy swirling around her.

"Hi, I'm Gina Schmidt. You must be Nick. I can't tell you how happy I am that Robin has a friend like you to help her with finding Mitch's killer. I'm so sorry I never got the chance to meet him. I think we would have gotten along fabulously. What do you think of the U.P.? Have you been here before? How long have you known Robin? I hope you two are careful in Miami. She tends to get herself into trouble, if you know what I mean. Did she tell you about my little problem? You see, I have this student named—"

"Aunt Gina!"

She looked stunned, took a deep breath and giggled softly.

"Sorry, I babble when I'm upset."

Nick smiled warmly. "It's okay. I like talkative people. Saves me the trouble of finding topics of conversation. Besides, you remind me a little of my mother. She talks a lot when she's trying to take her mind off something."

Aunt Gina rolled her eyes. "Great! Now when I meet a handsome young man, he tells me I remind him of his mother. There used to be a time when he'd ask for my phone number. It's hell to get old."

He laughed. "Well, I wouldn't want to make Robin uncomfortable by flirting with her very beautiful and vivacious aunt."

She blushed. I winked at Nick. Her demeanor was already relaxing a bit. Maybe now she would make some sense.

"So what's the deal with Kyle? Why don't you want to call his parents and let them handle this since it's their camp?" I asked.

She fidgeted a bit and played with a copper filigreed ring on her right hand. "Remember I said Kyle is very bright, if a bit troubled? Well, his parents got divorced a few years ago. His mother met someone on the internet. Apparently there were weaknesses in the marriage. One thing led to another; and she decided she would be happier with this other man in Arizona. His father is a neurologist at the hospital in Marquette. He's at a conference in Naples, Italy, right now."

"So soon after the holidays?" I asked.

Nick nodded. "Sure, southern Italy is glorious this time of year."

"How come I never get to go to conferences in places like Italy in January? Never mind," I said as I waited for one of two stoplights to turn green in Gladstone, the next town north of Escanaba on the way to the Hiawatha National Forest. The roads were snow-covered and slippery, causing traffic to slow, but just a little. It took serious ice or a blizzard to make Yoopers stay off the road.

"Maybe Kyle took off to visit his mother," I said. "Classes at Bay don't start for another week and I'm sure the weather in Arizona would be more to his liking right about now. What makes you think something could be wrong?"

She ran her fingers through her long strawberry blonde curls and sighed. "I doubt he would go to his mother. He hasn't spoken to her since the divorce," she said with a shake of her head. "I'm sorry to derail your plans. I know you probably need to leave for Miami as soon as possible. I just have this terrible feeling about this kid; and I don't want to face this alone."

Nick turned in his seat and gave her a devastating smile. "Don't worry, that's what friends and family do where I come from—they provide back-up."

She blushed again.

Once the highway hit Rapid River, U.S. 2 made a lazy right and then it was fourteen miles to Federal Forest Highway 13. It had been several years since I'd been to my best friend's family camp on Boone Lake, but I remembered it was some twenty miles north of U.S. 2. The Sullivan family was a couple doors down from the O'Bryans on the northeast edge of the lake. Nick and Aunt Gina chattered a bit about New York for a while, but once I turned on to 13, we all silently contemplated the gray hardwoods that lined the road. Their branches canopied the car, like bars in a bird cage. An ominous atmosphere had settled upon us. I tried to think of something to say, but suddenly I felt I didn't have the energy to deal with more problems. Why are we doing this, I wondered. The kid was probably on a three-day bender with a bunch of buddies and, if he didn't pass out in a snow bank and freeze to death, he'd have some great stories to tell in his old age.

I turned left at County Road 440 and followed a gravel road for a few miles and then turned down yet another gravel road. I knew the route by heart, having spent dozens of summer weekends swimming and many more winter holidays snowmobiling and snowshoeing through the woods. In the summer, the sounds of children playing and boats skipping across the water mingled with the pungent smell of barbecues and campfires. Winter usually meant hordes of snowmobilers converging on the camps that lined the lake, but the lack of snow this year had dampened their spirits and kept them at home. The wide lake was gray and placid, its center not yet frozen, stark against the fresh snow still falling softly. Passing the turn-off to the O'Bryan camp, I saw a cut-out metal sign announcing the entrance to the "Sullivan Family Retreat." The original camp appeared to have been built sometime in the 1940s but had been added on to at least twice to make way for ever-growing families. The one-story log structure had two wings extending to the east and west, neither of which blended well with the original structure. Stained a burnt sienna color, the cabin had spruce green shutters and a new green metal roof designed to handle the heavy snow load that fell during a normal winter in northern Delta County. This was no normal winter, though. I parked in a lot that ordinarily would be hemmed in on three sides by four-foot banks of snow by this time of year but was now covered with just a few inches of fresh snow. The Jack pines that dotted the property provided a welcome bit of green among the gray trunks of beech and maple interspersed throughout the yard.

As I got out of the car, I felt a cold wind knife through me. It was more than the weather. Somehow I knew something was wrong. There were no birds chirping and no signs of deer or rabbits, which usually crisscrossed the properties around the lake on days when humans were scarce. Belle whined softly from the back seat. Nick seemed to sense it as well, his cop instincts kicking in as he scanned the property.

"Stay here," he ordered my aunt when she opened the car door. She started to protest and then nodded and settled back into the seat.

The back of the cabin looked secure. I stepped onto a small cement slab that served as the back porch and jiggled the door handle. It was locked. The small windows, situated about five feet above the ground, were shrouded with thick curtains. Slowly making my way around the front of the cabin on to the deck that overlooked the lake, I had to remind myself to breathe. Nick was silent behind me, his footsteps barely making a sound in the snow. The air was still, no smoke rose from the chimney. Not a good sign. I stepped onto the deck and jumped a little when it creaked. I threw a glance over my shoulder at my aunt, who sat watching me with a palpable intensity from the safety of the car some twenty feet away.

" Kyle?" I called. No answer. I spoke a little louder. "Kyle, are you here? I'm a friend of Dr. Gina Schmidt."

Nothing.

The front windows were huge, meant to take in the view of the lake and the woods. I tried to peek between a gap in one of the drapes but saw little that was recognizable. Nick tapped me on the shoulder and motioned for me to stay behind as he opened the screen door and knocked. Again, no answer. The door knob turned easily under his gloved hand; and, casting a weary glance at me, Nick pushed it open. We stepped inside. As the screen door wheezed shut behind us, I heard the sound of a car door open and close. Ignoring my aunt for the moment, I looked around the room in disgust and growing trepidation. The place was a mess, with furniture overturned, at least two lamps shattered and miscellaneous household knick-knacks scattered around the floor.

Somehow I knew what I would find in the kitchen before I even saw him. There was a young man, sprawled between the sink and a mammoth pine table, obviously dead from a very severe beating.

"Aunt Gina, get back in the car. Now!" I yelled when I heard the screen door open.

"What's wrong?" she shrieked.

"Please, go!"

"But . . ."

I ran from the kitchen, grabbed her by the shoulders and shoved her out the door.

"I don't suppose you have the key for this place?" I asked once we were outside.

"Of course not. I haven't been here in 40 years. It's not like we slept here," she said and then looked chagrined when she realized what she'd said. I eyed her with suspicion. She threw up her hands.

"Look, Kyle's father and I dated for three years in high school."

I shrugged. "So what? Why the secretiveness?"

She looked uncomfortable as a gust of wind swirled around the corner of the cabin and riffled her hair around her pale face. I waved her off and said, "Never mind. We need to call the police. I wonder if cell phones work here."

Nick spoke up behind me. "Yes, I just called. They're on their way."

"What's wrong?" Aunt Gina wailed. She was holding back tears now, but not fighting as I maneuvered her back to the car.

"He's dead, isn't he?" she cried.

"Yes, I'm sorry." My own voice was shaking, as were my hands.

"Oh no, I was too late," she murmured and covered her face with her hands.

I put my hands on her shoulders and said, "You can't blame yourself for this. You couldn't have known." She ignored my touch. She needed some time to compose herself so I shut the door and walked back to where Nick stood on the porch staring at the lake, snow flakes collecting in his thick black hair.

"What a mess," I said.

He turned to look at me and leaned against the railing, crossing his arms over his broad chest. "You haven't seen many dead bodies, have you?"

"Too many lately, and in some pretty weird situations, but I've never seen anything that gruesome," I said.

I had seen photographs of victims who had been beaten to death but, as with most moments in life, photos didn't do justice to the real thing. Kyle's once youthful face had been smashed to a pulp, almost unrecognizable except for the thick thatch of blonde hair that fell over his brow in blood-soaked chunks and the copper stud earring in his left ear. From the smell, I guessed he'd been dead a few days before we'd discovered his body. I tried to think of anything that would block out the image of that kid dead on the floor in a pool of dried blood and vomit. I realized I was shivering and wrapped my arms around my body. Nick stood on the deck like a sentry guarding the crime scene. Tears streamed down my face. I swiped them away and cursed. It seemed like everywhere I looked in the last year, dead bodies peered back at me.

While the three of us waited outside the cabin for either the Delta County Sheriff's Department or the Michigan State Police to show up, the snow continued falling, burying any clues that might have been left in the dirt.

My aunt had been tempted to go back inside, but I'd convinced her it was a bad idea.

"You want to remember him as he was when he was alive, not like this. If you've ever trusted me for anything, please, trust me on this," I said.

She leaned against the car and sighed. The snow and wind were dissipating enough to make it comfortable to stand outside and not freeze.

"My God, how will his parents handle this? They're going to have to deal with a mountain of guilt," she said, skillfully twirling a curl between her index finger and middle fingers.

"What's that old saying? Something about don't invite trouble. How Kyle's family handles this is not your problem. The most important task right now is finding out who killed him and why," I said.

She gave me a strange look, as if she wasn't sure what to make of me. "You're right, to a certain extent. Of course whoever did this needs to be brought to justice, but his father is still very important to me," she said and then dug her fingers into her mass of curls. "This is crazy. This man's been out of my life for forty years and now I'm in the middle of his son's murder."

She quit fiddling with her hair and began picking invisible lint off her purple wool coat. When she finally raised her head and looked at me, her gray eyes were gleaming with tears. "Robin, I know this is a lot to ask when you're tracking your fiancé's killer, but will you please help me with this?"

Before I could answer, Deputy Lee Grenville drove up in a white Chevy Tahoe emblazoned with the Delta County Sheriff's Department logo. I waved and waited for him to get out of the truck. I'd met Grenville, a good-looking blonde with sharp green eyes and medium build, the prior summer when he was working the graveyard shift as a security guard at the paper mill just outside of Escanaba. He'd since been hired by the sheriff's department, but was still very green when it came to law enforcement. His tan and brown uniform looked a tad too crisp and clean.

"Good grief, Robin. Things just seem to happen around you, don't they?" he said, slamming the door and *eyeing* my aunt, huddled next to the car, and Nick, striding from the woods across the road where he had disappeared a few minutes before, presumably to take advantage of Mother Nature's facilities.

"Hey, Lee, believe me, I'd rather not be around when this sort of stuff happens. This is my aunt, Dr. Gina Schmidt. It was one of her students at Bay College that we found inside," I said and then motioned to Nick. "This is my friend Nick Granati. He's a homicide detective with the Chicago Police Department."

They shook hands and nodded. The cop greeting.

"He didn't know the deceased and neither did I."

Lee cocked his head at the cabin. "What's it look like in there?"

Nick took over the conversation at that point and explained my aunt's "bad feeling" and what we'd found inside the cabin.

"This was more than just a sharp conk on the head done in haste," Nick said. "Whoever did this was either very pissed or wanted to send a message."

"What kind of message?" Grenville asked.

Nick shrugged. "If what Dr. Schmidt said is correct about this young man being involved with drugs, it could be a deal gone bad, a snitch issue or any number of things. I just know that kid's body took one hell of a beating."

Aunt Gina shuddered and turned her face to the gray sky, as though searching for an escape, or an answer to why this had happened. Neither was forthcoming.

Grenville took a look around inside the cabin, perhaps to confirm that the person inside was indeed dead and that there weren't any other nasty surprises. He radioed some information to dispatch, where someone indicated that "Vale", the medical examiner and the crime scene processing team were on their way.

"Vale" was Detective Thomas Vale, a twenty-five-year veteran with the department who had considered running for sheriff for about five minutes about a decade ago and decided it would involve too much politics, i.e. tact, something Tom seriously lacked. The crime lab team was attached to the Michigan State Police and worked out of Negaunee, about an hour and a half from the cabin on a good weather day. The lab's jurisdiction included the entire Upper Peninsula, a vast area with more trees than people. Even so, they did their job as well as any urban outfit.

While Nick helped Lee string yellow crime scene tape through the trees and roped off the property, my aunt and I watched from the car in silence except for Belle's rhythmic panting. Finally my aunt pulled the owner's manual for the Outback out of the glove compartment and began fanning herself.

"Robin, crack a window. This little sweetheart's breath is giving me flashbacks to the New York garbage collector's strike."

I chuckled, turned the key in the ignition and opened all four windows an inch. Belle promptly tried to stuff her huge snout through the gap and snuffled deeply.

"She probably needs a pee break," I said and got out. Nick and Lee looked over when they heard me retrieve Belle from the back seat and slam the door.

"She needs to go to the bathroom," I called and they waved.

We walked east along the north side of the gravel road where Belle made a few business stops and then caught whiff of a scent. She jerked at her leash and pulled me off the road into the dead vegetation that lined the gravel and then into the woods.

"Where are we going?" I yelled as Belle strained against the nylon strap and snuffled her nose over the dead leaves that carpeted the ground just beneath the snow. She zigged left for about ten feet, and then zagged right for about twenty feet before coming to a stop, digging furiously in the snow and letting out a deep woof. I leaned forward, bracing myself against the trunk of a beech tree, and peered around Belle's stout body. It looked like a stick about an inch in diameter with both ends buried under dead leaves and fresh snow.

"Oh, for heaven's sake! Belle, it's just a twig. Let's go," I grumbled and pulled on her leash, but she wouldn't budge. Instead, she dug her nose under the leaves and began uncovering one end that had some gooey substance stuck on it. I bent down, shifted a few more leaves and snow away with a finger and felt the bile rise in my throat. It was a tire iron covered in fresh blood with bits of skin and hair stuck to its rusty surface.

"Lee! Nick! Come here quick. Belle found something," I shouted and pulled Belle away from the weapon, likely the one used to kill Kyle Sullivan. I gave Belle a scratch behind the ears. "Good girl. Good job. Remind me to give you a treat when we get home."

As Lee trotted toward us with Nick close behind, a parade of police vehicles sped down the road and stopped in front of the cabin. Detective Tom Vale stepped out of an unmarked white Ford Crown Victoria just as a lake blue Chevy Suburban belonging to the Michigan State Police pulled up alongside him. Lee turned and waved to the officers to follow him as he continued to where Belle and I stood.

"What's up?" Nick asked when he and Lee were within ten feet of us. I pointed to the tire iron.

Lee knelt in the snow and studied the tire iron for a moment, "Well, well, well, what have we here? Hey, Tom, check this out."

Vale's long legs covered the distance in a matter of seconds.

"HappyNewYear,Robin.Gettin'theyearofftoagreatstart,eh?"hesaidwith a scowl.

Ignoring his jab, I stepped back to let Lee take over the conversation before I made a snide remark and got myself banned from stepping foot inside the sheriff's office, something Vale had been known to do to reporters he didn't like.

While Grenville filled him in on what little he knew, Vale brushed a hand over his steel-gray crew cut and nodded, his eyes never leaving the tire iron.

"Alright, leave everything as it is. The crime scene crew is on its way from the crime lab. Dr. Hunter is about twenty minutes behind me. She was in surgery when the call came in to dispatch. Damned inconvenient for a medical examiner to be the last one to a crime scene," he said and then looked from me to Grenville, shaking his head. "We're getting too damned many dead bodies lately. Three overdoses in the last six months, four suicides and now this. I'm thinking I should have retired last year when the county and the sheriff offered me the chance."

He growled in frustration and then bobbed his head at me. "I want to talk to you first. Then I want to talk to the professor—What did you say her name was?"

"Dr. Gina Schmidt," I blurted.

"Right. Who the hell is this?" he asked as he began walking back to his patrol car and pointed at Nick, who lifted one thick, straight black eyebrow.

"Nick Granati, friend of mine from Chicago. He's just along for the ride," I said as I followed in his wake as he grunted in reply.

"Grenville, you work with the professor and start tracing this guy's whereabouts. I know some of the goons he hangs with, but we'll go over all that later," Vale said, dismissing Lee with a wave of his long gloved hand.

"Wait a minute, you know Kyle?" I asked.

"Yeah, I know, rather, knew him. He's managed to avoid jail on two separate occasions in the last few months. Too bad, maybe he would have been safer there," he said with a snort. "C'mon. I want to check out the scene and then we'll sit in the patrol car where it's warm. You look like you're freezin' your tooties off."

I wasn't sure what a "tootie" was in his world, but he was right about me being cold. I suddenly realized I was shivering again. I shuffled to his vehicle and leaned against the front bumper and waited for Vale to see what he needed to see. It was starting to snow again. Nick stood in front of me, seemingly oblivious to the weather.

"What do you make of all this?" he asked me.

Shaking my head slowly, I replied, "I don't have enough information. I didn't know Kyle at all. I remember a little boy playing around the cottage when I was at my friend Mick's camp down the road, but I didn't know the family. They didn't exactly mingle together, which is kind of odd for this area. People tend to invite the neighbors to family gatherings. Neither of them ever did as far I know. Frankly, I don't think the Sullivans and the O'Bryans thought much of each other."

"Why wouldn't they?" Nick asked.

I laughed thinly. "The U.P. isn't any different than Chicago when comes to class differences. Michaela's dad worked at the paper mill just outside of Escanaba for thirty-five years. You heard my aunt. Kyle's dad is a neurologist. Sometimes that doesn't matter. I think it mattered to the Sullivans, though."

"Hmph" was all Nick said.

Lee Grenville was talking to my aunt, jotting notes on a pad and nodding encouragement. She was composed now, probably doing her best to recall every last detail she could in the hope that it would provide a clue.

I turned back to Nick and said, "This area's changed a lot since I left seven years ago. There've always been issues with drugs. But lately the cops are making bigger busts with harder drugs and more guns and cash. Prescription drug abuse is a huge problem. Vale's right. We've had more than a few overdoses this past year. It's not the same small town feel that I enjoyed as a kid."

Nick sat next to me on the bumper, causing the nose of the car to dip noticeably. "You don't know that this is drug-related."

"No, but I wouldn't be surprised. Aunt Gina described Kyle as troubled. Troubled people often turn to booze and drugs to make their troubles go away."

Nick looked back at the cabin, now shrouded in snow and crime scene tape. "His troubles are over now."

Chapter Three

$\mathcal{A}$s crime lab technicians scoured the Sullivan property and the surrounding area for clues, Detective Tom Vale questioned my now frazzled-looking aunt. I could tell she was tired of talking to cops, and I was tired of standing around watching her talking to cops. So Nick and I went for a walk to County Road 440 and headed east toward the federal forest highway. The only sound beyond the shuffling of our feet through the fresh snow and wind through the pines was the distant whine of a snowmobile speeding down a nearby trail.

Sick of being alone with my grisly thoughts, I asked Nick, "What are you thinking?"

The intensity in his eyes was startling when he turned to face me. Finally he asked, "Robin, why did you come back here when Mitch died?" His tone was hard to pinpoint, somewhere between accusatory and curious.

"What you really mean is why didn't I stay behind to do my own investigation into his murder."

He shook his head vigorously. "No, that's not what I mean. I could understand needing to come home for a few weeks to get your bearings, but why did you move back here? I'll admit it's a beautiful place, but there's nothing for you here. I've made a living out of studying people and places and figuring out what fits and what doesn't. You stick out like a fat man at a vegan festival. You may have been born and raised here, but this isn't your scene. You were at the top of your game at the Tribune. You had friends. You went to museums, galleries, shows, clubs. You sure as hell dressed better." He eyed my faded twill pants and Sorels with disdain. "You used to style your hair. Christ, it looks like you haven't even had it cut in a year. Even your bangs are crooked."

I touched the tip of the fringes hanging in my eyes and winced. "Wow, you really know how to cut a girl," I said.

He put his arm around my shoulder. "I'm not trying to make you feel bad. I just see such a change in you that it's alarming. Remember, I haven't seen you since the funeral. I think the months in between have been harder than you thought," he said.

I continued playing with my hair, feeling the jagged ends and wondering how I hadn't noticed something so obvious. What had happened to me? I thought back to the exact sequence of events that had brought me north again after Mitch's murder.

"My first thought after he died was not of escape. I couldn't even picture life without him so escape wasn't an option. All those plans we made . . . We were going to get married this year at the Presbyterian church a few blocks from the *Daily Press*," I said, my voice trailing to nothing. "Anyway, I guess it was about a week after the funeral when my dad called to say the *Daily Press* publisher had talked to him about an opening and thought I might want to come home. It seemed like a good idea at the time. I disobeyed the first rule of grieving that you should never make any major decision for at least a year. In hindsight, it was a terrible move for my career; and it certainly hasn't helped me get over Mitch. If anything, it's made it harder because there's no one here who knew him so I can't really talk much about our life together. I can't even visit him."

We turned and started heading back to the crime scene.

"The one good thing is that I've reconnected with my aunt."

Nick nodded. "Yeah, she's pretty cool. I had a criminal justice professor like her, cared about her students beyond the books and grades," he said. "Listen, I want you to know I'm here for you. This is my way of giving you a wake-up call. As I said, this is a beautiful place, and I'm sure it has lots of up sides. But you left here because you were ambitious and focused on making an impact in journalism and you wanted a broader experience than the *Daily Press* could provide. You found it in Chicago. I remember you telling me all this when I first met you five years ago. The Tribune, although far from perfect, was a good fit for you. Now you're back here. Change is great as long as it's for the right reasons."

I made a "hmpf" sound. "I cried when I cleaned out my desk. At the time I thought it was because of Mitch. Maybe there was more to it," I said with a shrug.

We were almost within earshot of the cops and crime lab people milling purposefully around the cottage and its perimeter.

He gave my shoulders a squeeze, let his arm fall and said, "There's nothing wrong with taking a step back once in while and evaluating the situation, as long you remember to eventually start moving forward again".

We'd reached my Outback. My aunt was ready to leave.

"Are you okay?" I asked.

She nodded and smiled thinly. "There's nothing more I can do here so we might as well go. We can stop by my house so you can drop Belle off with my Yorkies. Then you can take me back to work and you can be on your way to Miami," she said and then cocked her head. "Are you okay?"

I shook my head. "No, I think I'm about as far from okay as you can get. My boss is going to kill me. Do you realize that it never even occurred to me to call the Press and tell them what happened? What the hell kind of reporter am I?" I said, digging my cell phone from the pocket of my parka.

Aunt Gina and Nick rolled their eyes collectively and got into the car while I talked to the news editor and relayed what I knew. Someone else would have to follow up on the case, but at least now they knew about it. Bob Hunter would be mad that the paper didn't have photos of the scene. Somehow, I just didn't care anymore.

After I said a tearful goodbye to Belle and left her with the two Yorkies at my Aunt Gina's house near Rapid River, we headed back toward Escanaba. Nick was drumming his fingers on his knees and eyeing the dashboard clock. It was already past two in the afternoon; and we had at least a six-hour drive (if the weather held) to Chicago. The plows and salt trucks had been out so the highway was now wet with a few slushy spots. In the backseat, my aunt stared out the window in silence for a while and then asked me about my faith in the capabilities of local law enforcement. She had always been ambivalent about the New York Police Department but was in awe of their resources, something the local cops severely lacked.

"Don't worry. These people are professionals. They may not handle as many murders as the NYPD, but when they do, you can trust them to do a good job. They take it personally when someone gets whacked in their jurisdiction," I said.

"They've called in something called NOMIDES to help with the case. What in heaven's name is that? It sounds like a chemical company," she said.

"The acronym is a bit much but it stands for the Northern Michigan Drug

Enforcement Squad. They're a cooperative effort on the part of city, county, state and federal law enforcement to combat the local drug problem. I think the team was formed about 15 years ago in response to some homemade drug called methcathinone. They eradicated that from the U.P. but now they're battling coke, heroin, large-scale pot operations and methamphetamine labs. They're ridiculously underfunded and understaffed considering they have to cover most of the Upper Peninsula, but they've actually had a lot of success," I explained.

For Vale to call on the drug team for help just a few hours after finding the body, he must have had a strong notion that drugs had played a role in Kyle's death. I said as much to Nick and my aunt.

"That's just one of the many, many things bothering me about all this. I feel so, I don't know, guilty, I guess. I mean, I should have said something to someone when I suspected something weeks ago," she said, shaking her head.

Nick turned in his seat and replied, "You know you can't help people who don't want help. It's one thing to care and to extend a helping hand, but there's no point in mulling over what should have been."

She smiled knowingly and said, "That's true. It's time to redirect my energies if I'm going to help find out what happened to Kyle."

I cast a weary glance at her in the rear view mirror and started to ask what she meant by that comment, but we had reached the college. She unfastened her seatbelt and leaned forward to kiss my cheek.

"Be careful, Robin. Call me tomorrow. I love you," she said and was out of the car and striding down the snow-covered sidewalk without a backwards glance.

"You be careful, too," I whispered and drove away.

Nick and I returned to my apartment. While he was making the flight arrangements from Chicago to Miami, I exchanged the parka for my trench coat and packed lightly—just a few toiletries, a makeup kit I hadn't cracked open in months, some underwear and a five-year-old Ann Klein skirt suit I'd bought on clearance at Macy's. I'd never been to Miami and had no idea what was considered stylish in the tropics in January. Besides, I was too nervous to think about frivolities like fashion. What if when I came face to face with Joey Leeds he actually admitted to me that he killed Mitch? I couldn't imagine staying "cool." I could, however, see myself leaping across the skinny little tables they have in nightclubs, digging my fingers into his neck and squeezing until his last breath was a plea for forgiveness. I wasn't ready to forgive.

We loaded the Outback and headed down highway 35 toward Green Bay. Charlie Baker called my cell phone about halfway between Appleton and Milwaukee.

What's this I hear about you being at the scene of yet another murder? Drumming up business for a slow news day?"

"Not funny. The victim was one of my aunt's students. She was worried about him so we went looking for the kid at his family's cottage in the Hiawatha National Forest. We got there too late," I said.

"So I gathered. How's your aunt?" he asked. He'd grown fond of her, often joining us for lunch and listening intently to her theories about reincarnation, clairvoyance and the power of the human mind.

"She'll be okay, as long as she lets the cops do their job. I'm a little concerned that she may try to do something on her own," I said.

Charlie guffawed. "Are you serious? Why would she think we could possibly solve this case without civilian assistance when you have proven so many times just how inadequate we are in the realm of criminal investigation?"

"Who bit off a chunk of your ass today?"

"Never mind. Who's the cop with you?" he asked.

"Boy, you don't miss a thing, do you?"

"That's why I'm a de-tec-tive as opposed to just a uniform."

"I'm sure they love being referred to as 'just uniforms'," I said. "I've told you about Nick Granati. He may have something on my fiancé's shooter so we're on our way to Chicago and then Miami to try and flush him out."

"Wow, you be careful," he said, the sarcasm now gone.

"Don't worry about me. Listen, Charlie, I'd like to hear your opinion of Vale. He's already called in NOMIDES. That makes me think he knows a lot more about Kyle than his family did in the last few months."

"Robin, NOMIDES has been keeping an eye on Kyle Sullivan for a while. He's been hanging around with a group of people we know have connections to dealers in Green Bay and Chicago," Charlie said. "As for Vale, he had a problem with booze quite a while ago, but I've always found him to be on the level. He's not the type to try to make evidence fit a theory. In fact, I'd say him seeking investigatory help from NOMIDES is a good step. It means he knows he's in over his head and doesn't have enough resources in the sheriff's department to handle this."

The Delta County Sheriff's Department only had about a dozen road patrol personnel to cover more than 250 miles of Lake Michigan shoreline, hundreds of miles of roads and about a dozen little residential enclaves.

"This is nuts! How did this kid get mixed up with drug dealers? I mean, his old man's an MD at Marquette General. He shouldn't need the money," I said.

"Who knows," Charlie replied. "Maybe he's taking advantage of Daddy's connections to get prescription drugs. There's a huge market for painkillers around here. Maybe he met someone who turned him on to some substance and he started down that path of searching in vain for a bigger and better high. Whatever you do, don't make too many assumptions. Maybe he wasn't using. He could have been a courier. It's way too soon to jump to any conclusions."

"Well, whatever it is, I'm leaving this one in the hands of the police so you don't have to worry about me interfering. As I said, though, keep an eye on my aunt for me while I'm gone, okay?"

"Sure. Anything I can do to help with the deal in Miami?" he asked.

"Not right now. You'll be too far away to bail me out if I get into trouble this time," I said.

He was quiet for a moment, probably struggling to come up with a sarcastic comeback. He failed. "I know," he said quietly, adding, "Can you trust this Nick person?"

I glanced at Nick, seated next to me reading a Robert B. Parker Spenser novel and pretending to ignore me.

"Yeah, I can trust him. I'll be fine. Don't worry."

"I always worry about you," Charlie said and hung up the phone.

Chapter Four

*T*he strangest feeling came over me once I hit the Cook County line at about ten that evening. It was like reconnecting with an old but close friend. It was my favorite of all the cities I'd visited on vacations, student trips and professional conferences. I hadn't been back since leaving last May with a U-Haul trailer attached to my Jeep, but seeing the lights of the Sears Tower and John Hancock building as we neared Nick's apartment on West Huron Street made me realize just how much I missed the city—from the Magnificent Mile Lights Festival at Christmas and the Chicago Blues Fest in June to the irony of the Chicago Fire Academy standing on the spot where Mrs. O'Leary and her infamous cow once lived.

As we'd planned, I dropped Nick at his apartment a few blocks off the Kennedy Expressway and a couple of blocks from where I'd lived for five years, and then drove out to Oak Park where Mitch had been raised and his parents still lived in a four bedroom, four square Edwardian house. Mitch's mother had insisted I stay the night with them when I'd called her on my cell phone on the way down. The porch light was on when I pulled into the driveway. They were both out the door and halfway down the front steps before I could exit the car. It was a bittersweet reunion that lasted several hours as we reminisced and caught up on the gossip of the last seven months, remembering the man we'd loved. I'd always adored his parents and upon seeing them again, was sorry I'd put so much distance, physical and emotional, between us after his death.

Thrilled that there might be a break in the case, they were still worried about me getting hurt, but after plenty of reassurances that I'd be careful, they let me leave the next morning with a hug and a promise to visit me in the spring. (The Upper Peninsula's reputation for death-inducing winter weather was just too scary for "southerners" to fathom braving until May.)

After leaving the Montgomery home, I found a gas station, fueled the car and then parked on the side of the shop and called my aunt from my cell phone. It was nearing eight-thirty in Rapid River, an hour ahead of me. She answered on the first ring and reported that Belle was enjoying the company of Victoria and Albert, it was snowing and it was still rather dark outside but she didn't mind. It helped her "focus her thoughts internally."

"What the hell does that mean?" I asked. My aunt often used mystical expressions to describe her state of mind. It took some getting used to, especially since I wasn't particularly attuned to my own state of mind.

"It means I need to clear my head of all external disturbances and use my mind to get in touch with Kyle's essence." Good thing she couldn't see me roll my eyes.

"Aunt Gina, I thought we'd agreed that we'd leave this case to the police."

"Nonsense. I agreed to nothing. Besides, maybe I'll learn something helpful. You should never underestimate the power of the mind, Robin. You can roll your eyes all you want, but I know you've experienced things you can't explain. It's a gift that runs in our family, but everyone can get in touch with that sixth sense if they just let themselves relax and open up to the world."

I started to ask how she could see my facial movements and then decided I didn't have time to get into that discussion. Instead, I asked, "How are his parents handling this?"

She sighed. "His father will get back from Italy late tonight. He called me from the airport in Naples last night. He's devastated. I guess Kyle's mother is flying in from Arizona today. Neither of them seems to have had a clue about Kyle's involvement with drugs."

We talked for a few more minutes and then hung up as she had to get ready for work and I wanted to visit the Crescent Police Department and see if anyone had learned anything relevant to Mitch.

Before I headed north for Crescent though, I stopped at the Forest Home Cemetery and placed a single red silk rose next to Mitch's marble headstone and sat on the frozen ground for several minutes listening as the wind whispered through the bare branches of the surrounding hardwoods. When we'd buried him in late April, the trees had been in nearly full bloom, arching over his grave as though sheltering him from nature's fury. Now they resembled the claws of the Grim Reaper reaching for yet another victim. The sky was as gray and hard as the ground where I sat, unyielding to the permanence of death. My aunt would have argued that death is simply the end of one life in preparation for the next life. For me though, Mitch was gone—forever. The late night conversations over hot chocolate spiked with peppermint Schnapps, the long walks through snow, rain and heat with Belle, the hours spent cuddling on the couch watching old horror movies—it was all gone. I let the tears fall and lost myself in memories until suddenly I felt a nervous sensation. I had company.

I looked around the old, vast cemetery and saw a few vehicles parked near plots or moving slowly along the maze of narrow roads that wound between the graves. No one seemed to be paying any attention to me, and yet, something was wrong.

"I have to go, Mitch," I said aloud, standing and digging a Kleenex from my jacket pocket. I angrily wiped my face and nose and vowed, "I promise I won't quit until the person who put you here is …" What? Brought to justice? What was justice? Prison? Death? "Well, we'll see what happens. Nick is helping me so we'll get it done. Just remember I love you."

Tears threatened again so I turned and walked back to my car, still feeling an unseen pair of eyes watching my every move.

I left Forest Park and headed north for the Crescent Police Department, a two-story brick building on land left vacant when an arsonist destroyed the abandoned brewery that had stood there for nearly a hundred years. The crazed young man had set fire to about a dozen buildings in the mid-nineties before he was finally caught late one night by an alert rookie cop fresh out of college and eager to make a difference in the world. Mitch's parent's still had the certificate of merit he'd earned for his work on that case hanging on their living room wall along side a photo of him in his dress uniform, the one in which he'd been buried.

The new station wasn't going to win any architectural awards but it was functional and had plenty of space for offices, interrogation rooms, files and a jail in the basement. I hoped to catch the chief, Rex Harper, in his office but his secretary said he was at a meeting at city hall. Other than Rex and a female lieutenant named Sharon Carter, I knew few other people at the department. I had kept my distance when Mitch was alive out of fear that someone would accuse him of leaking information to a reporter.

I was walking back to the parking lot east of the station when a gray unmarked Chevy Impala patrol car stopped behind my Outback, effectively blocking it. The driver side window swooshed down. I caught myself just before I groaned aloud as Dave Whelan, a uniformed officer who should have retired about five years before, stuck his face in the opening.

"Well, well, well. Robin Hamilton's back in town. Haven't seen you since the funeral. How's everything in Upper Michigan?" he asked with a grin. His eyes were a tad bloodshot and a few specks of dried blood had congealed on his cheek where it appeared he'd cut himself shaving. I'd never liked Dave. I found his sarcasm hurtful, not funny, and I didn't like how he'd always referred to Mitch by the highly original moniker "Four Eyes," because he couldn't wear contact lenses to correct his near-sightedness. I could understand why Whelan's wife had left him about two years ago. I probably would have filleted the man after about two days of marriage.

I drew the belt of my trench coat tighter around my waist and tried to smile.

"I'm fine, Dave, just looking for the chief. How have you been?" I didn't feel like making chit-chat, but my small-town upbringing wouldn't let me be rude.

He shrugged. "Fine as frog's hair. Still haven't caught the bastard that popped young Mitchell, though."

"I know. That's why I'm here. There might be a break in the case."

He looked surprised. "Really? I hadn't heard. What kind of break?"

I'll never know why I chose that moment to lie, but I concocted a story that sounded plausible and said, "A woman called one of my sources and said her ex-husband had a grudge against Mitch for arresting him a few years ago. I guess it really messed up his life so she thinks he might have been the shooter."

Whelan nodded. "I can see that. Sounds like a good tip. Who's following it? I thought the state cops had taken over the investigation from us in case there was a conflict of interest, and I've even seen a few feds sniffin' around here."

I was saved by the crackle of his radio as a dispatcher called for him. He grunted, rolled his eyes and pressed the button on the small radio receiver clipped to the shoulder of his dark blue uniform jacket. I breathed a sigh of relief when the dispatcher told him to respond to an accident at a busy intersection a few blocks away. Whelan sent me a two-finger salute with his left hand, revved the engine and drove off in a cloud of exhaust.

"What a jerk," I muttered and turned to get in my car. Another vehicle approached from behind and drove around to the back of the building where staff and officers parked. It was the chief. I ran across the asphalt and caught him just as he was exiting a patrol car similar to Whelan's.

"Robin! This is a surprise," he said and extended his hand in greeting. Rex Harper was tall and built like a long distance runner, with close-cropped gray hair and clear blue eyes the color of Lake Michigan on a sunny day. He was respected in the Illinois law enforcement community and was thought to be an intelligent investigator and fair supervisor, but Mitch had always felt he was too lenient on guys like Whelan who took every available opportunity to abuse the system.

"What brings you back to Crescent? Oh, of course. I shouldn't even ask. I'm sorry but I haven't heard anything more about Mitch's case. I keep in regular contact with Captain Talbot in Springfield, but they're worried the trail is getting cold," he said and motioned for me to follow him into the building.

"I just saw Whelan. He said the Feds have been here. What's that all about?" I asked as I tailed him into his office and shut the door while he hung his wool coat on an antique wooden coat rack.

"So Whelan told you that, did he? Let me warn you about listening to everything Dave Whelan tells you," he said and sat down behind a large oak desk and leaned back in his old, worn leather office chair.

I plunked down in a wooden arm chair across from him and sighed. "What's going on, Rex? Why are the state cops saying the trail is getting cold but Whelan is saying something different? I don't get it. I would think these guys would be stumbling over each other to solve the murder of one of their own. Maybe I'm wrong, maybe nobody seems to give a damn except me and Nick."

Rex's eyebrows narrowed. "Nick Granati?"

I nodded.

"Be careful of getting too close to that one. I'm still not sure which side of the law he considers his vocation," Harper said.

"Rex, you're trying to stall a reporter. It's not working. What the hell's going on here? At this point, I couldn't give a damn if Nick was working for the KGB, if they even exist anymore, just so Mitch's killer is found, whether that means prison or death."

Harper sighed and folded his hands over his belt buckle, eyeing me with defeat. "Alright. You actually hit upon it earlier. We're all stumbling over each other—this department, the state, the DEA. Everybody's pointing fingers at everybody else. There are just too many unknowns in this case.

37

Mitch left us too few clues."

I waited for him to continue, but he just sat and stared at me.

"That tells me absolutely nothing. Clues about what? We went over this a dozen times the week after he died. He never told me about any case he was working that could possibly get him killed. What does the DEA have to do with anything? I wasn't even aware that Crescent had much of a drug problem."

Harper shook his head slowly and leaned forward, spreading his hands on his green desk blotter. "Robin, this isn't easy to say, and I wasn't going to mention it, but since you insist, fine. Here it is. This all started about a week before Mitch died. One of the guys came to me and said he'd seen Mitch talking with a known drug smuggler in the region, but it wasn't an arrest situation, and Mitch wasn't on any investigation through this department. It made this particular officer wonder if Mitch had gone to the other side."

I was up and out of my chair before he'd finished the word "side."

"That's insane. You can't possibly believe Mitch was dirty. Who supposedly saw him? Where? When? How do you know he wasn't working a source?" I yelled.

He waved at me to sit down and be quiet.

"Robin, I know this sounds crazy to you, but there's more. I'm just not at liberty to talk about it. It's why I can't just walk into the squad room and dispel those rumors because I'm not convinced they aren't true. I brought you in here because I want you to understand that I'm walking a tightrope. All I can say is Mitch was into something he couldn't handle, something big, bigger than this department could investigate. Something went wrong and now the rest of us are left to try to piece it together. In all honesty, we're failing miserably. I know Nick Granati has been digging into this mess on his own. I told him to knock it off two months ago because he's getting in the way and possibly scaring off witnesses. There's a whole other layer to this case and once we uncover that layer, I'm confident we'll find out who killed your fiancé. You just have to trust me."

I shook my head in disbelief. "That's the biggest load of crap I've heard since I became a reporter. I thought you were better than that."

He sucked in his lips but didn't argue. "I'm sorry, Robin. It's part of my job. If you really believe Mitch was true to his profession then you have to believe that he would want you to be patient and let us handle this investigation our way."

He got up and walked to the window that overlooked the public parking lot. We were both quiet for a minute and then he said, "I assume you've come back to do your own legwork. I've already warned you about Granati. My advice to you is to turn around and go home, before you get hurt."

I stood and joined him at the window. The sky was threatening snow. "It's too late for that now," I said and left him to watch me drive away.

I found Nick in as foul a mood as myself.

"My boss just called," he said when I walked in the door of his apartment. "He wanted to know where I was going and why, said the head of the detective bureau was on his case about me, said he might have to cancel my leave. I told him to take it up with my union steward because I was taking my time."

I plopped onto his brown overstuffed couch and said, "That's probably my fault. I just had the strangest conversation with the Crescent police chief, Rex Harper. He mentioned you and said he had told you to butt out of the investigation. I wouldn't be surprised if he made a few phone calls after I left his office."

"Did you tell him anything?"

"No. He sure had some interesting things to say, though. I found out the DEA is looking into this. He also confirmed what you said before about the whole damn department thinking Mitch might have been dirty. Some cop supposedly saw Mitch with a known drug smuggler about a week before he was killed. Apparently they're trying to tie that to his murder. Do you know anything about this?"

Nick sat in a matching chair across from me and ran his hands through his hair. "Yeah, I heard the drug thing but most of the cops think it's bullshit. I guarantee the whole department doesn't think Mitch was dirty. I couldn't find anything solid, though. The only piece of information I could get was the name of the shooter, Joey Leeds, but no one knew why he was hired. I tried all the usual drug angles, like I told you before, and came up with nothing. Nobody had ever heard of Mitch. It was a dead end."

"Nick, do you think Harper might be dirty himself and trying to cover his tracks?"

Nick shook his head. "No, I don't. He's trying to weasel out of something, but I don't think he's dirty. I checked into his background a little using my old military connections. The guy's strictly by the book. He especially doesn't like outside interference. That's why he's trying to chase you and me out of town."

I looked at my watch. "Well, it worked for now. We have to get to the airport," I said and headed for the door.

Nick lived about twelve miles from O'Hare and traffic was heavy so we spent a lot of time waiting and mulling over what Harper had said. Nick couldn't help but wonder if the rumors were started because of jealousy.

"Mitch was a natural investigator, but he was terrible at office politics," Nick explained. "That department is notorious for being home to a bunch of prima donnas. He found that out early on but was too idealistic to abandon ship for another department. Actually, I think Harper convinced him to stay. He seemed to have something in mind for Mitch. Whether it worked out or not, I don't know. Mitch quit griping when he was promoted to sergeant."

Mitch had often talked to me about some of the officers not working as a team and that there seemed to be an every-man-for-himself attitude prevalent among some of them. I'd never thought much about it because I'd seen the same thing at the Tribune when the budget cuts had begun a few years back. It was simply human nature.

"Do you think it's possible that one of the cops could have hired Leeds?" I asked. It sounded ridiculous, but so had everything else I'd heard in the last three days.

He shrugged and said, "Sure, it's possible, but I don't have any idea who would have done it or, more importantly, why. The person who was promoted to sergeant after Mitch was killed deserved the job and would have gotten there sooner or later when one of the old guys retired. No, Mitch was hit by a pro in a well-orchestrated hit. Something like that evolves from a lot more than petty jealousy."

I had to agree with his logic, but added, "Well, Rex obviously knows a lot more than he's saying. It makes me wonder if we're wasting our time on this Leeds character. Maybe we should stick around here and shake a few trees to see what falls out."

"The trees are bare. No, my gut tells me Leeds is our man. We get him to talk, we get the person behind it."

I thought carefully before making my next statement but decided it was best to get everything out in the open now.

"Nick, Harper also suggested he thought you might not be staying on the right side of the law."

Nick smiled. "What is the right side of the law? I work with more crooked cops than you have hairs on your pretty head. I come from a long line of people who just do what they need to do to survive. There is no law, only honor."

We finally made it to O'Hare and, as we walked toward the terminal with our luggage in hand, I said, "You know, it just occurred to me that neither of us might make it out of this alive."

"That's right," Nick replied, his back straight and his eyes focused ahead on something no one could see. "And yet you're planning to get on that plane and come with me."

"I'm looking forward to it," I said, gripping the handle of my suitcase a little tighter.

"Ain't nothing like the thrill of the chase to make you feel alive, is there?" he said with a cold smile.

"Beats sitting behind a desk all day," I replied as I bent my head against the icy wind whipping down the tarmac and wondered if I'd ever see Escanaba again.

I was exhausted by the time the lights of Miami filled my little window shortly before ten that evening. The 747 made a couple of lazy circles around Dade County and then touched down with a soft thud that worked to send a jolt of energy through my system. I wasn't in Miami for a vacation, but I couldn't help feeling excited at being in one of the most vibrant cities in the world on the adventure of a lifetime. Nick, on the other hand, appeared unaffected by the colorful shops and people we passed on our way from the air-conditioned gate to the steamy pick-up zone just outside the terminal. A black Buick Lucerne quietly rolled to a stop in front of us as soon as we hit the sidewalk. A tall, thick-necked man with a deep tan and short dark hair jumped out from the front passenger seat as an unseen finger pushed the trunk release and popped open the lid.

"Tony, how's it going, man?" Nick said, grabbing the other man's hand in both of his. Tony's sport coat did little to conceal the forty-five semi-automatic pistol in his shoulder holster as he reached to slap Nick on the back.

"Everything's on track, Nick. Uncle Rudy's waiting for you both and has made some arrangements," Tony said.

"Fantastic," Nick replied and turned to me. "Robin, this is my cousin Tony; he just left the Chicago P.D. Tony, I'd like you to meet my friend Robin Hamilton. She's the bait."

I balked at his characterization of the situation but let it pass. Tony took my hand and bowed gracefully. "It's a pleasure to meet you, Ms. Hamilton.

Welcome to Miami. Have you ever been here before?"

I shook my head and smiled in spite of myself. Everything about this guy screamed danger, bodyguard, man of the world and every other bad Hollywood cliché, but I couldn't help but be charmed. "No, I've never even been to Florida, but I think I'm going to like it. The weather is certainly an improvement from my hometown." The city was in the midst of a heat wave and felt downright balmy, a slight breeze blowing off the ocean ruffling the ends of my long fine hair. Lights of the city overwhelmed the stars, but I took a minute to study the sky anyway while Tony and Nick loaded our luggage into the trunk. It was a habit I'd acquired as a teenager when I most needed guidance from my late mother. I would often go outside at night, look up and tell her what was bothering me. Oddly enough, I almost always came away feeling better or least knowing what course of action to take. I now asked her one simple question—would I be okay? I took a deep breath and closed my eyes. Suddenly every muscle seemed to relax and a soft breath of air against my face swept my mind clean of doubt. Yes, I would be just fine. Someone was watching out for me.

"Yo, Robin, we're holding up traffic," Nick yelled.

I slid into the back seat and sank into the soft black cushions, smiling to myself. I knew when I left Escanaba that there would be no going back. I'd given the police a chance to find Mitch's killer. Now it was time take matters into my own hands. Maybe Nick was right. There was no law, only honor.

Chapter Five

Rudolph Granati lived on a yacht that he kept moored at the Miami River Marina at night and sailed around the Keys during the day. It was about sixty feet from stem to stern, white as a blizzard and taller than my house in Escanaba. As we approached it from the rear I glanced at the boat's name painted in shimmering emerald Old English script.

"Morghanna?" I whispered incredulously. Tony, who was walking in front of Nick and I, turned and winked at me.

Nick grinned. "My Aunt Crystal named it. She's half Irish. Morghanna is the Celtic sea goddess. You'll get a kick out of Crystal—sort of a cross between Elvira and Snow White."

We'd reached the ramp extending from the starboard deck to the dock where a striking, sixtyish man wearing dark slacks and a white flowered Hawaiian shirt met us with a warm smile and a wave of his hands.

Nick leaned down and whispered, "My Uncle Rudy."

"Welcome, welcome weary travelers. I trust you had an uneventful trip. Robby, bring their bags from the car. They'll be spending the night on the boat with us," he said, nodding to the thick-set young man who'd driven the Buick from the airport. I saw Tony raise an eyebrow in surprise but he said nothing.

Nick and his uncle embraced and then I was introduced and greeted with a kiss on the back of my hand.

"Such a lovely lady to have endured such tragedy. My sympathies on the loss of your fiancé. My nephews Nick and Tony and our friends will help you right this terrible wrong," he said.

I thanked him and had to resist the urge to curtsy. For people who carried guns and didn't seem too concerned about danger, they certainly were polite.

Rudy led us to a luxurious lounge filled with deep blue, thickly-padded chairs and couches and a bar along one wall. A large, square glass coffee table with a porcelain sculpture of two dolphins frolicking in waves was the focal point of the room. Rudy asked us to sit while he made up a batch of margaritas. Robby passed by the starboard entry and popped his head in the door. Without looking up from the blender, Rudy said, "Put them in the two port-side guest rooms and shut the door."

"Yes, sir," Robby said and pulled the door shut without a sound.

Rudy jerked his head at the door and rolled his eyes. "My wife's brother's son. Good kid, but he's green as a tree frog."

Nick stretched out his legs from where he sat on the couch next to me and said, "I thought we were staying at the Best Western on the beach tonight. Why the change in plans? Trouble?"

His uncle stepped out from the behind the bar with a silver tray in hand and four margaritas, glasses garnished with sea salt and a slice of lime. He said nothing until each of us had been served and he'd taken a seat in a large easy chair, like the commander in chief taking his position at a cabinet meeting. After savoring a sip of his drink, he set it on a coaster and looked at Tony, who sat across from him in a similar chair.

"I don't know if we've got trouble or not," he finally said. "Let's just say I think it is prudent that we take precautions. One of our connections at the hotel called while you were on your way here from the airport. It seems a woman called the front desk and asked for Robin Hamilton's room number. It's silly, really. Everyone knows hotels don't give out that kind of information."

"Your aunt?" Nick asked me.

"No, Aunt Gina would call my cell phone. Besides, how would she know where I was staying? I didn't even know until you told me on the plane."

Tony loosened his tie and said, "Does the hotel keep a record of incoming calls? Maybe we can trace it that way."

Nick leaned over and slapped him on the knee. "You should never have left the force, man. You were a great cop."

Rudy smiled indulgently. "Yes, until that Granati temper got the better of him."

"So, how are you all related?" I asked, noting the strong family resemblance in the three men.

Tony grinned. "There are three Granati brothers. Uncle Rudy here is the youngest. Nick Senior was the oldest. He died about twenty-five years ago. My old man is in the middle. It's an interesting story of how we all came to be here with Uncle Rudy, but that's for another time."

"Yes," Rudy intoned. His chiseled Mediterranean features and smooth voice would have easily landed him a job in the movies in the Golden Era of Hollywood. He picked up the French phone on the small glass and silver table next to him and dialed a number. "Leslie Hanover, please." He waited a moment and then spoke in Italian for a few minutes before putting the receiver back in its cradle, a grin on his face.

"Good thinking, Tony. She said it will take about an hour to access the information she needs. Fortunately for us, the clerk who took the call was still there and recorded the time the call was received at the front desk so she knows what to look for."

"Is Leslie another relative?" I asked.

"Employee. We own the hotel," Rudy said. "Now, who is interested in knowing where you're staying in Miami, my dear?"

I let my head fall back against the cushion and thought about my feeling of being watched at the cemetery in Forest Park and my encounter with Dave Whelan outside the Crescent police station.

"My experience has been that if your gut tells you something is off, then it probably is," Tony said after I explained what had transpired earlier that day.

"Who knew you were coming down here?" Nick asked.

"Just Charlie, my aunt and my editor. My dad's on a cruise so I didn't want to bother him," I said.

"Charlie's a detective in Escanaba," Nick explained to the others. "I don't see a connection between any of those people and this case. We must be missing something. Somebody in the Chicago area probably has a contact up north keeping an eye on you."

"Who's this other cop in Crescent, this Dave Whelan?" Tony asked. He'd been gazing at me from time to time, as though he were curious about some unique creature he was seeing for the first time. I normally didn't like being studied like a specimen, but I didn't mind him at all. In fact, I found myself gazing back quite often. Although substantial in stature, there was something about him that spoke of gentleness and depth of spirit. My aunt would have noted that his aura was clear, but soft. He reminded me of Mitch, minus the eyeglasses over pale blue eyes and wavy brown hair. Tony's eyes were brown with flecks of gold, like chocolate pudding with butterscotch sprinkles.

I considered Whelan for a moment. "He's one of those guys who's been on the force for a couple of decades and really should retire but can't because he doesn't have enough money or doesn't know what to do with himself outside of a patrol car. He and Mitch never really got along, but I can't imagine Dave would have him killed, not through a hit man."

Rudy sat forward and clasped his hands under his chin. "Alright, let's proceed from this point knowing you are being watched and that there are several people working behind the scenes. That makes this whole endeavor a lot more dangerous because we're dealing with so many unknowns.

"Robin, here's the plan. Joey Leeds hangs out at a club in South Beach. It's a hip place so my wife will take you shopping tomorrow to get you the right clothes, hair and make-up. I have some concerns that Leeds may recognize you as someone connected to one of his victims so we want to transform you into someone your own family wouldn't know up close. Tomorrow is Friday so you're likely to find Joey at the club. I'm still trying to set up a firm meeting. I've made arrangements for you to get past the doorman. Tony will be within earshot at all times. You will approach Leeds and tell him you would like to talk business. I assume Nick told you the setup to get him to admit to killing your fiancé?"

Marveled by how much had already been organized, I merely nodded.

"Good. He'll probably give you his terms and then you'll arrange a meeting. Try to make it a marina, just not this one. I don't want unnecessary attention brought upon us. Once you've made contact with him, we will move in and take care of the rest."

I straightened and asked, "What does that mean?"

Nick patted my arm. "Robin, the less you know, the better. Our goal is to get to the bottom of this. This guy's eluded the best cops in the world for years now. It's time to try another tactic."

"What makes you think he'll even agree to do the job?" I asked.

Rudy smirked. "My dear, the man kills for sport and money. We've gone to great lengths to make your identity as the jilted wife real. He's already checked your references and smells the fragrant odor of cash."

Sighing heavily I sank back into the couch. Somewhere in the back of my mind I heard that old proverb about if you lie down with dogs, expect to wake up with fleas. I felt an itch already.

Despite the excitement of the last few days, I fell into a sound, dreamless sleep and was awakened only by a soft tapping on the door. I pulled myself into a sitting position and peeked between two slats in the blinds. Sunlight glistened magnificently on the turquoise water. Paradise. I told the tapper to come in and gaped as the most fantastic-looking woman I'd ever seen stepped into the room and shut the door behind her. Long, sleek black hair fell straight to her slim waist while a soft fringe of bangs framed her creamy white skin and emerald eyes. Her lashes were thick, long and black, her lips and nails were painted red and her curvy-yet-tiny figure was clad in a silk sapphire jumpsuit that fit like it had been tailored just for her. This had to be Aunt Crystal, although the word "aunt" sounded too pedestrian for this woman. Elvira and Snow White, indeed. In the midst of all that glamour, though, was a face more striking for its inherent kindness than its structure.

"Hi, Robin, I'm sorry to wake you," she said with a sheepish smile and walked across the small room to the bed. "Do you mind if I sit?"

I shook my head dumbly as she perched on the edge of the mattress, tucking her right leg under her fanny. She held out her hand. "I'm Crystal Granati. Rudy's wife." Her hand was warm, soft and small, almost as small as mine though she was a good two inches taller than my five-foot-three-inch frame.

"Rudy tells me our plan for the day is to transform you into a maneater."

I laughed out loud. "That ain't gonna happen," I said, giving her another once-over and then picturing how I must look in my discount-store cotton nightgown and dull ash blonde hair hanging in my face.

She waved a manicured hand at me. "Honey, beauty has almost nothing to do with what you see in the mirror first thing in the morning and almost everything to do with attitude. Look at me. I'm forty-three and proud of it, I just don't need to look it. I just take what Mother Nature gave me, highlight the best and say to hell with the rest. I'd say Mother Nature gave you plenty.

"Now, how about you get dressed, and Tony and Robby will drive us out to the big mall north of Miami for a day of fun." She patted my leg, shot me a dazzling smile and left. Wow, I thought, forty-three? I hadn't seen any signs of Botox, but she probably hadn't spent more than five minutes at a time in the sun without a hat and sunblock.

About a half hour later the four of us were in the Lucerne heading north on Biscayne Boulevard to the Aventura Shopping Mall, which would cover most of downtown Escanaba if placed on top of it. We entered near the star-shaped fountain across from the Crate and Barrel and found a restaurant open for breakfast for refueling and then Crystal led Tony, Robby and me to a little boutique on the upper level. The store catered to the nouveau riche, whom Crystal described as "women with too much money and too little common sense to know the difference between trendy and trashy. That's exactly the look we want for you, my dear."

While Robby kept watch for trouble outside the store, Tony faded into the circular racks of dresses, bustiers and tight pants, trying to remain inconspicuous in search of would-be assassins. As Crystal explained to the saleswoman what she had in mind for me, I wondered just how much danger I was in. The idea of needing a bodyguard made me nervous but it went with the territory. If I was going to take matters into my own hands regarding Mitch, I had better be prepared to defend myself. Unfortunately, I wasn't prepared beyond knowing a few self-defense moves that would do little harm considering my small stature. I relaxed a little and told myself to be thankful for Tony and Robby's presence. Besides, it was way past time for Mitch's murder to be solved. The police had made such little progress and almost seemed to be stalling. Why? Mitch's parents hadn't been kept updated on anything and I had to show up at the police station to even get anyone there to talk to me. Did they have something to hide? Was the chief the dirty one? I could not picture Mitch getting involved in something illegal. I'd seen him pick up change from the sidewalk and drop it in charitable collection tins numerous times. The whole reason he'd become a cop was his sense of justice. I had sometimes teased him about being idealistic and naïve for believing he could change the world by setting a good example and showing people an alternative to crime. He would have made a great social worker. That made it especially hard to fathom why someone would want him dead. It would help if I knew who had allegedly seen him talking to a known drug dealer and the identity of that dealer.

"Robin, hello, are you in there?" Crystal was waving her hand in front of my face.

"Sorry, I have a tendency to get lost in my head."

"Well, if these don't bring you back to the real world, nothing will," she said and gestured ala Vanna White to a dressing room full of colorful, shiny dresses designed to maximize the wearer's assets and visibility in a crowd.

I laughed and shook my head. "I don't think I could wear any of those and not look like a little kid playing dress-up in her mother's closet."

"Remember, it's all about attitude," Crystal said and pulled me into the dressing room. "You're playing a role—the pissed-off, semi-trashy wife of a man with too much libido and not enough brains. Here, try this one first." She took down a black strapless garment that resembled an inner tube and waited while I removed my shirt and pants. I struggled into it, turned and looked in the three-way mirror while Crystal watched from behind. We both burst out laughing at the same time.

"No, no, that will definitely not work. You look like a piece of linguine that's been dipped in roofing tar," Crystal said.

We tried a flowered number with puffy sleeves—too eighties; a hot pink two-piece set with a bare midriff—too Playboy bunnyesque; and then a black-and-white hounds-tooth suit with red trim that brought to mind jokers in a deck of playing cards.

"This is ridiculous," I wailed. "Who wears this stuff?"

"Honey, when you step into that club tonight, you will enter a whole new world of fashion where wearing stripes with plaid is the least offensive fashion faux pas," Crystal said as she studied the remaining items on the rack. She whipped out a jade green sleeveless sheath with gathered seams and tossed it me. "This just might work if we give you red hair."

"Red hair?" I mumbled as I pulled the dress over my head. Once the seams were adjusted, we stepped back and look at my reflection.

"Wow," I said, eyeing my newly-found curves with wonder.

"Ta-da! Perfect!" Crystal said with a flourish of her hands. "See what I mean about highlight the best? Our next stop is Victoria's Secret for the right foundation garments to maximize those curves even more."

I glanced at the price tag. "Four hundred and eighty-nine dollars?" I squealed.

"Relax, it's on me," she said with a wink.

"Crystal, this isn't about money, it's the principle. This is more than my monthly rent payment," I said as I changed into my street clothes.

She made a face as she threw the dress over her arm and headed for the cash register. "Do you live in a dumpster?"

"No, actually I have a view of Lake Michigan. Housing is cheap in the U.P. compared to this place."

It took another forty-five minutes to find the perfect padded push-up bra and bodyshaper to add a few inches in all the right places and bring the dress to the next level above "wow." Then we headed to Crystal's beauty salon which, in addition to providing two-hundred-dollar haircuts and four-hundred-dollar highlights, also sold wigs.

Tony was beginning to look annoyed as Crystal explained to Todd, her stylist, what she thought would look best. She pulled the dress out of the bag and held it up to my face.

"I'm thinking curly, long and red, but not too red. More like Rene Russo in 'The Thomas Crown Affair,' not Jessica Rabbit."

Todd pulled my hair back from my face, hooked a thumb under my chin and turned my head this way and that, scrutinizing every detail and looking as though he didn't like what he saw.

Finally, he said, "Too pale. We could do a fake-bake but will it look just that—fake. How about Nicole Kidman in 'Practical Magic?'"

Crystal snapped her fingers and lit up. "Yeah, that's great. Todd, you're wonderful."

"I know. I'll be right back," he said drolly and disappeared behind a thick red velvet curtain at the back of the salon.

I looked around for Tony and saw him leaning against a pillar outside the salon. He winked at me and then went back to people-watching. Crystal nudged me and whispered, "I think he likes you." I just smiled.

Todd swished back into the salon about five minutes later with a foam head adorned with a light auburn wig made up of perfectly tousled spiral curls, quite similar to how my aunt wore her hair, except hers was natural. He sat me down in his chair and stuffed my hair under what looked like a Nylon stocking before fitting the wig onto my head. I was immediately transformed. The color brought out the green in my eyes in a way I'd never seen. I couldn't help but grin.

"I like it," I drawled.

"Now, remember, Crystal, don't overdo the make-up or she'll look like a marionette," Todd instructed. "You do have that tendency after all."

She fluttered her false eyelashes at him and laughed.

We left the salon with some makeup and all the necessary items for care of the wig, and then hit one of the many shoe stores for strappy stiletto-healed sandals to match the dress and a more practical pair of sandals I could wear if Leeds and I had a second meeting. By this time, I was tired, Tony was sick of shopping and we were all hungry so we found the car and prepared to drive back to the yacht.

We'd just pulled onto Biscayne when Bob Hunter called my cell phone. I groaned because even though I'd promise to call him every day to keep him updated, I hadn't called once since leaving Escanaba Tuesday afternoon.

Bob was upset, but not about my lack of courtesy. "Robin, the publisher just stormed out of my office. He said you have to be back at the paper Monday morning or I have to fire you."

"I don't get it. Why is Sam being so hard about this? He's never had an issue with me taking time off without pay before," I said, thoroughly puzzled.

"I know. I don't get it either. He just said the company will not allow it and that you have to be here. Will you?"

"No. I'm sorry, Bob. I can't promise you anything. I'm down in Miami right now and I have no idea how long this is going to take," I said.

Bob was incredulous. "Robin, we're talking about your job!"

"Bob, I'm well aware of that, but I'm not destitute. I'll be okay. How about this, just so we make it a clean break, how about I resign effective last Tuesday? That way you don't have to go through the mess of justifying a firing to the unemployment people," I said.

He reluctantly agreed, but I could tell this wouldn't be the end of it.

When I clicked the phone off Crystal asked me what the problem was. "Sam Burns, my newspaper publisher, just ordered my editor to fire me. It's so odd because on Tuesday they were ready to give me a promotion, but I guess the company won't allow me to take any more unpaid time off."

Crystal patted my arm and said, "I'm sorry. Will you be alright? You don't seem too upset."

I shrugged. "I'm not upset. I'm not happy in that job. Besides, Mitch made me the beneficiary of his life insurance policy through the city of Crescent. I haven't touched the money yet so I'll be just fine. It will give me some time to think about what I want to do next. Anyway, I'm too tired to worry about it. Who knew shopping could be so exhausting," I said as I sank into the backseat cushions.

"And boring," Tony cracked from the front seat.

"Hmph, if I left you to your devices you'd be walking about Miami in a plaid flannel shirt and jeans," Crystal replied.

"Sounds like you'd fit right in up in the U.P.," I said.

"Tell me about your home. What's it like?" he asked.

"It's a lot different from here or Chicago—very rural, isolated, not a lot of culture or shopping," I said and nudged Crystal.

"Sounds dreadful, especially the culture part. I love modern art," Crystal said.

"Actually, it's wonderful if you're into outdoor activities. There's even a thriving arts community. Most of the time, it's peaceful and beautiful. It's a good place to relax and get in touch with yourself—if you let nature work its magic. But it has its issues, too. Good jobs are tough to find. The weather can be rough and the problems of the big city are creeping north."

My mind hit on the image of Kyle Sullivan sprawled dead on the floor of his cabin and I wondered if my aunt was spending time with his family and staying out of Detective Vale's way.

As soon as I got back to my room on the boat I called her office, cell and home phone numbers, but got no answer. A little ball of worry began to form in my stomach as I recalled her words about redirecting her energies "to help find out what happened to Kyle." Had she decided to play amateur sleuth? I certainly wasn't setting a good example with my own escapades.

My thoughts were interrupted by a knock at my door.

"Come in."

Nick poked his head inside and asked, "How ya doin'?"

I sat down on the bed and waved my cell phone at him. "I'm tired and worried about my aunt. I can't reach her."

Nick came in the room, closed the door and sat in a chair in the corner. "She's a big girl and capable of taking care of herself. You need to focus on the task at hand. Tonight will require all of your senses to be on alert so my advice is to get something to eat, take a nap and then get dressed and ready to party. From what Tony said, it sounds like you guys found the perfect get-up."

I smiled wickedly. "You're gonna love it! So, while we were out shopping what were you up to?"

He stood and frowned. "I tried to find out who was looking for you last night. The call came from a payphone in Wetmore, Michigan. Does that sound familiar?"

"Are you sure? Wetmore is at the north end of the Hiawatha National Forest where Kyle was murdered. That doesn't make any sense," I said. "Why would someone up there be calling for me here? I don't even know anyone who lives there."

Nick mussed my hair and said, "Don't worry about it right now. Uncle Rudy is serving up some savory steaks so let's go eat. Your rendezvous with Joey Leeds is set for ten so it's going to be a long night."

Chapter Six

The sun had long since set behind the Miami skyline when Robby, Tony, Nick and I stepped off the *Morghanna* and walked to the black Buick. I had to concentrate on keeping my ankles straight in the four-inch-heeled sandals.

"Damn!" I yelled when a heel caught in a hole in the cement, twisting my ankle.

Nick caught my arm before I fell. "You obviously don't wear heels much, do you?"

"Function over fashion is my motto," I said.

"Actually, you look pretty hot. I'd ask you out, if I didn't know you so well," he said sarcastically.

"Please, I get enough abuse from Charlie back home."

Tony raised an eyebrow at me and held open the back door of the car. "Is that cop your boyfriend?"

"No, more like an obnoxious big brother," I said with a snort as I struggled to get into the back seat without my dress riding up over my butt and without knocking my wig askew.

"What if this thing comes off?" I'd asked Crystal while she'd applied my makeup.

"It won't, as long you don't do the alligator on the dance floor," she'd replied.

Nick slid into the seat beside me and reviewed the plan for the night as Robby drove to the club in South Beach on the other side of the island. "Tony will be within ten feet of you at all times, Robby will be at the bar and I will be in the car so you don't have to worry about Leeds attacking you. Just remember the script we rehearsed earlier. Relax, try to have fun. If you're nervous, he'll smell it in a second and get suspicious. Pretend you're onstage giving the best performance of your life. Strut a little, like your sleazebag husband doesn't know what he's losing."

53

My Aunt Gina's voice suddenly filled my head, telling me to take a few deep breaths and remember why I was doing this. Mitch. The man I was about to meet had pulled the trigger and ended my fiancé's life and, along with it, my life as I'd imagined it. Joey Leeds had eluded the police for years. Maybe I could bring about his downfall.

I was in a relative state of calm by the time Tony, Robby and I were strolling toward the bouncer, walking past the line of young, nubile, scantily-clad people eagerly awaiting approval for entry. Tony took the lead and approached the bouncer, a tall, bald, handsome black man with straight white teeth. The bouncer nodded as Tony leaned forward, whispered something in his ear and passed him a green roll of paper. Tony stepped back. The bouncer pocketed the money without looking at it, smiled, and lifted the rope for us to enter, ignoring the protests from the crowd. I smiled at him as we passed, eliciting a quick wink.

Once inside, I stood near the door and marveled at the scene. The last time I'd been to a dance club was New Year's Eve the previous year. Nick, Mitch and I had joined some friends from my neighborhood and spent the night partying downtown. My guess was that all dance clubs were pretty much the same—loud, colorful and filled with people at varying stages of intoxication. Techno music thumped from the speakers as we stood on a balcony that overlooked the lower level. To the left of us a long bar lined the wall and small circular tables were scattered around the balcony that circled the dance floor. Two glass and metal spiral staircases fed traffic from each side of the room down to the dance floor. A deejay stood on a raised platform in the corner below, encouraging the already-gyrating crowd to "pump it up" and raise their fists in the air. Robby tapped Tony on the shoulder and indicated he was moving into position by the bar.

I leaned toward Tony and yelled above the music, "Do you see him?"

He nodded and discreetly pointed diagonally from us. At one of the small round tables sat a small, thin man with his back to wall. His blonde hair was faded and his sharp, calculating eyes took in everything around him. He was alone. His pale blue Bermuda shirt lent him an almost effeminate glow.

"He looks like a rat in drag!" I said.

Tony laughed. "Yeah, I can see that. But don't let this appearance fool you. He's an assassin, a damned good one. One of the reasons he is so good is that he can blend into any crowd. You don't want someone like Crystal doing contract work. Too conspicuous."

"Right," I said and patted my wig to make sure it was still in place. "How do I look?"

Tony's eyes roved over me, taking in the entire package. "You look like a self-centered wife more interested in money than love, which is exactly what we need."

"Wow, that's not much of a compliment," I said and rolled my eyes.

"*You* are beautiful. I prefer the natural look, never did go in for all that make-up and skanky clothing. Guys who fall for that bit are always surprised they take home a ten and wake up with a two. It's all for show."

I couldn't resist stretching and giving him a peck on the cheek. "You're really something, you know that?" Then I adjusted my dress and said, "Well, it's showtime."

To make sure Leeds saw us, I sashayed down the steps in front of us and weaved through the writhing crowd, feeling Tony close behind me. As I moved, I felt myself relax and mentally step back as my new alter ego, Lisa Rollo, took charge. Smiling brightly at a young waiter in a white waistcoat at the top of the opposite set of stairs, I moved to let Tony in front since he would be making the introductions.

Leeds appeared to be surveying the dancers below but I could tell he was watching us from the corner of his eye. When we reached his table he stayed seated and simply raised his eyes in greeting.

"Mr. Leeds, this is Mrs. Lisa Rollo," Tony said and stepped back. Leeds nodded and stuck out his hand.

"I'm very pleased to meet you, Mrs. Rollo. Please, have a seat," he said in a crisp British accent.

The moment our palms touched I saw a flash of Mitch's face. It was dark save for the glow of lights from the dashboard in front of him. Then the image was gone. I was so rattled by it that I nearly lost my composure. I smiled thinly, withdrew my hand and sat down in the chair to his right.

"Lisa, it's just Lisa. I don't want nothin' to do with being Mrs. Rollo anymore," I sneered in my best Brooklyn accent.

"So I hear from Mr. Smith over there," he replied, dipping his head at Tony standing against the railing across from the table. "What is he to you anyway?"

"He's my assistant. Now, let's get down to business. I have other places to be tonight." I tapped my new fake russet-painted nails on the glass table and frowned. "I hear you're good at what you do—clean, no witnesses, no clues. Smitty there says you did a cop in Chicago last year. That's pretty gutsy, don't you think? How'd ya get away with that one? I'd think the cops would be all over you."

My guts felt like they were going to leap through my dress any second. Would he confess?

Leeds looked down at his drink (Scotch?) and then back at me. "I succeed, Lisa, because I select my clients with extreme care."

Well that didn't tell me anything.

"Fine. You got any references?" I said.

Chuckling, he replied, "Do you?"

"You know I do, but fair enough," I said, capitulating for now. "Smitty there probably told you my husband has a million dollar life insurance policy. I'll pay you one-third once I have the check in hand. You know how fussy insurance companies can be so it's gotta be clean."

Leeds was a tough person to read because his eyes never came to rest on a subject for more than a second or two. He didn't even blink when he said, "That is unacceptable. For that kind of work I will require a fee of five hundred thousand dollars with one hundred thousand up front, in cash."

I slapped my hands on the table and yelled, "Are you nuts? That leaves me with just half a mill."

"Lisa," he hissed, drawing out the name, "I'm sure your husband has other assets—a nice home in Miami Beach, perhaps a sports car or two, maybe even a vacation home in Maine." So he had checked the references laid out by Rudy Granati's network of associates. Was Leeds bluffing or had nothing seemed out of place to him, I wondered. If he wasn't bluffing, it proved that he could and did make mistakes. "I am also sure you will lead a comfortable life with your husband out of the way. If you really want him gone, find the money, now. I don't like to stretch things out for long periods of time. This has already taken several days too many."

I shifted in my chair and twirled a curl of hair between my fingers. After pretending to consider his counteroffer, I said, "Alright. You gotta deal. How do we work this?"

Leeds had the waiter bring another drink—Scotch—and asked if I wanted anything. To sound legitimate I ordered a screwdriver. I didn't know what it was, but I didn't plan on drinking it anyway. Once the waiter was gone, Leeds said, "Meet me at eight tomorrow morning at the Bayside Marketplace. I'll be waiting near the Port Boulevard entrance where I will arrive by speedboat. Look for a white boat with purple and gold detailing.

Bring several photos of the intended and the cash, nothing larger than a fifty."

The waiter brought our drinks. Leeds downed his in one gulp and then stood, shook my hand again and nodded at Tony. "It's been a pleasure. Good evening," he said and walked toward the bar and disappeared into the crowd, which was much larger and louder than when we had arrived. Tony grabbed my arm and said, "Let's get out of here. I don't trust that guy."

Robby met us at the front door. Nick was behind the wheel of the Buick and waiting in front of the club for us with the engine idling when we stepped outside.

"How'd it go?" Nick asked once we were all secured in the car and on our way back to Rudy's boat.

"We have a deal, but he admitted nothing. He certainly didn't deny killing Mitch though," I said as I slipped off the sandals and pulled off the wig, which made my scalp itch. Then I filled him in on the entire conversation, word by word.

Nick's jaw clenched. "He's definitely our shooter. Now we just need to get him to tell us who hired him."

"This guy's cool as a corpse and about as emotional. I think it will be tough to frighten him into a confession," I said. "If he's a former MI6 agent, he's been trained in tactics to resist torture so pulling out his fingernails won't help, if that's what you had in mind."

"We'll see," was Nick's only comment.

Robby asked, "What's the next step? Do we just show up tomorrow and grab him when you go to meet him with the down payment?" It was the first time I'd heard Robby speak all day.

"That might be too hard if he's planning to arrive in a speedboat," Tony said. "That's an effective mode of escape. He could disappear in minutes with all the islands, coves and little harbors down here."

Nick nodded. "We'll have to have the marketplace entrance to the marina covered. He'll probably want you to get on the boat. I'm not crazy about our chances if that happens so avoid that if at all possible. Keep an eye out for cops and people trying too hard to act casually. We want to avoid any attention from the law at this point. They'd just get in the way."

Once we were all back on the boat and settled in the stateroom, Rudy and Crystal joined us, the latter breathlessly asking how it all went down as she sat on the arm of Rudy's chair. When I told her about the image I got when I first shook hands with Leeds, she gasped.

"Wow, you must be a clairvoyant. How cool. My mother was one too," she said.

Tony and I briefed them on the plan and how Leeds had checked my fake references.

"You all must have done a great job of setting up my background. I was worried he would see right through me," I said and then wondered aloud, "Do you think he knew anything about Mitch's personal life?"

"You mean did he know about you?" Tony asked. "I doubt it. He probably learned all he could about Mitch's job and saw an opportunity there. It really was the perfect setup."

That last word triggered something in my memory. "Mitch wasn't supposed to work that night. He'd already worked eight afternoons in a row but the emergency officials figured the approaching storm would be fierce and cause considerable damage so they needed all the help they could muster. I remember now because we were going to meet at his apartment to go over some plans for the wedding. He called me at work to tell me he couldn't make it."

Nick leaned forward, startled. "Robin, that could be very important. That means someone within the department could have been feeding Leeds information. How else would he know to find Mitch on patrol?"

Tony shook his head and said, "Slow down, guys. You all would make lousy hit men. I'm sure Leeds had been watching Mitch for days, waiting for the right opportunity."

Nick smiled sheepishly. "Oh, right, yeah. I thought we had something there for a minute."

Grinning, Rudy said, "You earned your keep once again, Tony. Now, let's focus on tomorrow. We'll get the *Morghanna* maneuvered into position about a quarter-mile south of the marketplace by seven-thirty. Nick, Dr. Franklin retired down here last year. He has a Stinger speedboat that you will pick up at the marina in Bal Harbor around six and cruise the water near the Port Boulevard Causeway just north of Bayside. There's a channel that Leeds will have to shoot if he tries to bolt north. Robby, you will take your father's cabin cruiser and position yourself in front of us. Tony, you and Crystal will accompany Robin to the rendezvous."

I looked at Crystal in awe. She smiled and winked. "I can pack and whack with the best of them, if necessary."

"Where did you learn that?"

"I'm from Belfast, Northern Ireland. We moved to the U.S. when I was twelve. My father was a British soldier of Italian descent. My mother was Protestant Irish. Our life was, um, interesting."

Rudy patted her knee. "She can take care of herself. I'll also have a few more boys to stand watch at the marketplace. Sound acceptable?"

Everyone nodded except me. "What about the money?" I asked.

"It's already taken care of; I anticipated this," Rudy said and rose from the chair. "It's late, get some sleep. I have some phone calls to make."

Crystal also stood and took the wig from my hands. "C'mon, let's fluff this wig and figure out what you'll wear tomorrow."

When I was finally alone again, my face clean of makeup and my own hair falling around my shoulders, I stretched out on the bed and tried to absorb the craziness of the last few days. I didn't get too far because I heard a faint beep in the room. It took me a minute to realize it was my cell phone. I had set it to "vibrate" mode and tucked it into my purse before leaving the boat earlier in the evening and then tossed the purse on top of my suitcase when we'd returned. The beep meant I had a message. It was from Charlie who said to call him at home no matter how late. Now what had gone wrong?

"I'm beginning to think your whole family is nuts," he said when I returned his call.

"Why?"

"Because I just had to bail your aunt out of jail," Charlie snapped.

"What! How did she end up in jail?"

"Vale arrested her for trespassing. She crossed the crime scene tape at that student's apartment and went inside. Someone saw her and called the cops so Vale ordered her arrested. Robin, she's not going to let this thing go. I think she found something in there, but she's not saying squat to me," Charlie said.

I sank onto the bed and groaned. "Alright, I'll call her and try to talk to her. She's not going to listen, though."

Charlie chuckled. "Good luck with that. Why would she listen to you? You're doing the same damned thing down there in Miami. By the way, how's it going?"

"I don't know. I met the shooter. He definitely did it. It's almost like I saw it when I shook his hand," I said and thought about the vision that had flashed through my mind when we'd touched. "Anyway, the hard part comes tomorrow when we try to catch him. The people helping Nick and me are prepared. I can't figure them out, though. Nick's uncle is an accountant and Nick's cousin is an ex-cop from Chicago, but they sure seem to know a lot about criminal strategy and tactics."

"Comes from being a cop. Cops make some of the best criminals." Charlie oozed sarcasm.

"I don't mean that way. I guess I don't know what I mean."

"Are they with the mob?" he asked.

I was quiet for a moment and then replied, "I'd be naïve if I didn't believe there was some connection there. It doesn't really matter to me, though. I trust them. Hell, they might even be able to straighten out my aunt."

Charlie snickered again. "I doubt that. Keep me informed and take care of yourself."

As soon as I hung up, I dialed my aunt's home phone number, prepared to lecture her on the boundaries of the law. Unfortunately, she didn't answer. There was also no answer on her cell phone or at her office. It was past one in the morning. Where in the heck was she, I wondered. My aunt may have spent more than thirty years in Manhattan, but she was no match for murderers hell-bent on covering up their crimes.

Chapter Seven

*F*riday dawned clear with the sun casting a soft peach glow over Miami Beach as I stood on the deck of the *Morghanna* and enjoyed the solitude of a tropical morning. I'd been awakened by the low rumble of the three diesel engines when the pilot had started them at about five-thirty. We were now gliding out of the Miami River Marina heading west. The Coast Guard station and the MacArthur Causeway were on the starboard side where I was leaning against the railing, savoring the gentle movement of the yacht. We then skirted the northern side of Dodge Island where the cruise ships docked. A few of the mammoth liners were in port, quiet before the onrush of eager vacationers. As the boat rounded the northwest edge of the island and pointed her nose toward the Bayside Marketplace on the mainland, footsteps approached from behind. I turned and smiled as Tony joined me at the railing and handed me a cup of coffee.

"This is my favorite time of day," he said and drew in a deep breath of salty air.

I nodded and sipped the strong brew. "Mine too. It's so serene. You can almost imagine a life without worry—just peace."

The boat slid into a visitor's slip at the Bayside Marina next to the marketplace. Tony, Crystal and I would have to disembark soon, but I wasn't ready to break the solitude just yet. I liked Tony. Not only was he smart, but he seemed unafraid of life, not just that he was cool under fire, but that he was free to love and care about those around him, and show it. I wanted to know more about him.

"What are you doing with Rudy? Do you work for him?" I asked.

He leaned his elbows on the rail and shrugged. "Not really. He's my uncle and Nick's my cousin. We're a tight family. We've been through a lot together. When Nick called and said he needed assistance, I came down from Chicago and helped Uncle Rudy set this thing with Leeds in motion. I quit the force right after Thanksgiving so I had some time on my hands."

"That's right, I'd forgotten about that. What will you do once this is done?" I asked.

"I'll probably find another law enforcement job. It's not like I have a bad record, I just got sick of the crap some of the cops were pulling. They all had excuses, but I couldn't stomach it. I didn't get into law enforcement to make money or hold power over people."

He looked down at his cup, swirled the liquid and then gazed back at me. "It would probably sound nuts to Nick but I'd love to live in a place like the U.P. or northern Wisconsin. I like the woods, the water and the slower pace. I haven't told any of them yet but I got a job offer from the public safety department at the university in Superior, Wisconsin. Do you know where that is?"

I nodded. "It's on the other side of the river from Duluth. It's a nice area, maybe five hours from Escanaba," I said.

Tony grinned. "I like the sound of that."

I started to respond when Crystal popped her head out the side door to the lounge. "Hey, Lady MacBeth, it's time to get into character again."

Groaning, I handed Tony my cup and said, "I hate that wig. It may look great but it's itchier than starched wool underwear."

Forty-five minutes later I morphed back into Lisa Rollo, black widow wanna-be, wearing the wig, too much makeup and an orange jumpsuit that was only a little less conspicuous than what deer hunters wore come November 15 in the U.P.

"I feel like a walking pumpkin," I said, checking my reflection in Crystal's full-length mirror. She, of course, looked fabulous, with her long glossy hair pulled up at the sides and falling softly across the back of her white satin blouse and faded hip-huggers.

By seven-forty-five, Tony, Crystal and I were strolling through the Bayside Marketplace, still quiet and devoid of shoppers. While I clutched the handle of the black briefcase full of money, Crystal carried a white handbag, her right hand buried inside around the grip of a .357 Magnum that "kicked like a captured leprechaun" she'd teased when I watched her stash it in the purse. Two men dressed like Tony, in dark slacks and short-sleeved shirts that hung loose over their waistbands (presumably to hide more weapons) stood at the northeast end of the marina, waiting to radio Tony as soon they caught sight of Leeds. I couldn't see them but I knew

Nick was floating north of the Port Boulevard channel while Rudy and Robby were keeping watch in the water south of the marketplace.

My nerves grew more tense with each minute. I glanced at my watch for the hundredth time.

"I don't like this. He's already ten minutes late," I said. "This guy doesn't strike me as the type who would be late for an appointment."

Tony's two-way radio finally crackled with Nick's voice. "He's going into the channel now. Be prepared, he's got a go-fast boat."

"Roger, clear," Tony responded and motioned for Crystal to hang back at the edge of the marketplace.

I got into character mentally and strutted toward the rendezvous point at the northern edge of the marina that hugged Port Boulevard where it began its ascent over the Miami River toward Miami Beach. Leeds rounded the corner of the dock, cutting a deep swath in the water. When Nick had said Leeds had a go-fast boat he wasn't being flippant. The growl of the massive twin engines underneath the rear cowling filled the air as he maneuvered into a slip. At nearly forty feet long, it was white with metallic purple and gold stripes and had seats for five people but there was no doubt this thing was built for speed, not pleasure-cruising. I heard Tony whistle behind me.

"Now that's a boat," he said. "Bet he's doing a little runnin' from the Coast Guard in his spare time."

If I'd known anything about boating, I'd have been concerned by how loosely he tied the craft to the mooring. Instead, I stood with the briefcase and waited anxiously for him to step up onto the dock. When he was finally beside me, he stood close and eyed the briefcase.

"Open it," he ordered.

I clicked open the locks and gave him a peek at the greenbacks inside. He fanned one stack, nodding with satisfaction. "Excellent," he said with a sly smile.

Meanwhile, Tony and the two hired hands moved in and prepared to spring. Leeds was ready. He tossed the case into the boat, pulled a .40 caliber semi-automatic pistol from his waistband and wrapped his left arm around my throat before I had time to react. He first pointed the gun at my head and then at Tony.

"Now, Mr. Smith, if you will kindly step back, Miss Robin Hamilton and I will go for a little ride."

I'm in trouble, I thought, as I was pushed from the dock into the backseat of the boat. Leeds jumped in front, fired up the engines and pulled away from the dock without bothering to untie the loose rope. He somehow managed to keep the gun pointed at me and steer toward the channel under Port Boulevard. Tony, Crystal and the other two men were running toward the end of the dock, guns drawn, but we were already out of range. I thought about jumping but I wasn't a strong swimmer and he'd probably shoot me in the water. I'd have to bide my time and be ready for an opportunity to escape.

I didn't have long to wait. As we started to turn left to enter the channel I saw a flash from the top of a large building on Dodge Island and heard a high-powered gun blast. I hit the deck, waiting for another shot. When none came after about five seconds, I poked my head around the portside front seat. Leeds was slumped over the wheel, a bullet hole where his right eye had been. I screamed and then panicked when I realized the boat was headed straight for the cement east wall of the channel. I pulled Leeds to his left and tried to remember all those episodes of *Miami Vice* I'd watched as a kid, where Sonny Crockett skillfully maneuvered cigarette boats around Miami. I grabbed the wheel, steered through the channel, missing an oncoming cabin cruiser by just a few feet, and pulled back on the throttles, finally bringing the boat to a stop. In his own speedboat, Nick roared up along the port side and yelled for me to wipe down the wheel and controls with my sleeve, grab the money, and then jump into his boat.

"What about the cops?" I yelled as I wiped any fingerprints from the boat.

"Never mind. Let's go!"

I grabbed his outstretched hand, jumped into the cockpit of his boat and fell backward when he hit the throttles, roared through the channel and headed south for the Keys.

"Jesus Christ!" I screamed. "Why are we running? We didn't kill him! Did we?"

Nick shook his head furiously. "No! Leeds was hit by a high-powered rifle. They might have been aiming for you. The cops can't protect you from a sniper."

I suddenly felt like I was melting into my shoes. As I sank to the floor of the boat, a mantra began to drone in my head—"Mitch, what the hell were you into? Mitch, what the hell were you into? Mitch, what the hell …"

❋

We joined Rudy around eleven after docking the boat at a private residence at Newport on Key Largo and boarding the *Morghanna* at a nearby public marina. Somewhere along the way Rudy had retrieved Crystal and Tony, who seemed relieved that I was still functioning, although I felt far from whole mentally.

"What the hell happened today? How did he know who I was?" I asked and ripped off the wig. "Did he know all along? Who killed him? Were they trying to hit me? Why did they quit firing when he went down? Am I fugitive now? I can see my face in post offices across the country. Robin Hamilton, public enemy number one!"

Nick sat in his chair in the lounge and stared at me in amazement. "I'm glad to see you're taking this so calmly, kind of reminds me of your aunt."

"Sure, crack jokes. I just saw a guy's head get drilled and you're making like a comedian. Great. Where's the laugh track? Is David Letterman going to pop out from behind a curtain?" I yelled as I paced the floor, the spacious yacht suddenly feeling cramped.

Tony just shook his head and threw his hands up. "We missed this one by a mile. We knew there was another player but none of us anticipated this. That shooter was on the roof of the Marine Spill Recovery building, which means he had to be using a sniper rifle and was trained to use it because it's pretty damn hard to hit a fast-moving target a few hundred yards away."

"Did anyone see anything?" Nick asked.

"A couple of people saw a tall, thin, pale man with a Dolphins ball cap, jeans and dark green long-sleeve shirt on the roof when the shot was fired. Then he was gone. The Dade County Sheriff's Department found the clothes in a garbage Dumpster nearby." Tony paused and pointed at me and said, "Nobody paid any attention to you. They saw the boat Nick was driving but couldn't identify it."

I flopped down next to him on the couch. "Well, that's a relief. How did you learn all that?"

"It pays to have a friend in every port," he said, stretching his legs out and smiling. "So, what do we do now, Cousin?"

Nick tapped his fingertips on the arm of his chair and stared at the ceiling for a moment before standing and walking to the portside wall of windows that now looked out over the southern edge of Key Largo as we headed back toward Miami. Finally, he turned to all of us and said, "My guess is

Leeds was tipped off between last night and this morning. He might even have been set up by someone else. I don't think he suspected you were anyone other than Lisa Rollo last night. There actually is a couple named Nick and Lisa Rollo here in Miami; they're friends of mine and agreed to let us assume their identity for a couple weeks. That made it easy to see if Leeds was serious about taking the job by checking references. He called the company where Nick Rollo works, he checked with their neighbors, everything. I'm convinced he bought the cover, so someone had to tip him off."

"But who?" I asked. "Was it the person who called for me at the hotel? You said that call came from a woman at a pay phone in the Hiawatha National Forest. There aren't too many payphones in that area. The only one I can think of right now is outside a little grocery store on the federal highway that runs north-south through the forest. The odd thing about that is a student of my aunt's was murdered there this past weekend at his family's cottage about six or seven miles from that store."

Tony cocked an eyebrow and straightened his solid frame on the couch. "Really? That's interesting."

Speaking for the first time, Rudy waved his hand in disagreement. "No, it's not. Think about it. It's probably some neighbor of the student's who heard you were involved, called your office, found out you were on your way to Miami and tried to track you down," he said.

I had to laugh. "You have no idea how logical that sounds, especially for Yoopers. That's probably exactly what happened. I'll call the news clerk on Monday morning and see if anyone called for me. I didn't tell her where I was going but I'm sure my editor would have told her," I said and then looked at Nick. "Back to Chicago?"

Nick nodded. "For me, yes, I have few things I want to check regarding Leeds' activities around the time of Mitch's murder. Tony, I want you to go to Escanaba with her," he said, pointing at me. "I have a hunch we poked a stick at this snake and made him angry. He may come after you, Robin."

My usual I-can-take-care-of-myself-just-fine-thank-you attitude failed to materialize. Instead, I agreed to everything Nick planned. Although warm and sunny, Miami was turning out to be a dead-end and I was worried about my aunt. Besides, I didn't think I'd mind Tony's company.

Chapter Eight

N̄ick, Tony and I braced ourselves against the wind and light snow howling across the parking lot at O'Hare International Airport after being delayed one day by lousy winter weather. We'd spent Saturday stuck in the Miami airport waiting for a flight to somewhere within a hundred miles of Chicago. Now that we'd made it that far, we had to search for my Subaru Outback, seemingly miles from the terminal. We finally found it under a foot of drifted snow.

"This sucks!" Tony yelled above the wind. "How the hell did they even manage to land the plane?"

As Nick loaded our luggage into the cargo area, he replied, "The flight attendant told me the worst of the storm had passed by about ten this morning. We got lucky."

"This is lucky?" Tony growled.

"C'mon guys, let's move it. We've already lost a whole day," I said as I brushed the snow off with my arms.

I was anxious to get back to Escanaba and check on Aunt Gina so I dropped Nick at his apartment and stopped at Tony's place so he could trade his Miami clothes for flannel shirts, jeans and a parka. As I drove north through intermittent flakes, we talked about Mitch and me meeting after the murder of a wealthy young woman in Crescent. Tony had seen my fiancé a few times with Nick but hadn't known him well.

"Nick was really fond of him, though," Tony said. "He seemed to bring out something paternal in Nick, like he was his little brother or something. It really tore him up when Mitch was killed. We did a lot of legwork that first month afterwards but got nowhere."

I looked at him and scowled. "I wonder why Nick never mentioned you were helping him," I said.

Tony shrugged. "I don't know. Nick and I have always been close but we're very different men. He had a much rougher upbringing than I did.

His old man did some work for the higher ups in the mob. Nick Sr. pissed off the wrong person somewhere along the way and was run down in the street outside his house when Nick was fourteen. He saw it happen. It definitely wasn't an accident but nobody would say a word about it. Ever since then Nick's been waging an internal battle between staying on the right side of the law and joining the Outfit."

"Where does your Uncle Rudy fit in all of this?" I asked.

"Rudy's the brains in the family. He was a senior partner in one of the big accounting firms in Chicago until he retired two years ago. He figured he had enough money and wanted to spend more time with Crystal. Anyway, Rudy helped raise Nick. The rest of the kids, two girls, were grown and out of the house when Nick Sr. was killed. Rudy saw all that aggression and encouraged him to go into the military and then law enforcement, hoping to channel some of that energy into something worthwhile. The problem is that the majority of Rudy's business involved laundering mob money in the seventies and eighties by buying legitimate businesses. The Outfit has appeared clean as a bleached towel for a long time now, thanks in part to my uncle's efforts. That connection is like a blood-bond, it can never be broken. That's enticing to a guy like Nick who would like nothing better than to get the guy who killed his father."

"Wow, sounds like the plot of a movie. How come your family didn't step in for Nick?"

"My dad tried for a while, but he didn't approve of the mob associations. He's a retired high school history teacher and has spent his life with his head buried in a book. I'm a lot like him in that I love to read but, like Uncle Rudy said, I still have the Granati temper and that tends to make me unsuitable for academic pursuits. I get frustrated with bullshit. The public schools around Chicago are smothering in it," Tony said with a grim chuckle.

"Just before we left Chicago, Nick said something I'm still trying to digest—that there is no law, only honor. Do you believe that?"

Tony looked at me intensely. "Do you?"

I gripped the steering wheel and thought about the difference between the code of law and the code of honor. "The world would certainly be a better place if everyone lived by a code of honor rather than a maze of laws."

"Sounds almost Biblical, doesn't it?" Tony said. "That was the gist of Jesus' teaching. Justice is in the eyes of the person wronged."

I wasn't too big on discussing religion so I suggested we stop for lunch just north of Green Bay. The snow had stopped, the roads were clear and I was hungry so it seemed the ideal time to take a break. We found a little family restaurant just off U.S. 41 and enjoyed a buffet dinner as people around us speculated about the Packers' shot at another Super Bowl title the following season. As we were getting back in the car, my cell phone rang. It was my aunt calling from her office.

"Where the hell have you been?" I asked as soon as I hit the connect button. "Charlie called me two nights ago and said he had to bail you out of jail."

She actually giggled. "You know, that was really sweet but I could have handled that myself. Besides, it was worth it. I don't want to talk about this on a cell phone, though. Where are you?"

I told her a little about what had happened in Miami and who was with me now, leaving out the part about almost getting shot.

"Great! Come straight to my house. You two can bunk there for the night and we can talk."

It was going on six-thirty Central time, an hour behind Rapid River, so we wouldn't be at her house until nearly ten but she said she didn't mind. "I'm too excited to sleep," she said and hung up the phone.

Tony looked at the exasperated expression on my face and cocked an inquiring eyebrow at me.

"My aunt. She and Crystal just have to get together."

Aunt Gina was waiting at her front door when Tony and I pulled into the driveway, freshly plowed of snow. I parked in front of her two-car garage and jumped out to greet Belle who waddled quickly to meet me. She covered me with kisses while I laughed and scratched her floppy russet ears and thick body.

"This must be the dog Mitch got you for Christmas two years ago," Tony said and knelt down to pet her. Belle gave him the once-over with her snout, apparently approved of what she smelled and lapped him a few times on the face.

My aunt stamped her feet on the porch and yelled, "Get inside! It's freezing out here."

The temperature had dropped throughout the day and was now sliding below the zero mark. As we retrieved our luggage from the rear of the Outback, I asked Tony, "Are you sure you want to move north? Florida may be crowded but it's a heck of a lot warmer."

Tony grinned and took my suitcase from my hand. "Nah, weather like that makes you soft."

A half hour later we were situated in front of a soothing fire in my aunt's living room eating homemade fried chicken and sweet potato pie.

"Where did you learn to cook such great southern food?" Tony asked.

She chuckled and said, "My roommate in college was from South Carolina, descended from slaves. She now runs a huge chain of restaurants down south and still sends me recipes."

I studied the crispy, well-seasoned coating on a leg and said, "I think preparing and sharing food is a way of saying you care, a form of therapy. I always feel better after eating a home-cooked meal."

"That's the point, dear," she replied and patted my leg. "So, tell me what really happened in Miami."

With Tony filling in some of the behind-the-scenes details, I reviewed my initial meeting with Joey Leeds at the club and then his shooting the next day. From her large jade silk pillow on the floor next to my chair, she gasped and said, "That means whoever killed him is still out there and probably looking for you."

"Maybe. One thing has been bothering me though. Why not just kill me if they're so concerned that I might learn something?"

Tony shook his head as he wiped his fingers on a cloth napkin. "They can't. Too many people are involved now. They'd have to eliminate all of us and whoever is behind this likely thinks that Uncle Rudy has connections with the Outfit. I don't care who you are in the crime world and how tough you act, you know better than to mess with them if you want to stay alive."

"What's the Outfit?" Aunt Gina asked with a frown.

"The Chicago mob that traces its roots back to Capone," Tony explained.

She turned to me and grabbed my hand. "Are you enlisting the mob? Good heavens, Robin, do you realize what could happen simply by associating with those people? When I lived in New York there were always stories in the news about people with mob connections getting shot or vanishing without a trace."

Tony leaned forward from where he sat in the corner of the couch and said, "That is not going to happen here because the Outfit is not directly involved in this case. All I'm saying is that my uncle allegedly has some loose connections to them. That simply means that there is a perception that Robin is protected. For now, that perception may be what's keeping her alive."

My aunt sighed and threw up her hands. "I don't like this at all but I guess there's nothing I can do. It sounds like Mitch made some very powerful enemies."

I stood and began pacing the floor. "It also means we're back to having no idea who might have hired Leeds. Nick's theory that it could be that disgraced bank VP is losing value. That guy's not going to have the physical resources to track both me and Leeds and then have Leeds killed. I think we need to look at large-scale criminal operations."

Nick had already ruled out mob involvement so I asked Tony what was left?

He rubbed his chin and considered the question. "I never worked narcotics, but I have to believe it's tied to that. For one thing, Leeds was driving a boat that is notorious for drug running in South Florida. Also, you had said something about Mitch being seen with a dealer about a year ago. Officially, he may not have been working a case, but what if he was working a lead for someone else?"

"Like who?" Aunt Gina asked.

Tony rubbed his hands together and replied, "Well, it's not unheard of for the state or feds to work with local police departments on specific investigations."

"Don't you think the chief of police would know about it though?" I asked.

"Not necessarily, not if the chief is under investigation. Besides, I doubt that guy—what's his name, Harper?—I doubt Harper is telling you everything he knows."

"He did say the various jurisdictions were tripping over each other," I said and stopped pacing to sit on the floor next to Belle, stretched out on her side in front of the fireplace. "Harper sure doesn't trust Nick so he probably wouldn't be straight with me now that Nick and I are working together. So how do we get around this? Nick already tried talking to the Crescent cops and got nowhere."

Tony replied, "They probably don't know anything, anyway. Look, since we're here, let's see if we can find out who called for you from that little grocery store in that national forest. Maybe that's a clue."

I looked at my aunt. "Any ideas?"

Shaking her head, mystified, she said, "I don't know anyone who lives around there and I didn't tell a soul where you were going so I can't imagine this has anything to do with Kyle's murder."

As I stroked Belle's side and felt the comfort of her rhythmic breathing, I said, "That reminds me, what were you doing in Kyle's apartment? You know you can't enter a designated crime scene without permission."

She grinned slyly. "I'd love to tell you what I've been up to since you've been gone, but ..." she said and then eyed Tony with doubt. "Do you have an open mind?"

Oh brother, I thought, this ought to be good, but Tony burst out laughing. "Are you kidding? My family is Sicilian. We're just about the most superstitious people around. My great-great-grandmother was supposedly the village wise woman back in Sicily."

Aunt Gina beamed. "How wonderful! So was mine, except she lived near Hamburg, Germany." She jumped up and trotted to her bedroom. When she returned, a little black address book was clutched in her hands. She tossed it to me. "That's what got me arrested," she said.

"What is it?" I asked as Belle sniffed the book. It smelled faintly of cigarette smoke, liquor and something I couldn't identify. The cover was sticky from traces of adhesive tape.

"Let me start at the beginning," she said, repositioning herself on her pillow. "You know those shows on television about the police enlisting psychics to probe crime scenes and see if they get any visions? Well, I figured the best way to get in touch with Kyle was to go to his apartment. It was Friday so I figured the police would have gone over the place and removed the tape, but they hadn't done so. I didn't want to wait so I let myself inside the same way I did before, credit card. I looked around and didn't see anything different from when I was in there before he died. It's a studio apartment with a kitchenette and a sofa bed that was pulled out. I sat on the bed, closed my eyes and focused on his face and voice in my mind. That's when I smelled the marijuana smoke in the bedding, like there had been large-scale partying going on in that apartment. Kyle had recently bought a new car, I mean a brand new car, a Pontiac something-or-other. He worked at the hardware store in the mall so he didn't make much money and, from what he said about his relationship with his parents, I didn't think they'd bought it for him. That made me wonder if he was maybe dealing pot. I started exploring every piece of furniture, cupboard and floorboard for a hiding place for the dope. That's when I found that."

She pointed at the book in my hand.

"It was taped to the bottom of a few floorboards under the corner of the carpeting, which had been lightly tacked into place. I had every intention of turning it over to the police until I looked through it. Check out page forty-eight."

I flipped to the page and saw the name Sean Vale. "That's Detective Vale's son," I said and then studied the entry. It contained his name, a phone number and a series of numbers and letters that formed some sort of code. Glancing through the rest of the pages, I saw a few more names I recognized and the same format. "It almost looks like a customer list."

"Exactly," she said. "How could I give that detective the book if his kid was listed in there? It might disappear into the incinerator."

I had more faith in Vale than that but I couldn't deny the possibility that he would try to protect his son even if the guy could shed some light on a murder case. "How did you manage to hang on to it? The police must have searched you when you were arrested."

"Easy, my coat pocket had a hole in it so I pocketed it as soon as the police arrived and then when they led me downstairs, I ripped the fabric a little more and let the book drop to the ground once we were outside. Then I kicked it under a Dumpster. I retrieved it later that afternoon when Charlie sprung me from the clink."

I rolled my eyes and Tony suppressed a smile.

"And here I was, worried I would be Public Enemy Number One when my aunt is putting Bonnie Parker's memory to shame," I cracked and began to study each page of the book. When I flipped to the next page after Vale's I blinked at the name Steve Wojokowski, who most people recognized as Steve "The Breeze" Sampson (his middle name), the longtime manager of the only hard rock/heavy metal radio station in the area. A note next to his name read "Tu 1 ER".

I tapped Steve's name and said, "I know him. He's been rumored to be an addict of some sort for decades. Heroin would be my guess considering his spacey behavior. I would bet a month's pay that you're right about this being some sort of record of people buying drugs." I then handed the book to my aunt and asked if she recognized the handwriting. She scrunched up her nose and shook her head.

"No, this certainly isn't Kyle's writing. His was much more legible."

"Did he have a roommate?" Tony asked.

She nodded and said, "Sort of. He was dating a girl who spent a lot of time at his apartment. I never met her. I think her name is Shasta."

I just about choked on the chamomile tea I had been sipping. "Shasta Burns? That's the only person I've ever met with that name. It's got to be her."

"Is that some relation to your publisher?" Aunt Gina asked.

"Yes, that's his daughter. The last time I saw her was about two months ago. She was at the mall buying a party dress. She looked like hell, with her hair a bleached mess and dark circles around bloodshot eyes, like she was coming off a three-day drunk. I almost didn't recognize her."

"Certainly sounds like drugs to me," Tony said and reached for the address book. As he paged through it, he nodded. "Kind of like something bookies use—that was my line of work with the CPD, vice."

"What were you planning to do with this information?" I asked, dreading the answer.

"I want to find this Shasta person and talk to the Vale kid. I figure I have some leverage. "Tell me what this is all about or I'll go to your father," she said.

Tony laughed quietly. "You sound like my uncle's business associates. I have a better idea though, how about Robin and I work that angle while you ask around the college. Classes must be starting soon."

She nodded but looked disappointed. "Classes start tomorrow. I have a few students I can approach, although I was kind of looking forward to playing the heavy."

"Where are you getting these ideas?" I exploded. "You're going to get yourself killed. If Kyle's death is related to drugs, you could be dealing with some major dirtbags. I've already lost one person to scum, I have no intention of losing another."

She sighed. "I suppose you're right, but you have to promise to tell me everything you learn."

Tony pocketed the address book and winked. "Sure thing."

"There's something else," Aunt Gina said, shifting on her pillow. "This will probably sound odd. Well, maybe not, considering the source. I couldn't help feeling someone had died in that apartment recently."

Just what we needed—more dead bodies.

74

Chapter Nine

*W*e were all up early and out the door by eight the next morning. From her bungalow in Rapid River, I drove behind my aunt but within sight just to make sure she went straight to her office at Bay College in Escanaba. Since classes were starting she would have little time for extracurricular investigations but I wanted her to know that I was keeping an eye on her.

"So what's our first step, boss?" Tony asked with a grin as soon as we left the house. He looked like he was ready for anything. I, on the other hand, wearied at the prospect of more adventure.

"I would feel a lot better if at least one local cop knew what was happening," I said. "My friend Charlie Baker is a detective/sergeant at Escanaba Public Safety and is the most trustworthy person I know. He'll have some ideas how to handle the info in that address book."

"I am so glad to hear you say that. I don't like playing the rogue cop, especially since I still want to be a cop for a long time. That sort of thing doesn't look good on a work record. Besides that, it's dangerous," he said.

At the college, we watched from a distance as Aunt Gina parked her black Toyota Prius in the lot closest to her office. She waved in our direction before disappearing into the building.

Tony laughed. "She's great. I like her spunk."

"Nick said she reminds him of his mother," I replied as I pulled back on to the highway and drove toward the public safety department on the near north side of town.

He nodded. "Yeah, I can see that. She had to be spunky to handle Nick."

Charlie's SUV was in the parking lot behind the building, as was his unmarked brown Chevy Malibu. We waited in the lobby until he finished a phone call and then followed him back to his office when he came out to greet us. The room was small, with antique metal furniture left over from the department's location in the old city hall back in the sixties but he didn't seem to mind.

I made the introductions and sat back to listen as Charlie and Tony swapped background information.

"Vice detective, eh? That must have been interesting. Why did you quit?" Charlie asked.

"It's a long story, but it comes down to me just needing a change of scenery. The day I was promoted to sergeant was the same day I found out my lieutenant was taking bribes from a gambling ring. It was too much for me so I told him off and turned in my badge." Tony waved his hand as if to dismiss the whole episode. "Anyway, I'm taking some time to think. I have a job lined up with the police department at the university in Superior, Wisconsin. I can start the first Monday in February. Until then, I'm helping Robin and my cousin Nick."

Charlie nodded approvingly. "Sounds like a good move. I know I couldn't see myself working in a big city," he said and then looked at me quizzically. "I know you didn't come here to socialize so what's going on? Why aren't you at work?"

I told him about getting fired/quitting while in Miami.

"What the hell got into Sam Burns? That doesn't sound like him," Charlie said.

"I don't know. I'll be paying him a visit today, too. The reason I'm here is you were right when you thought my aunt had found something in Kyle Sullivan's apartment." I told him about the address book and its cryptic code.

He threw his hand up and snorted with disgust. "Great, just great. Do you realize that's a felony? How the hell is she planning to explain that one to Vale?"

"She didn't turn it over to the police when she was arrested because she found a name in there that made her think they might intentionally misplace the book," I explained.

He raised a reddish-brown eyebrow and adjusted his tie. "Go on."

"Sean Vale. Isn't that Tom's kid?" I asked.

Charlie heaved a sigh and nodded. "I'm not surprised, but I had hoped that when he started classes at Bay this past fall, he was turning his life around. You remember Greg Connor from last summer's bit of excitement?"

I nodded. Connor had met an untimely end due to some unfortunate associations.

"Well, Sean and he were buddies all through high school and afterwards. They got into a fight over your former publisher's daughter about a year ago, which is why Sean was out of the picture when Greg got into trouble."

"Who ended up with Shasta?" I asked.

"Sean."

"That's convenient. My aunt said Kyle was providing shelter to her occasionally these last few months. Maybe we have a motive for Kyle's murder—jealousy," I speculated.

Tony spoke up. "The sooner we find this Vale kid, the better, not to mention Shasta."

"Wait. There's more," I said and told Charlie about the radio station manager, Steve Sampson.

"That's another thing that doesn't surprise me," he said. "Everyone in the county knows he's a doper but we haven't been able to pin anything on him. Any other treats in that little book of tricks?"

"A few names I recognize but nothing special," I replied.

"Where's the book?"

Tony looked at me and I nodded. He pulled it from his shirt pocket and tossed it to Charlie who paged through it, committing its contents to memory. When finished, he ran his fingers over the still-tacky cover.

"It was taped to the bottom of some floorboards," I explained. "What are you going to do with it?"

Charlie leaned back in his chair and glowered at the tiny black book.

"You're aunt put us in a hell of a jam. She means well, though, so I don't see any point in making things worse for her. That said, this book," he tapped the cover with a long forefinger, "could contain key evidence in a murder investigation so I'm going to make sure it's clear of our fingerprints and drop it in the mail, addressed to the sheriff so at least someone else sees it before it gets to Vale. It will probably arrive tomorrow, giving us a little time to sniff around quietly and try to come up with something on Sean Vale and Shasta, just in case the good detective tries to cover for his son."

Tony nodded. "I like it. Are you free to help us on this?"

Charlie shrugged. "Things are quiet for now. I've got a few break-ins to look into, but I can spare some time. What about your fiancé's case? Is that resolved?

"I wish," I said and explained what had happened on Saturday. "I'm back here to follow up on that phone call from the grocery store while Nick tries to track down more information on the shooter's movements when Mitch was killed. We may be facing a dead end, though. These people have done an excellent job of covering their tracks."

Charlie tapped his mustache and narrowed his eyes. "Maybe, maybe not. The location of that phone call is curious. You know, the U.P. has long been a hideout for criminals from Chicago, Milwaukee and Detroit."

I laughed skeptically. "You mean the people behind Mitch's death could be right here? That's absurd." I stood and touched Tony's shoulder. "C'mon, we've got work to do. I'll see if I can track down Shasta through her father. Do you have an address for Sean?"

Charlie turned to his computer and clicked through a couple of screens before he grunted and said, "This address is about five months old so I don't know if it's accurate. These kids move around a lot." He wrote it down on a yellow Post-It note and handed it to me. Sean lived on some obscure side road near Rapid River.

"Where is this?" I asked.

"Got me. The Rapid River zip code covers a lot of territory," Charlie said.

"Good thing my car gets decent gas mileage," I replied and opened the door to the hallway and then turned back to Charlie to add, "Let's meet back at my aunt's house at seven tonight. Do you remember where it is?"

Charlie nodded.

"Good." To Tony, I said, "Let's find Sam Burns."

Sam's truck wasn't parked behind the newspaper even though it was past nine, but that didn't deter me. He would have a month-end and year-end report to prepare for the corporate suits and often liked to work on those at his home office, free of interruptions. As we drove to his house about two miles past the small county airport, I showed Tony my apartment and the one-story house where I'd grown up. My dad wouldn't return from Europe until the end of the week but the neighbor had kept the driveway and sidewalk free of snow. The sun was bright today but it was bitterly cold. I tuned in Steve Sampson's morning show just as he was giving the weather report—continued cold, highs around zero, with a huge storm system moving down from western Canada. If it moved over Lake Michigan, we could expect more than a foot of snow in a few days.

Steve "The Breeze" had adopted George Carlin's Hippy Dippy

Weatherman to his own radio persona, except it wasn't much of a stretch for him. I listened for a few more minutes as he traded risqué quips with the news director and turned it off, annoyed by the prattle.

"How do you want to work Shasta's father, if he's home?" Tony asked.

"Solo," I said. "Something in my gut tells me it wouldn't be a good idea for him to see you."

"Right. Since the airport is on the way, drop me off there. I'd like to call Nick and then check out who keeps private planes there. Sometimes that can be valuable information."

I did as he asked and then found Sam at home in his large tan brick ranch house with a huge front yard on highway M-35 and a wide backyard that bordered an ice-covered beach and deep blue water beyond.

Sam's shock was evident when he opened the door. "Robin! What are you doing here? Did you go back to work?"

"No, Sam, I meant what I said to Bob. I have to quit. I just wanted to let you know it's nothing personal. I understand it's a company thing," I said and fumbled for the right way to ask about Shasta. As always, I stuck with the straightforward approach. "Sam, I also need to ask you some questions about Shasta."

He sighed and rolled his eyes, stepping back to let me enter. I followed him down a hallway to the left of the front door and into his study. A wall of glass provided a splendid view of the lake, but the sun's glare off the snow was blinding. Sam, however, didn't seem to mind as his desk was situated such that his back was to the window. How odd, I thought, as I sat in a brown velvet Queen Anne chair in front of his desk. He sat behind the massive cherry desk and spun around to face the water. After several seconds of cold silence, he said, "Now what's she done?"

"Did you know she was dating Kyle Sullivan?"

"Who?"

"That kid who was beaten to death in the Hiawatha National Forest about a week ago," I said. Why wouldn't he look at me?

He finally turned to face me, scowling behind his thick-framed spectacles.

"No, I didn't know that. Did she kill him?"

Stunned, I stuttered, "No. I don't know that. I don't think so. I mean, do you think she's capable of murder? This was one ugly crime scene."

He stared at me, ice in his eyes. "Robin, have you ever met my daughter?"

"Yes, at a picnic at Camp Harstad about eight years ago," I said.

"What did you think of her?"

I squirmed in the chair and hesitated.

"Well, um, she seemed like a typical teenager. I remember she really hated her first name—Emma right?—and wanted to be called Shasta. I only talked with her briefly so my impression might not have been entirely accurate."

He laughed bitterly.

"That's why you're such a good reporter. You know how to BS your way in and out of situations to get the story," he said and then clasped his hands in front of him on the desk and looked me in the eye. "I'll tell you what you thought of Shasta. You thought the same thing everyone else does except her mother—she's an inconsiderate, obnoxious snot. I'm sure it's strange to hear that kind of statement from a father but let me clue you in on a bit of family history since it will help you understand the situation."

He settled back in his chair and stared at the space above my head for a few moments before launching into the semi-sordid tale of Shasta Burns.

"By the time we moved to the Upper Peninsula so I could take this job, Sam Jr. was eleven and Shasta was four so no one knew that I had adopted Shasta. In fact, you're only the second person I've told since coming here nearly eighteen years ago. Janet and I just felt it was no one's business. You see, my first wife, Sam's mother, died in a car accident when he was seven. She was a second grade teacher and was driving to school one morning when some idiot who had been driving all night, fell asleep, ran a stop sign and plowed into her doing about seventy miles an hour. She was killed instantly. Sam was in the back seat and somehow survived with just a few bumps and bruises.

"I met Janet a year later when I stopped by her wine shop for a good bottle of Chardonnay. Her life up to that point had sounded like the plot of a soap opera—born to rich parents who showered her with clothes, cars and money, but little attention; married a talented but self-centered plastic surgeon in suburban Chicago who dumped her and their two-month-old baby when his well-endowed receptionist captured his fascination. Rather than wallow in self-pity or run back to her parents, she learned everything she could about the sommelier business and started her own shop in Evanston, catering to the same crowd that her ex-husband nipped and tucked. We married a year and a half after we met. Shasta's father agreed to me adopting her since it would release him of any financial obligation and he never planned to be a part of her life. Sam seemed to enjoy having a little sister, although, unfortunately, he and Janet weren't bonding well. I was head of the advertising department at the Arlington Heights Daily Herald when I saw the advertisement for the publishing job up here. We decided a change of pace would be good for the whole family so we didn't hesitate when I was offered the position. Janet took time off to raise Sam and Shasta and then started another sommelier shop here, which I might add, has been immensely successful, something we weren't sure was possible in such a rural area," he said with a shake of his head and then fell silent.

I waited for him to tell me how Shasta fell in with a crowd that did drugs, but he seemed lost somewhere.

"Sam, yoo-hoo," I called and waved at him.

"Oh, sorry," he said but he just looked at me as though he'd lost track of where he was going.

"What happened with Shasta along the way that made her turn to drugs?" I asked.

Sam took off his glasses and rubbed his eyes, which were ringed with bluish purple circles along the lower lids.

"I've asked myself that question about a million times over the last four years," he said, adding when he saw my shocked expression, "Yes, this has been going on for at least four years. It started with drinking, then she moved on to marijuana and now she's doing God-knows-what, although she does seem to have backed off the hard drugs lately. Janet has been in denial. 'It's just a phase. Don't worry about it. If we nag her, it will only make it worse,' she has said so many times the words play over and over in my head. I tried to talk to Shasta, I tried to let her know I wouldn't judge her if she came to me with problems, I tried to support her when she wanted to try a new sport or hobby. All I ever got were smart remarks about how no one understood her and she wished she could go live with her 'real' father. Keep in mind, this was a man who had nothing to do with her until she was about 13 and then, after suffering a mild heart attack, decided he needed to rectify his past wrongs and develop a relationship with Shasta. It was after spending a month with him in Chicago that she came home with an even worse personality and demanded to be called Shasta. She even wanted to take his last name, Wolf, again."

"Wait a minute; they named her Emma Shasta Wolf? Were they hippies?" I asked.

He chuckled, the first genuine laugh he'd emitted all morning. "I wouldn't call them hippies since both of them are focused on money. Mainly they just wanted to name her something different. Apparently they honeymooned somewhere near Mount Shasta in California so I guess it was appropriate," he explained and then grew serious again. "Anyway, after about two years of this nonsense with her, I have washed my hands of the whole thing and now let her mother deal with her."

Addictions are often passed from one generation to the next but I knew Sam didn't use drugs. He rarely drank more than a glass of wine with dinner when I'd seen him out on the town. I hardly knew Janet but she was always so full of energy and charm that I had a tough time picturing her needing to get high on an artificial substance. Sometimes people just fell into the trap of substance abuse for no reason other than stupidity and human weakness. Unfortunately, knowing Shasta's background did little to help me figure out what, if anything, she had to do with Kyle's death. I said as much to Sam.

"I can't help you when it comes to him. I never met him. But I will say that Shasta is a very attractive young woman, at least she used to be, and can be quite charming when she wants to be. She's never had a problem attracting men, but she never seems to keep one in particular around for too long," he said and then paused, narrowed his eyes and finally added, "To be honest, I haven't seen much of her in about a year. My son got married four years ago and lives in the Houghton area where he's working on his PhD in mechanical engineering at Michigan Tech. He and his wife had twins a year ago. I made it clear that if Shasta wanted to see her niece and nephew when they visited, which is quite often, she would have to clean up her act. She told me to do something which is anatomically impossible. Now she only comes around to beg for money from her mother when I'm not around. Although, as I said, the last time I saw her, which was Christmas, she was looking more alert, more 'with it.' I don't know, maybe Janet's right, maybe it is just a phase and she's ready to grow up. I just hope and pray she had nothing to do with this young man's death."

Sam slumped in his chair. I felt like putting my arms around him and telling him everything would be alright, but I didn't know if it would be alright. Instead, I said, "I'm so sorry, Sam. I had no idea you were dealing with all this. I never knew about your first wife either. To be rejected by Shasta like this, after everything you've done, must be very hard."

He looked up at me with glistening eyes. In a thick voice, he said, "Yes, it has been hard, but it's my burden, not anyone else's. Please keep this to yourself."

"Of course. None of this is relevant to Kyle's case right now anyway," I said and shifted in my chair before I added, "But, Sam, you must know that if it turns out she is involved in some way in his death, the police will find out and they will release it to the media."

He sighed heavily and nodded. "I know, I know. Listen, I'm sorry you felt you had to quit. You have no idea the pressure I'm under right now. Sometimes I'm very sorry I moved here."

"I'm sorry too, Sam," I said and showed myself the door when he turned back to the lake, lost in turmoil.

Chapter Ten

*T*ony was waiting at the edge of the parking lot in front of the small terminal at the Delta County Airport. He jumped in the car and rubbed his gloved hands together and then held them up to the heater vents.

"How did it go with Sam?"

"He claims he doesn't know where Shasta is and that he doesn't care. Apparently, she's been a wild child and he's done playing zookeeper," I said. "He looked terrible, like he hasn't slept well in days. I know ad revenue is down at the paper. I wonder if his job is at stake."

"We've got our own problems. That bank VP? He moved to Seattle last week to work at some big bank out there. Nick said it's clear that Mitch arresting him may have ended his career at LaSalle Bank, but he landed on his feet so we can scratch him off the list of suspects."

"I never liked that idea anyway. Like I said before, he doesn't have the resources," I said. "What else did Nick say?"

"He took an Interpol photo of Leeds to various bars and neighborhoods around Crescent last night. He got a positive I.D. at a bar three blocks from the police station and at the house across from Dmitri Karastova's house."

"The hundred-year-old Russian arms dealer?" I asked.

Tony laughed. "He's not quite one hundred, more like eighty-five. The neighbor said the old man is an invalid but a woman in her early fifties has been showing up periodically for the last four or five years to check on him. Seems that this neighbor saw Leeds at the house two, maybe three, times last spring. He's not sure, but he thinks that every time Leeds was there, so was the woman."

"So who's the woman?"

Tony shook his head. "Nobody knows. She shows up with a suitcase about four times a year, usually in a different vehicle each time, stays a week or two and then leaves. Nick tried to finesse the hired help at Karastova's house but they pretended they didn't speak English. She could be his daughter. She'd be about the right age."

"What's the daughter's name?" I asked.

"Nobody knows. The kids were already grown when the old man and his wife bought that house in the mid eighties, right around the time the oldest son died in that boating accident in Florida. The old lady died about five years ago."

"That's when the woman showed up. Maybe she's a mistress," I said.

"Nah, a mistress would spend more time there and they have a live-in nurse. My guess is that it is the daughter, probably estranged from her mother, came back when the old woman died," Tony said and then rubbed his stomach. "I'm hungry. Let's grab some grub and sit someplace where we can talk."

We stopped at one of Escanaba's myriad fast food chains, ordered the healthiest things we could find on the menu and found a parking spot in the line of spaces west of the Sand Point Lighthouse at the northern tip of Ludington Park, just a few blocks from my apartment.

Little Bay de Noc had yet to freeze over, but the water snaking up between Escanaba and Gladstone looked frigid, lapping at ice crusted near the shore as we ate and sipped our drinks, diet soda for me and milk for him. From late March until December, ore freighters would deposit coal for the nearby power plant and pick up iron ore pellets delivered via rail from the mine to the north near Marquette. Today, though, all that broke the surface of the water was the occasional whitecap stirred up by a northwest wind and a few seagulls diving for a bit of dinner.

I asked if he learned anything interesting at the airport. Tony scowled and said, "Not really. They're mostly small single engine planes, not something you would use to get across the country quickly. One guy told me to check at Sawyer International Airport south of Marquette. He said they've got some private jets."

"Okay, let's move on and say for the sake of speculation that this woman is Karastova's daughter taking over the family business and Mitch caught wind of it," I said. "What business are we talking about? Is she an arms dealer? Drugs? How do we find out who she is?"

Tony munched his chicken sandwich and shrugged.

"Does Nick want us to come back down to Chicago?" I asked.

"Nope. He still wants us to work on that phone call. I had him check that address Charlie gave you on Google. He came up with a map and e-mailed me the directions. I've got them on my cell phone. The house is off a county road several miles west of the forest highway. What's say we head to that grocery store first and then the kid's house on the way back before we meet up with Charlie?"

"Sounds like a plan," I said and finished my salad before putting the car in gear and heading back to the highway.

I wasn't expecting to learn much at the Hiawatha General Store since the call to Miami had been placed at eight thirty-seven, more than an hour and a half after the store closed. Fortunately, the owner lived across the highway from the business and kept a close eye on people using the payphone in the parking lot after hours.

"We've been broken into so many times in the last twenty-five years that I've lost count," said the grizzled-but-amicable storekeeper. Hooking his thumbs in his hunter orange suspenders, he rocked back on his heels and told us about the late night caller.

"The wife and I had a big floodlight installed a long time ago so we got a real good view of that parking lot. There were two people in the truck—a red and black or dark gray Dodge, older, little bit of rust around the wheel wells. I don't know who the people were but I know I've seen that truck around here before. One person got out of the passenger side of the cab and used the phone, not too long, maybe ten minutes. The person had a list and dialed several times."

"Could you see whether they were male or female?" I asked. We already knew the caller was a female but maybe the question would trigger a memory in the old man.

He shook his head and tugged on his beard. "Couldn't tell one way or the other. Both of them was wearing toques. But, you know, I can't be too sure but it looked like maybe the one making the calls had long hair tucked into the collar of the coat, like girls sometimes do." He pointed at me and I touched the back of my hair where the hood of my parka covered it at the neck.

"Any ideas?" I asked Tony.

He shook his head. To the storekeeper, he said, "We would really appreciate it if you would give one of us a call as soon as you spot that truck again." He wrote our cell phone numbers on the back of one of his old CPD cards. The storekeeper turned it over, read it and eyed us with curiosity.

"This a criminal thing?"

"It's possible," Tony said. "We're not sure yet. It would help if we could talk to those people, though."

The storekeeper agreed to let us know if he saw the pickup again so we left and drove the twenty-five miles back down Federal Forest Highway 13 to U.S. 2, both feeling perplexed.

"I don't understand any of this," Tony said. "Why would anyone up here care if you were in Miami unless they needed to track your movements? It just doesn't make any sense. It sounds like the caller was going off of a list of hotels and just happened to hit on Uncle Rudy's. The only reason I can think of is that someone up here knows a lot more about your fiancé's murder than you realize."

"I doubt it, but I do have a theory that might be less of a stretch. What if it was Shasta Burns, Kyle Sullivan's girlfriend? What if she heard I was at the crime scene and wanted to talk to me?"

"How did she know you were in Miami?"

"I'll call the news clerk at the *Daily Press* and see if she talked to anyone," I said and dialed the number but it was another dead end. Amy was more interested in learning why I really quit, although I did finally get her to tell me that not a single person had called for me since Tuesday. The message light on my phone wasn't even blinking.

I cursed and flipped the phone shut. "Nothing."

Using the directions Nick had sent for Sean Vale's address, we finally found it after a half hour driving down an endless string of gravel roads. The mobile home looked abandoned. The driveway hadn't been plowed and two windows on the ancient trailer were shattered.

"That was a waste of time," I grumbled as I prepared to turn the car around.

"Not necessarily. At least we know he's not here," Tony replied. Always the optimist.

Sean did have one elderly neighbor, a woman about a quarter-mile down the road who said "the kid" had moved about two weeks prior, taking a few boxes and the TV and stereo and leaving the rest for the wild animals to claim for nests. She said Sean never caused any problems and even cut her grass a few times. He had lots of friends who came to visit at all hours of the day and night but they were quiet. "No wild parties."

Back in the car, Tony asked, "Now what? It's only a quarter to four."

"Good question," I replied, stalling.

While I plotted our next move, Tony watched the landscape change as we hit the main highway across the southern U.P. and headed west toward the town of Rapid River. Open fields mingled with stands of hardwoods and evergreens while the occasional modest house provided a glimpse of civilization. Some of the houses dated back to the turn of the last century when farming and logging were the lifeblood of the local economy. Logging was still important to the area but, other than a few dairy or potato farms, agriculture employed few people. Like everywhere in the nation, the population was aging and getting fat so health care had taken over as a key jobs-provider in the region. That thought made me wonder what the medical examiner had to say about Kyle Sullivan's death and if the autopsy was complete. Delta County no longer had a pathologist so it took longer to get autopsies done here than in more urban areas.

"Maybe I should check with Detective Vale and see if there's anything new on Kyle's case. We don't seem to be getting anywhere with Mitch and Joey Leeds," I said.

"What about his son?" Tony asked.

"I'll play dumb. Heck, he might not even see me since I'm no longer a working reporter."

Vale didn't seem to know or care if I was still with the Press when he met me at the front desk of the sheriff's department, but he had no new developments to report. The autopsy had been completed, confirming that Kyle had died of blunt force trauma and that his blood contained traces of uppers and downers. Vale's frustration was evident when he said, "No one's saying a damn thing. That's odd for our local scumbag population. Every agency in the county has been ordered to question anyone they arrest about the murder. Usually you can find one or two who will spill the beans on some other scumbag in order to get a break, but nobody is saying anything. Two of our deputies said they arrested a drunk driver early this morning that obviously knew something but denied ever hearing about the case. They said the guy acted scared out of his mind when they started asking him about it."

"Maybetheguywasjustafraidthecopsweretryingtopinthemurderonhim," I said.

"I thought of that, but one of the deputies was Lee Grenville, that new guy. He has a real friendly, easygoing manner that proves especially useful in questioning suspects. They get careless around him because they see him as a friend," Vale said.

"Any confirmation that it's drug related?" I asked.

Vale ran a hand over his balding head and seemed to be debating how much to tell me. He jerked his head to the door at the end of the counter that led to the offices and the jail. After we were in his office with the door closed, he seated himself behind one of the neatest-looking desks I'd ever seen and stared at the wall behind me for a few seconds before saying what was on his mind.

"Robin, as I said before, I have a lot of respect for you as a journalist. You really know what you're doing and you've never done a thing to jeopardize an investigation," he said.

"Thanks, I appreciate hearing that, but I no longer work at the *Daily Press* so don't bother trying to flatter me," I said, squirming under Vale's intense gaze.

He waved a hand and said, "Whatever. The Burns clan isn't too high on my list of favorites anyway. But, hey, you might want to do some stringer work for Milwaukee or Detroit, if this story turns out to be as big as I think."

He leaned forward and lowered his voice, "As soon as I heard the victim was Kyle, I figured it was drug-related because most of his friends were in the business either as users or pushers, or both. As for trying to flatter you, maybe I was, but we can help each other out here. Let me clue you in on what NOMIDES and the local departments have been working on lately. Maybe between us we can put some pieces together."

"Tom, you've never asked me for help before. Why now?" I asked.

"I'm desperate. I don't like to admit that, but it's true," he said and shifted in his chair.

"Do you know Steve Sampson?"

I nodded. This interview was turning out to be a lot easier than I expected.

"Sampson's a dealer, fairly high up the ladder in terms of local power. We've been watching him for about a year and have traced some pretty significant buys for everything from coke to methamphetamine all the way up to him. We were just about ready to nail him when this Kyle Sullivan bought the farm. So obviously we're holding back a little now to see if maybe we've got something to bargain with, you know what I mean?"

I frowned and shook my head. "Not really. I'll admit that when it comes to drugs, I'm pretty much out of the loop. My friends and I never got into that scene. I follow that maybe if Steve is involved with Kyle's death, you can use that to get him to roll over on his suppliers, but where do I come into the picture?"

The detective leaned over his desk, clasped his hands in front of him and fixed his gaze on me. "As far as we know, he doesn't have a clue that we're on to him. He's been dipping into his own stash a bit too often lately and is getting careless, if you know what I mean. We can't go undercover with him because he's been in the U.P. too long. He knows too many of the cops. So I want you to go talk to him, feel him out, see what he offers."

"Are you serious? I'd have to go to court and testify, just like you. The defense would rip me apart," I said.

Vale was unmoved. "We'd fit you with a bug and have NOMIDES there as back-up."

How could I even consider this? Hadn't I just failed at undercover work? Should I tell Vale the last guy I tried to set up was murdered? On the other hand, what if Steve Sampson had ties to the people behind Mitch's murder? That possibility was beginning to sound less far-fetched.

"Alright, I'll do it."

I agreed to show up at the sheriff's department at eight the next morning to get briefed and fitted.

"What about that Chicago cop that was up here last week? Is he available?" Vale asked. "I'd feel better if you had a pro go into the radio station with you."

"No, Nick's not here right now, but I have another friend who might be able to help, a former Chicago cop," I said. "By the way, what did you mean when you said the Burns family didn't rank too high on your list right now? Are you referring to Shasta?"

Vale fiddled with his already-loosened knit tie and shrugged. "Yes and no. Shasta hangs with the same crowd as Steve and is probably a runner for him. When we went to her parents' house yesterday, her mother told us to beat it. I've known Janet for quite a few years and, to be honest, I always found her to be a bit hoity-toity. For Christ's sake, a wine shop in Escanaba? What's next, a Tiffany's? Will Northern Motors start selling BMWs?"

"I don't know her, but from what I hear, the shop's doing okay so somebody must be buying the stuff," I said.

"It's not that I don't like wine. I don't like that citified attitude that says 'I'm better than you because I'm from Chicago.' Tell it to someone who cares, I say," he said with a wave of his meaty hand. "I've never had any issues with Sam Burns, though. He seems like a good enough guy, if a bit stand-offish at times. Probably can't get a word in edgewise with that wife around."

"Getting back to Shasta," I said, "do you suspect she was there when Kyle was killed?"

"You make sure and ask her if you find her before I do."

As I left the building, it occurred to me that this morning Sam had said nothing about the police visiting the day before. He'd even denied knowing Shasta was seeing Kyle. He probably hadn't been home and his wife hadn't said anything about it since he was estranged from the girl, I told myself and joined Tony in the car. He smiled at me and said, "Nick's on his way. He said you may have some important information in your possession. He wouldn't say what though."

Puzzled, I said, "I can't imagine what it would be. Anyway, he can help me play wannabe drug addict."

"Say again?"

I explained Vale's idea as we stopped at my apartment for some fresh clothes and to pick up my mail (junk, bills and two postcards from my dad) and then drove to my aunt's house in Rapid River. Tony wasn't crazy about Vale's idea and said, "You do live dangerously. You fit right in with the Granati clan."

Aunt Gina was already home and preparing chicken cordon bleu when we walked in the door. Tony groaned and said, "I hope you have a treadmill or something here, otherwise I'm going to gain about ten pounds of flab."

She dropped the knife she was using to slice the chicken breasts, spread her arms wide and laughed. "A treadmill? Do I look like I use a treadmill?" she said and pointed to her slightly plump figure. "Honey, I strap on a pair of snowshoes or hiking boots and go for walks in the woods. That's the extent of my workouts."

"I've never tried snowshoeing," Tony said with interest. "Sounds like fun."

Aunt Gina grinned and pointed to the corner of the kitchen where a pair of metal frame snowshoes and ski poles leaned near the back door.

"Go on, give 'em a try. Robin and I can handle dinner. Just don't get lost."

Tony looked like a kindergartner with a new toy fire truck and said, "Cool!"

Tony and I went outside and got him ready. I'd never realized my aunt had such big feet, convenient for Tony since the straps, with a little adjustment, fit over his boots perfectly.

"Remember to float," Aunt Gina called from the back door as Tony faded into the crisp, cold night with Belle trotting along beside him on a wide trail through the woods, the only sound the fwish-fwish of the frames on the crusty snow. She shut the door and went back to prepping the chicken while I checked the potatoes boiling on the stove. My aunt didn't believe in using instant mashed potatoes.

"Tony seems like a good man," she said after a comfortable silence. "You seem to blend well together, as though you've known each other a long time."

I sat on a stool across from her and rested my chin in my hands. "I do feel a natural sort of closeness with him, but I just met him four days ago."

She smiled knowingly. "Sometimes that's all it takes."

I stirred the cordon bleu mixture absentmindedly. "I know what you're getting at, but I don't know if I'm ready. I still love Mitch."

She took the spoon from my hand and began efficiently stuffing the breasts. "You will always love him. That doesn't mean you can't open yourself to someone else. You have a great capacity to love. I can't believe Mitch would want you to spend the rest of your life alone."

"No, I know that," I murmured, now wishing I had gone with Tony into the woods, not because I wanted to avoid this conversation but because I liked being with him. But getting involved with Tony would mean Mitch was really gone. I felt a lump form in my throat at the thought of letting go. Shaking it off, I said, "What about Tony's family connections?"

"Alleged connections, dear," she corrected as she rolled the chicken in bread crumbs and put the pan in the oven. "Besides, that doesn't mean he's working for them. Every family has some dark clouds in its background. We each determine our own destiny apart from our families, if we're strong. Tony is strong. Don't use his family as an excuse to avoid something wonderful."

"So you approve?"

She laughed. "I approve. I think even your crabby old man will approve once he gets back from gallivanting across Europe. I still can't believe Sophie convinced him to go overseas. He hasn't been out of the country since he got back from Vietnam."

I showed her the two postcards from him, scrawled in his quick hand, saying he was having a great time but missed me. I could tell she was about to crack another joke about him when there was a knock at the front door. I looked at the unicorn-shaped clock above the stove. Ten minutes to seven. Charlie was never late. As I went to let him, I said over my shoulder, "Don't start planning my wedding just yet, okay?"

Aunt Gina gave me an angelic smile and went to work on the potatoes.

Charlie had just settled at the kitchen table with a cup of coffee when Tony clomped through the back door with Belle, snowshoes in hand and cheeks flushed with cold and exertion.

"That was great! There's no moon so the stars are bright as rhinestones on black velvet. Beautiful!" he extolled as Belle buried her head in her food dish.

Charlie got up and slapped him on the back. "We have a convert, a born-again Yooper."

We spent the next hour eating and sharing information. Charlie was stunned by Vale's request for help.

"They must really be low on resources, although he does have a point about Sampson knowing all the cops. There's no way any cop in the U.P. would get past him. He's been around too long and does broadcasts from events all over the region," he said. "Do you think Nick will help you with this?"

I looked at Tony who nodded. "Definitely. He lives for this stuff. He'll be here around eleven tonight, if that's okay with you," he said and glanced at my aunt.

She smiled wickedly. "Poor Robin and me, stuck in a house full of gorgeous men. Whatever shall we do?"

Tony actually blushed.

Chapter Eleven

Nick drove up in a black Mustang less than five months old and covered with road salt.

"Nice car but not very practical ," I quipped as I held the front door open for him.

"Style, baby. It's all about style," he said and ran a hand along his slicked-back hair. I stashed his suitcase in the corner of the living room and told him to sit and try not to mess up his hair while I got him something to drink.

Charlie had left a few hours before Nick's arrival and Tony was watching the eleven o'clock news with my aunt and the three dogs. Before departing, he'd left a photocopy of the address book my aunt had found in Kyle's apartment. As Nick made himself comfortable in the living room and got acquainted with my aunt's cooking, I explained both the address book and Detective Vale's plan to use us to get to Steve Sampson.

"Charlie thought you should take a look at that book in case you saw a Chicago connection. He said a lot of kids head south after high school, get in trouble and then come home to get straight," Tony explained.

"You recognize anyone?" Nick asked his cousin.

Tony made a zero sign with his left hand while he caressed Belle's head with his right.

"How's that detective going to react when he sees his son's name in that book?" Nick asked. "He's not going to be happy to get the damn thing in the mail."

"What else could we do? Auntie there put us in a bind," I said and sat next to Tony on the couch as my aunt innocently fluttered her eyelashes at me. "Anyway, Charlie seems to think Vale is fully aware of his son's issues."

I then explained what Tony and I had discovered that afternoon at the general store and Sean's former residence.

"For now, let's forget that damn phone call. It's not getting us anywhere. I'll help you with that Sampson guy tomorrow, for your sake, my lovely," Nick said with a smile and bowed his head toward my aunt who beamed. "Then we need to head over to your apartment for what might be a pretty painful task."

"What's that?" I asked nervously.

Nick stretched out his legs and studied his nails for a moment. "On a whim, I stopped by Mitch's parents' house. They're great people, so normal," he said and paused, lost in some memory. "His mother said she gave you the flag that had draped his coffin and a large shoebox full of cards, mementos and journals. We need to read those journals."

"I never knew he kept a journal," I said. Just how much had Mitch not told me? Suddenly I felt very cold. I pulled a magenta fleece throw around my shoulders and frowned. "All that stuff is in the cedar chest I got for my sixteenth birthday. I haven't even opened it since I moved here in May. I—I couldn't."

Tony put his arm around my shoulder and passed me a tissue.

"It'll be alright. Maybe it's time," he said softly.

"Maybe."

Early the next morning, after a long restless night where I got little sleep, Tony went to work with my aunt to mingle with the students while Nick and I drove to the sheriff's department. The temperature had risen to around ten degrees and thick clouds had formed overnight.

"What are we going to be looking for when we read those journals?" I asked.

Nick picked some dog hairs off his pants and said, "I'm not sure. I knew Mitch liked to write a little, but I didn't know he'd kept a journal either. I hope he recorded his thoughts about the job and not just some bad poetry and love letters to you."

The thought of love letters from the grave made me want to cry so I changed the subject. "Did you get a chance to look through the photocopy of that address book?"

He nodded. "I did, and I found one name that caught my eye, Mandy Miller, a woman I questioned who discovered the body of a fellow hooker on the Northwest side about six years ago. Mandy's probably from around here and came home to try and clean up her act. She had a nasty heroin habit when I knew her."

"If she's in the book then it doesn't sound like she's been too successful," I said.

Vale and two scruffy undercover detectives from NOMIDES were waiting for us when we walked into the building shortly after eight. Both detectives looked vaguely familiar and then I realized one was an Escanaba Public Safety office and the other a sheriff's deputy. They had taken temporary assignments with the narcotics team in order to get some investigative experience and develop an understanding of the local drug community. Trying to buy drugs when you looked like a cop wouldn't work so NOMIDES detectives typically grew their hair long and let mustaches and beards sprout on their faces to alter their appearance.

The five of us gathered in a conference room to review the plan they had developed. All I had to do was wear a small listening device clipped near the collar of my parka, introduce Steve to Nick and tell him we were in need of some pick-me-up pills for Nick's sister. Depending on whether Steve bought my story, the detectives might have use for me again later. The "bug" took just a few minutes to install and test and then Nick and I set out for the radio station in Gladstone. Vale and the detectives followed in the department's marked Chevy Tahoe and would park about a block away from the radio station, ready in case something went wrong.

I wasn't nearly as nervous as I'd been Friday night preparing to meet Joey Leeds. This was a simple conversation that wouldn't take much acting on my part. Tony and my aunt had been concerned but Nick would be at my side and Steve and I had always gotten along well so I didn't expect trouble. We had become acquainted when I started working at the *Daily Press* nearly ten years ago and our paths would cross at various media-oriented events. When I last saw him, he'd been in his late thirties with a long dusty brown ponytail, glasses and a thick flowing mustache that made me think of a pirate. He'd earned the nickname "The Breeze" because of his breezy informal delivery on the air. A native of the Detroit area, Steve had been working his way up the ladder to increasingly larger markets as a disc jockey and even had his own afternoon show during prime "drive time" in Milwaukee at one point. He had ended up in Delta County managing the small but profitable station at the eastern end of Delta Avenue in Gladstone, a pleasant residential community of about forty-five hundred people. Steve had never explained his trip back down the ladder of success other than to say he had "needed a different environment in order to thrive."

I'd long suspected he was abusing some substance because he seemed to suffer strange lapses in memory during normal conversations. Sometimes he would stop talking in mid-sentence, as though his mind paused, and then start talking about a different subject. We'd lost touch in the nearly seven years since I'd moved to Chicago so it would not be too far-fetched to have befriended the kind of people who were into drugs.

I parked the Outback in a diagonal slot in front a century-old red brick building on the 900 block and looked around. The downtown had undergone a makeover in recent years with new streetlamps patterned after the gas lights of the late 1800s and other quaint touches. The effect was attractive and inviting—if you were a fan of the Victorian era.

I was about to open the door to the station when it was pushed in my face, knocking me to the ground. A pale young woman with long blonde hair bowled past me, yelling over her shoulder, "Fuck you. You can't treat me this way, asshole."

Shasta Burns. She was awfully strong for someone who supposedly had a drug problem. Nick helped me up and I brushed off my pants as we watched her get into a rusty maroon Chevrolet Corsica and drive west toward the highway. No doubt, like me, she had come to see Steve. Hopefully, we wouldn't end up leaving in the same manner.

As soon as I opened the door again my ears were assaulted by Judas Priest's "Ram It Down." I remembered the song being popular when I was in high school; now it just gave me a headache. It was a good match for the royal blue shag carpeting and dark paneled walls. The station looked like some heavy metal hell with colorful, some even nightmarish, vintage concert posters plastered on the walls. The place smelled like my neighbor's apartment in college—like a beer and pot party had been held a week ago and no one had aired the place out since. But there was something else underneath that smell, like chemicals burning. I tried to resist breathing through my nose.

Steve, his hair now grayer and in an even longer ponytail, was standing in the studio behind a college-age guy seated at the control board. He was trying to explain how all the little buttons and knobs worked and what gauges to monitor. He caught a glimpse of Nick and me from the corner of his eye, started to smile, froze and then darted out of the studio and down a long hallway to the back of the building with Nick at his heels.

"Get some back-up! This guy's a fugitive!" Nick yelled over his shoulder.

I ran after them but the back door slammed in my face.

"Vale! Steve took off on foot as soon as he saw Nick. The guy's a fugitive," I yelled into the bug as I jerked the heavy steel door open and searched left and right down the alley for some sign of them. Then I spotted them. "They're running west through the alley between Delta and Minnesota, about two blocks from the station."

I watched in horror as Steve reached around and pulled a gun from the waistband of his jeans. I started to scream but Nick was ready. He dived behind a green dumpster with his .45 in hand. Steve fired blindly back down the alley and kept running. I screamed into the bug that Steve had a gun and then started to run after them but Nick saw me as he emerged from behind the dumpster, held up his hand and took off running again. He was a good six inches taller than Steve and in a lot better physical condition so it didn't take long to catch him. Steve turned and was about to fire again when Nick leaped and hit him square in the back of the knees, sending them both sprawling to the ground. Steve tried to fight but Nick had him in a headlock before he could get to his knees. Sirens wailed from every direction but a Gladstone Public Safety patrol car was first on the scene, screeching to a stop just as I caught up to them.

Steve's face was red and his faded Levi's were torn in both knees where he had skidded on the pavement.

"Fuckin' lousy pig. What the hell are you doing' here? You ain't got no authority in this town, asshole," Steve ranted.

Nick smiled sweetly and said, "My, my, my. Still a mouthy little bastard, aren't you?"

As Vale and the NOMIDES detectives jumped out of the Tahoe, the Gladstone officer yelled, "Would someone please tell me what's going on? Who are you?" He pointed at Nick as Steve was jerked to his feet.

Nick pulled out his badge and handed it to the officer. "He's right, I don't have any authority here. But this man is wanted in Chicago for two murders in the late nineties. His name is Steven Walter Kazansky. If you run his prints, you'll find a match," Nick said and shoved Steve in the direction of the patrol car.

"Steven Walter Kazansky? I thought your name was Steven Sampson Wojokowski," I said stupidly.

"Quiet! Is that true, Steve? Are you wanted for murder?" Vale asked.

Steve just glared at all of us.

"Okay, I guess that's good enough for me for right now. I'll bring him in and then we'll call the Cook County DA," the Gladstone officer said as he handcuffed Steve and put him into the back seat. Steve tried to struggle but the officer had about fifty pounds on him and was used to dealing with unwilling suspects. Leaving Steve to sulk in the patrol car, he pulled out a small leather notebook and turned back to Nick, Vale and me. "By the way, I'm Sergeant Dan Cheever," he said and shook hands with Nick.

"Detective Sergeant Nick Granati, nice to meet you."

Cheever looked at me and smiled. "I've seen you around the department. Robin Hamilton, right? You work for the paper. Getting quite a reputation for sniffing out trouble, I hear."

"That's me, never a dull moment," I said with a smirk, not bothering to tell him I quit the *Daily Press*.

Cheever wanted us to come back to the department and fill him in on more details about his illustrious captive. Vale, meanwhile, was as close to "hopping mad" as I had ever seen someone.

"This blows the whole goddamn case now," he yelled, froze in mid-gesture and then grinned like the Grinch on Christmas Eve as an idea popped into his head. "That is, unless he wants to make a deal."

"That's not up to me," Nick said, stepping back. "Down there, we leave that stuff up to the DA's office. Our job is just to haul in the garbage. They sort it out."

Vale ignored him, herded the detectives back into the Tahoe and followed after Cheever.

As Nick and I walked back to my car, I said, "You recognized that guy right away, even after all those years."

Nick shrugged. "It's part of the job. It's not so much memorizing faces as it is characteristics about a face. He looks quite a bit different than when I last saw him—longer hair, more gray, the mustache, but he can't hide that circular scar above his right eyebrow. Someone in Calumet City took one of those four-pronged tire irons and jabbed him with it about twenty years ago. He's lucky he survived. It must have given him a pretty nasty concussion."

I drove to the station on the northeast side of town and listened intently as Nick recounted his experience with Steven Kazansky, aka Steve "the Breeze" Sampson Wojokowski. It turned out that Steve had risen to the rank of a mid-level enforcer for a dealer out of Chicago in the eighties and nineties before the cops caught up to him.

"He was never the smartest guy in the bunch, just brutal," Nick explained. "He wasn't afraid to break kneecaps, and since he never went alone, his small size wasn't a problem. That's what makes him all the more contemptible. He doesn't even know how to handle himself in a good clean fight. The other guys didn't respect him much and finally somebody squealed when we picked up one of his helpers on an assault charge. Son of a bitch was leading a double life. Mister DJ by day, Chicago pusher and thug by night. I've got to hand it to him though; he eluded us for a long time. He must have hid out up here after we tried to corner him in Chicago. I never suspected he had a real job."

Cheever called the Chicago PD and the district attorney's office, confirmed there were multiple felony warrants out on Steve and that they would be sending someone to bring him back to Chicago in the next few days, after he'd been arraigned and the extradition papers put in order.

"Well, Nick, we do appreciate your help. Sorry your vacation couldn't have been more peaceful. It's amazing the things that can happen to you when you're a cop," Cheever said. "By the way, why were you going to see him anyway?"

Vale stepped in and said, "Long story. They were trying to help us on an investigation though. We can transport him to the jail, save you the time."

Cheever nodded. "That's fine with me. I bet he's already got a lawyer so I doubt he's going to talk, but maybe you've got something to bargain with now."

Vale thanked Nick and me for our help and released us from duty. He still wasn't happy with the surprise of Steve being a Chicago fugitive, but he probably had another surprise waiting for him at the jail when he saw that address book. Charlie said he'd included a note saying it was the property of Kyle Sullivan so the sheriff's department would have a frame of reference. Whether it led to anything remained to be seen.

As I drove toward the college to meet my aunt and Tony, I thought about how I was an eyewitness to a little too much crime lately. I said as much to Nick.

"You would have made a good cop. You handle yourself well when the heat's on. That's important."

"Don't you think I'm a little small for that job?"

"Are you kidding? Some of the best cops on the CPD are just little things like you. It's got nothing to do with size. The majority of police work nowadays is up here." He tapped his temple. "Those ladies who are on the small side just know to take a little extra back-up with them when they hit the streets."

After a while, I asked, "Nick, what do you think this means? Do you think Steve is still working for that party in Chicago?"

He laughed. "Nope, not possible. That bad boy took a bullet in the head before going for a little involuntary swim in the Chicago River about five years ago. His territory was taken over by someone else in Chicago, but we haven't been able to determine who."

"Are we talking the mob here?" I asked.

"Nah, most of the mob got out of that scene a long time ago. At least the smart ones did. They do a much better job putting their money into investments that are a lot harder to trace. They pretty much leave drugs to the Jamaicans, Mexicans and gangs like that. Those guys don't have no ethics. In the mob, there's a code you're expected to follow. Those that don't follow it, don't get return business, you know what I mean? Take Steve. He and his kind don't have no ethics. Mob wouldn't work with him. Steve's not our problem, though. If he can help in that kid's murder case, great. But he certainly didn't hire Joey Leeds to kill Mitch. That's our main concern."

How could I forget?

Chapter Twelve

*W*e found my aunt in her office nimbly tapping away at her keyboard.

"Where's Tony?" I asked when she looked up at us standing in the doorway.

"He said he was going to hang out in the cafeteria and pretend to be a prospective student," she said, removing her reading glasses and setting them on the textbook open next to her computer.

"Isn't he a little old for that?" Nick said with a laugh.

"Not at all," she replied. "Community colleges tend to attract older students who need a more flexible schedule and more practical training than a university can provide."

She then asked how our undercover assignment went. I let Nick explain since he knew the background.

"Wow, sounds like a quite a day and it's not even noon," she said.

Nick pointed at the black phone on her desk and asked if he could make a phone call.

She stood and stepped away from her desk, which was covered with papers and books of all sorts. Waving a hand at the phone, she said, "Certainly, go ahead."

"I have to call down to the department in Chicago and I didn't want to use a cell phone," Nick explained.

"Don't worry about it. Do what you need to do," Aunt Gina said and motioned to me to follow her out the door. "We can take a little walk. There's something I want to tell you anyway."

Nick raised his eyebrows at me. I shrugged and followed her out the door, closing it behind us.

"Is everything alright?" I asked as we walked down the hallway of offices. She took my hand in both of hers and squeezed.

"I didn't want to tell you this with Tony and Nick around, but I'm very worried about you. I had a terrible dream last night, a vision really. You were chasing a figure down a dark city street when it turned on you and attacked. You screamed and I woke up in a sweat," she said, still squeezing my hand.

"Aunt Gina, it was just a nightmare."

She shook her head. "No, no. You don't understand. I rarely have nightmares. My dreams are usually full of color and light and silliness. There was nothing silly about this dream. Robin, someone is looking for you and seeks to do you harm. You must promise me to be careful."

I nodded reluctantly. Ever since Mitch's death I'd had the feeling someone was after me. I'd just chalked it up to paranoia but Leeds' murder proved someone was keeping track of my movements.

Aunt Gina reached into the pocket of her purple blazer and retrieved a wad of tissue paper. With a solemn face, she handed it to me. "Robin, will you please wear this under your clothes and swear to me that you will never take it off until I tell you it's safe?"

I carefully pulled away the paper to reveal an inch-long shard of rose quartz with a black rope-like cord. "It's beautiful. Thank you."

She gave me a thin smile and placed it around my neck. "I wish you didn't need it. It's a protection amulet. I charged it this morning while you all were still asleep."

"Charged it?" I asked, turning it over in my fingers in search of some sort of plug or battery.

Laughing, she said, "No, no, not like that. It's a spiritual thing. I have a lot I would like to show you when you're ready, but now is not the time. Just know that I love you and that I will do whatever I can to help you get through this."

I hugged her tightly. "I love you, too. I'll treasure this, and I won't take it off. I promise."

We turned around and began to walk back to the office when a question sprang into my mind. "Aunt Gina, can you pick up any vibes from Nick, you know, like his aura? I know you've done that with other people."

She stopped and looked at me curiously. "You want to know if he might be the figure in that dark street."

I started to protest but she held up her hand to silence me.

"My first impression of him is that he is an honorable man, like Tony, but you must know that he is also a passionate and loyal man. Those are great qualities but you have to ask yourself why he is that way. Something in his past continues to propel him forward. That kind of passion can lead a person to not always use good judgment. I really wish he hadn't drawn you into tracking down this assassin. Don't rely solely on him for protection. Be prepared to face your danger alone."

She walked to her office and opened the door, leaving me standing speechless in the empty hallway.

Aunt Gina was seated back behind her desk and Nick was looking out the window when I rejoined them a few minutes later after using the bathroom.

"Well?" I asked, looking at Nick. "What did your people have to say about Steve?"

He turned to face me, looking like someone had kicked him in the stomach. "Robin, did you ever meet a woman named Angelica Davis?"

I shook my head. "Doesn't ring any bells. Why?"

Nick crossed his arms and leaned against the window sill. "She's one of the lead investigators at the DEA unit in Chicago. I've been working on getting her to trust me and give me a little insight into that tale of Mitch supposedly meeting with a known drug dealer. I called her again today to see if she knew anything about Steve Sampson or Kazansky or whatever the hell his name is. First of all, she knows him as Steve Charles. She said someone's moving heavy amounts of coke that has been trucked from the Mexican border to Chicago and then Steve's been moving it north, possibly to Milwaukee, Green Bay or even Canada."

"That's pretty gutsy of him to be hanging around Chicago when he's wanted for two murders," I said.

"That's not even the most interesting aspect," Nick said. "She finally admitted to me that Steve's the one Mitch was seen with last January, and our eyewitness is none other than Dave Whelan."

I removed a pile of books from the extra chair in Aunt Gina's office and sat down hard.

"Unbelievable," I said, shaking my head. "All this time, all this effort and it was him all along. But why kill Mitch?"

Nick walked to the door and shut it quietly. "I have a hard time believing that guy is smart enough to run a multi-national drug operation employing hundreds of couriers and dealers. He's an enforcer and a dealer, that's it. Someone else is behind all of this. Gladstone is probably Steve's base of operations for getting the stuff into Canada through Sault Ste. Marie."

"What is the DEA going to do? Are they coming up here to question him?" Aunt Gina asked.

Nick shook his head. "No, it doesn't work like that. Something else is going on that we don't know about. Angelica has been very cagey with me. I'm shocked as hell that she even said that much. She said they'll wait until Steve is on their turf, let him get a taste of life in the Cook County jail and then work him."

"You were right, we need to read those journals. Maybe Mitch talks about why he was meeting with Steve. Hell, maybe the meeting never even happened and Whelan was just trying to get him fired," I said.

"I thought of that," Nick said. "Angelica said the DEA is aware of that possibility."

"What does that mean? Are they investigating Mitch's murder or not? What about the state cops? Have you tried talking to them?"

Nick nodded. "I have a good friend in the main office at Springfield. He said they've been shut out of the investigation. It's all in the Feds' hands now."

My aunt tapped a pencil on the arm of her chair and said, "I bet that means someone suspects RICO-related violations within the Crescent Police Department."

I threw up my hands. "Mitch was not a criminal! He certainly wasn't involved with racketeering and organized crime. Nick, you said none of your mob contacts had even heard of him."

"Robin, there's a lot more to organized crime than the mob. Gangs of all kinds fall under the RICO statutes. I think your aunt might have a point," Nick said.

"Do you honestly think Mitch was taking graft from Steve so he could peddle drugs or transport drugs or whatever he was doing?" I asked, my voice cracking.

He shook his head again and said, "I don't know what to believe. What I do know is that giving Steve even one day to get messages to people could destroy any chance we have of finding the ringleader and clearing Mitch's name, if it even needs to be cleared. We need specifics about Steve's operation locally."

"Then we better track down Shasta," I said and then jumped when someone knocked on the door. It was Tony.

"Hey gang, what's the scoop?" he asked innocently.

Nick took five minutes to fill him in on what we'd learned about Steve.

"Can this thing get any crazier?" Tony said with awe. "Never mind, I withdraw the question. You know, from the time that call came from the U.P. I wondered about the connection. I'd say it's a safe bet that it was Shasta Burns who tried to find you that night. Shasta was Kyle's girlfriend. Kyle was getting into the drug business. Shasta works for Steve. Steve works for … That's our next piece of the circle."

"God, I feel like that's all we've been doing, going around in circles," I said.

Tony came over and knelt in front of me. "Well, maybe I have a lead on someone who can help. I met one of the nursing instructors in the cafeteria. I started asking her some generic questions about the area and then asked her about drugs. I told her I had kids and didn't want them exposed to that garbage, blah, blah, blah. Anyway, she starts telling me about one of the other instructors who lives in Rapid River and how she thinks there might be a meth lab on some adjacent property. I weaseled the name out of her—Heather Adams. She's also an ER nurse at the hospital."

"I know Heather. We went to high school together," I said.

"Do you want to see if she's at work before we head over to your apartment?" Tony asked.

Aunt Gina chimed in, "I know her. I'll call the hospital and make sure she's there."

Heather wasn't able to come to the phone but my aunt told the receptionist to let her know I would be stopping by to talk with her about something.

Tony patted my knee. "Who knows? If this Steve is running things locally and that really is a meth lab, odds are it belongs to his minions."

Nick and I looked at each other and nodded together. "Sounds like a plan. We'll meet you back at the house at six-thirty," I said and gave Aunt Gina a hug and a kiss.

She whispered in my ear, "Be careful, child. I love you."

As I drove the mile to the hospital, it occurred to me that I had yet to stop by the *Daily Press* to clean out my desk and turn in my key. In fact, it was odd that Bob hadn't hounded me for the key. I hadn't even bothered to read the newspapers from the last week to see who had handled the coverage of Kyle's murder. Maybe it *was* time for me to get out of the business.

Everyone seemed lost in their thoughts. I could tell from Nick's expression that he was worried. There were too many unknowns in this case, too many paths leading off into dark corners that shrouded too many dangers. In Chicago, he had a network of snitches, spies and sources to aid him, not to mention the entire metro police department. In the U.P., he was just one man who didn't know the players, the game or even the board layout and the moving pieces.

I found a spot at the edge of the visitor's lot across from the emergency room and parked the Outback.

"You guys want to come in with me?" I asked.

Tony sighed. "No, I'd probably just intimidate her since she doesn't know me. Get as much detail as you can. We'll sit here and keep thinking."

Nick added, "I feel like I'm missing something. If I just think long enough, maybe it will come to me."

"Or maybe you'll drive yourself insane," I said. "Why don't you give Charlie a call and mention that Mandy Miller, the name you recognized from that address book. Maybe he knows her." I gave him Charlie's office and cell numbers and then jogged across the parking lot to keep the cold from creeping too deep into my bones.

The woman at the admitting desk said she would check if Heather Adams was available and then disappeared around the corner. The door leading to the ER opened a few minutes later and Heather, all smiles, emerged. She'd been a year ahead of me in high school and my mentor on the track team, always cheering me during those last few laps of the 3200 meter run when I felt like my legs would collapse under me as I pushed to improve my position. Nursing was a great career for someone who lit up a room like a fluffy white kitten.

"Robin, I'm so happy to see you," she said and threw her arms around my neck.

"I hope I'm not interrupting anything important like an ingrown toenail or hangnail," I said.

Heather laughed. "Oh, you know this place. One crisis after another, gunshot victims, stabbings, poisonings. It never ends," she said and then sobered. "I guess I shouldn't joke about that. It seems you've caused quite a ruckus since you've come back to town."

"What do you mean?" I asked as I followed her back to an empty examining room.

"I read the paper and I'm close with the cops. I know you've done more than your fair share of playing Sherlock Holmes, sometimes getting too close for comfort to the bad guy," Heather said. She pulled a wheeled stool over from a table against the wall and pointed to a plastic chair where I could sit.

"Heather, you've lived here your whole life, right?"

She nodded, her highlighted blonde ponytail bouncing along the neck of her teal-colored uniform top.

"I know you're on duty so I'll get to the reason I'm here. What do you know about the drug situation in the county?"

She blinked in surprise, threw a glance over her shoulder and then rolled over to the wide heavy door leading to the hallway and shut it quietly. When she rolled back, her brow was knitted in concern.

"In a word—huge. I'm telling you, Robin, this area has major problems. We've had four people die from overdoses in the last year and several others come awfully close. We're seeing everything from heroin to cocaine and homegrown stuff like marijuana and methamphetamine. We've even got a few people around here who I'm sure are addicted to prescription meds. There's no way the local cops can keep up with this. I think there's something going on right near my house but my husband keeps telling me to butt out because he thinks if we call the police, something bad will happen to us."

I tried to remember where Heather lived but I was drawing a blank. She must've read the look on my face because she said, "Four years ago Craig and I built a house about seven miles east of Rapid River in Ensign Township. It's a great little community with a good school and decent neighbors."

"I know. My late mother's family was from Rapid River, but I guess you knew that since you know my aunt," I said.

"That's right. Gina Schmidt. She's a great addition to Bay College. The students really like her and she keeps the faculty on their toes with her enthusiasm, even after all those years teaching at NYU. Nice lady, if a little unconventional for the U.P."

"Yeah, you got that right," I replied. "So what's going on near your house?"

"About eight months ago, I was taking the kids and the dog for a walk down a path that winds through the woods. We have twenty acres. The trail keeps going beyond our property and meets up with what I'm guessing is an old logging road. We kept going down this road for maybe a hundred yards until Addie, my daughter, noticed an old camper parked deep in the woods. Now, we had walked this path many times the previous year looking for blueberries and whatnot and my husband hunted deer back there in the past but this was the first time we'd been down there after the snow melted. That camper wasn't there the year before. You could see where someone had driven down the road and cut some smaller trees to get it back into the woods. Well, right away I thought it might be a meth lab. The news has been full of stories about how those things are cropping up all over the Midwest. Addie and Rick, my son, wanted to go exploring around it but I said no and we hightailed it back to the house. Naturally I told Craig about it, and he went out there with his rifle and checked it out but there wasn't anyone around. I wanted to call the police, like I said, but he was afraid. He said as long as they aren't bothering us, we shouldn't bother them. Besides, we didn't have any proof."

"Have you noticed anyone coming and going from there?" I asked.

"Yes, usually after midnight. I've heard an inordinate amount of traffic back on that road, especially snowmobiles this past week but there aren't any designated snowmobile trails back there," Heather said. Then she sighed and pounded her fists onto the top of her thighs. "The thing is I know something is wrong. If they are making drugs back there, they could start the whole forest on fire. What if the kids are playing back in the woods and something happens to them? Robin, maybe you can do something. You can tell the police it's an anonymous tip."

"Where exactly is your house?"

She wrote the address and the description (light blue one-story modern ranch with a two-car attached garage) on a notepad advertising some obscure prescription drug. I stuffed the paper in my purse and asked, "How far is the trailer from your house?"

She bit her upper lip and shrugged. "I'm not good with that sort of thing but I'd guess maybe a half mile. The road actually hits the highway west of our property and then runs along the back. I have no idea where it leads, for all I know it just dead-ends somewhere back in the woods. One thing I know, I've never seen or heard any logging equipment back there."

"How deep is your property and who owns the adjoining land?"

"I think we have five acres of frontage on the highway so that would mean it extends back about four acres. If I remember the survey, the lot looks like a big rectangle. Various members of my husband's family own the land behind and all around us. They homesteaded it back in the mid to late nineteenth century. They've farmed it, logged it and hunted it at one time or another, but there're just three homes on the land now and they're all on the highway. I can't see any of them involved in illegal activity," Heather said and then shot a glance to the closed door. "I have to get back to work, but there's something else. I've noticed a big increase in activity back there in the last few days. I'm scared because Craig is out of town for a sales conference in Detroit until Saturday. What if they come to the house, Robin? I mean, I know how to handle Craig's hunting rifle, but what about my kids?"

Her fear was real and so was the potential for tragedy if it turned out there were drug dealers operating behind her property. From what Nick had told me about Steve's past crimes and the vicious way Kyle and Mitch had been killed, it was clear the type of people who had infiltrated our once quiet little community cared nothing about the lives they destroyed.

"Heather, can you stay with your parents or maybe Craig's parents, at least until he gets back? I can't go into all the details, but I do sense that something is brewing. It may be completely unrelated to what you've seen and heard, but until the police know for sure what's going on, it's not worth risking your family," I said.

She looked at the ceiling and expelled a sigh. "I can't believe this is happening. Why wouldn't Craig let me call the cops last summer? Damn," she said, slamming her fist into her palm. "I can stay with my parents. They still live on Garth Point Lane on the bay. What are you going to do, Robin? It sounds like you're working on another investigation."

I stood up and stretched, trying to combat the atrophy that had settled into my body thanks to too little sleep and exercise. "Yeah, I'm working on something, but I'm still clueless as to how all these pieces fit. What you've told me could be very important though. Would you mind if a friend and I camped out on your property tonight? I'd like to see firsthand what's happening there."

Heather rolled the stool back to the little desk in the corner of the examining room and said, "Sure, I don't mind. Just take care of yourself. Leave the heroics to the cops."

With a smirk, I said, "It's just not in my nature to sit back and take it easy. My fiancé was murdered last year and the people running the drug trade up here might have been involved. If that's the case, I have to do everything I can to help bring them down. Unfortunately, the local police just don't have enough resources to handle a large-scale investigation and I'm starting to wonder if some of the cops Mitch worked with have crossed to the other side."

Heather placed a hand on my shoulder. "Robin, I'm sorry."

"Thanks, I'll be okay. I've got a pretty good support system," I said, fingering my new amulet and thinking about how much Aunt Gina had added to my life since we had reconnected. I also suddenly remembered Nick and Tony sitting in my cold car. "I've got to get going but promise me you'll go to your parents tonight. Here's my business card with my cell phone number. Call me if you hear anything."

Heather took the card and gave me a hug. "Take care of yourself."

"You too," I said and dashed back to the car. Tony was still sitting in the passenger seat while Nick was in the back, both looking pensive. I got in, started the engine and began to relate what Heather had told me. When I was finished Tony rubbed his chin.

"Well, it certainly sounds like a clandestine drug operation. What do you think, Nick? Should we scope it out tonight?"

Nick nodded. "Yeah, but we need to let Detective Vale know what's going on," he said and added, "Robin, I talked to Charlie. He does know Mandy Miller. Apparently she's quite the local barfly and has a knack for attracting dirtbags fond of using women as punching bags. He was going to stop by the house where she lives with her latest creep and see what she has to say about Steve."

"That's great. Maybe we can find something out before Steve alerts his contacts," I said.

"Hope springs eternal," Nick replied. "I called Vale to see if he can meet with us right away. He has about an hour to spare. I'm anxious to let him know what Angelica had to say about Steve and what your nurse thinks is happening near her property. I'd also like to see if he has any idea what kind of people may have put down roots here. It could be one of Karastova's kids who's running things, switching from arms dealing to narcotics. If that's the case, I can guarantee that the local cops are underpowered."

"You think maybe his daughter is here?" I asked.

"Or his remaining son. Remember I told you I felt like I was missing something? I think I figured it out. I made a few phone calls when you in there," he nodded toward the hospital, "and learned some interesting things about his family. Karastova had three children, two sons and a daughter. One of the sons was killed in a boat racing accident near Miami in the late '80s. The other is an economics professor at Northwestern but supposedly has very little contact with his father. I don't buy that since he probably lives less than twenty miles from Dmitri so he's in a great position to run a smuggling operation around Chicago. The daughter is a mystery. She disappeared from the radar screen about the same time her brother died. There was speculation that she went to Mexico to continue the family business. She was supposedly a bright lady who inherited her ol' man's talents. If she is the one periodically visiting the old man, maybe she's doing more than just visiting. Either one of them has the brains to take over Daddy's operation. The question is, do either of them have the guts to kill when it's necessary? In that business, there always comes a time when it's necessary."

"Mexico's a long way from the U.P.," I said.

"Don't be too sure of that," Nick mumbled under his breath.

Chapter Thirteen

I put the car in gear and headed for the sheriff's department at the east end of town, all the while wracking my brain for a local connection to Dmitri Karastova and coming up with nothing. Det. Vale was waiting for us at the front desk when we arrived. After we introduced Tony, Vale led the three of us back to his office. Nick filled him in on what he knew about Steve Kazansky and then I related what was happening near Heather's house on the outskirts of Rapid River. When we were finished, Vale wiped his face with his hands and groaned.

"What a mess. I'm retiring May 31. Why couldn't this all have waited until after that?" he grumbled. "Alright, first things first. Nick and Tony, you realize you're out of your jurisdiction and, therefore, have no official authority in Michigan. However, since you've been willing to volunteer your services, I am more than willing to accept. You obviously have the experience and connections we'll need to nail this Karastova person, if he, or she, is behind all of this. Nick, does your superior officer know you're up here?"

Nick folded his arms across his broad chest and nodded. "He does now. I called him a little while ago. He's not thrilled, but he understands why I'm here. The equipment I brought belongs to me, not the Chicago PD, so there's no problem there. I'm not operating on behalf of the department, just assisting you in whatever capacity is most beneficial."

"What about you, Tony?" Vale asked.

Tony grinned. "I'm merely freelancing until the beginning of February. I don't have a supervisor, but I do want to stay clean, and alive."

"Understandable. Okay, then let's get down to business," Vale said and pulled out a yellow legal pad from his desk. "Let's start at the beginning and put down everything we know. When did Mitch allegedly meet with Steve Kazansky in Crescent?"

"That's one thing we don't know," Nick said. "He was killed on April 20

113

by a professional assassin. The assassin bought it four days ago in Miami when we tried to bring him in, bullet through the eye and out the back of his head."

Vale made a face and wrote a few notes while Nick filled him in on what he'd learned from the DEA, the Illinois State Police and the chief at Crescent.

"How were you able to find out about the contract?" Vale asked.

"I was born and raised in Chicago and, with the exception of four years in the Army, I've spent my life on the streets. I've built relationships with sources of all kinds. That's all I can tell you without further endangering someone," Nick said.

Vale nodded. "I understand. Then we have this mysterious phone call that might have been made by the not-so-lovely Shasta Burns, who was dating Kyle Sullivan, who was bludgeoned to death at his family's cottage. According to your aunt and his father, Kyle had been using drugs for several months." He stopped talking and opened his center desk drawer, pulling out the little black address book my aunt had found. We all had to feign surprise and interest.

"The mailman delivered this little gem to the department this morning. It is supposedly from Kyle's apartment and reads like a who's who in drugs in the U.P.," Vale tossed it on the desk. "Go ahead, leaf through it. In the Vs you'll find my son Sean."

Tony looked genuine when he said, "I'm sorry."

Vale looked at the ceiling, then at his desk and back at Tony. "So am I, but he's been in trouble since he was small. A lot of it is probably my fault, but I have two other sons who were on the honor roll, played sports, acted in school plays, went on to college and made something of themselves. What's that old Meatloaf song say, "two out of three ain't bad"? I guess that's how I look at it these days."

"That's pretty much how Sam Burns feels about Shasta," I said. "By the way, when your guys went to their house on Sunday to ask about her, was Sam there?"

Vale flipped through a thick file on his desk and nodded. "Sure, it says right here they questioned Sam and Janet Burns about their daughter."

"He lied to me."

"You probably would lie too if you had a kid like Shasta, or my son," Vale said, toying with his pen. "I can empathize with Sam Burns. It's tough to balance your public face with being a parent of a kid in trouble. My wife and I did everything we could to help Sean. I'm sure Sam did the same thing. Besides, I doubt Sam is running a drug smuggling outfit so let's focus on that."

He referred back to his notes and continued. "Today, you discovered that Steve Sampson was actually a fugitive from an old murder investigation and he was arrested, but not before you saw Shasta leave the radio station in a huff. Next, Robin here talks to a former classmate who's witnessed some unusual activity back in the woods behind her house—an old camper and lots of traffic on what's supposed to be private property," Vale said as he wrote down the facts on the pad. When he'd finished he looked back over the list. "The next step is to get a look at that camper tonight."

We all agreed, but before we began planning that escapade, I asked, "Tom, what do you know about Shasta besides her being an addict?"

Vale shrugged. "I don't really know much about the girl except she's always had a mouth on her. She and my son were in the same grade in school. Scott said she was smart but, I don't know, bitchy, like she thought she was better than everyone else because she came from money, just like her mother."

I laughed. "Money? I'm sure Sam makes a little over a hundred grand a year and Janet seems to be doing well with her wine business, but I'd hardly call them rich. Sam did tell me he thinks she's been using drugs for several years. Do we know for sure that Steve was her supplier?"

"Maybe we can get that question answered by someone else." Vale picked up the phone and dialed. "Kevin? It's Tom. Where are you? Great, can you stop by my office right now? I need some information. Thanks." He hung up and said, "Kevin Martens is a detective with NOMIDES. He was in court this morning when we hit the radio station. I just caught him in the parking lot getting ready to take off for the evening. Maybe he can help sort some of this out."

There was a knock at the door and then a scruffy man in ragged jeans and a red Budweiser sweatshirt stepped into the office. He looked young and relatively new to the department in the last couple of years, which made him a good operative for NOMIDES since he would be relatively unknown.

After more introductions Vale started firing questions at him.

"What do you know about Steve Sampson?"

Kevin grinned. "I'm not surprised that he's wanted for murder. I think he killed that Sullivan kid in the national forest. We've had some leads on him for a while but nothing concrete. His arrest this morning helps answer some questions. Basically, he's a dealer and has been since he came to Gladstone a decade ago. In fact, I'd bet that's why he moved here. He's working for someone, but we don't have any idea who. We don't know how he contacts them, we don't know how the drugs are moved, we don't know how he gets paid, nothing. But because we now know he has ties to the Chicago area, it's a good bet that's where his bosses are located."

"Maybe that's where this Karastova character comes in," Vale interjected.

"Who?" Kevin asked.

Nick explained about Dmitri Karastova and his children.

"Hmm, the plot thickens," Kevin said. "I never heard that name around here but it makes sense."

"What about Shasta Burns?" I asked.

"You know, I used to think she was just a coke head, but that girl's got some balls. Another detective has been working a lead to her and found out last week that she's been working for Steve. She's actually done a bit of enforcing herself, making people pay up. She's no shrunken violet. She may look like hell, but it's a vast improvement from a year ago. I think she's trying to kick the drugs so she can move into a position of leadership within the organization," Kevin explained.

Vale made some more notes on his fact list and then asked me to tell the detective about the situation near Heather Adams' property.

Kevin frowned when I'd finished and said, "That's a new one on me. I've never heard of anything going on in that area, but it sounds promising. Unfortunately, most of the team is working with the Marquette City cops on a bust tonight so I'm the only one available to do any kind of stakeout."

Vale closed the Sullivan file and said, "Okay, we'll set up camp around the perimeter of this thing. Let's meet in the Adams driveway at 10 tonight. Nick and Tony, I know I'm asking a lot but I'd really appreciate it if you'd be there to observe. You might recognize someone if we've got Chicago drug dealers working the area."

Nick and Tony gave each other a knowing look and nodded.

"What about me?" I asked.

Vale shook his head. "Too dangerous."

I cocked an eyebrow at him and stared him down. "I go where they go," I said and jerked my head at the Granatis, both of whom tried to suppress grins. Men!

Vale started to protest when Tony spoke up. "She'll be our responsibility."

"Fine," Vale acquiesced. "Kevin, you get in a four-wheel-drive truck, take the GPS and a digital camera and find the exact location of that camper, snap a few pictures and then hightail it out of there," Vale ordered. "Robin, you three check out those journals. Let's hope we can learn something worthwhile. Everybody dress warm, bring lots of coffee and prepare for a long night."

I left the safety of Vale's office reluctantly. I was already hungry and tired, now I had to go home and sort through painful memories of Mitch. It would indeed be a long night.

My cell phone rang just as we reached the Outback in the parking lot. It was Charlie.

"We found Mandy Miller."

"That's good. Did she have any light to shed on this mess?"

"She ain't talkin'."

My heart sank.

"I don't like the sound of that."

"Robin, the one thing about this job that I will never get used to is the smell of people who've been dead for more than a few days. I can't even begin to describe it. I won't be able to eat for a week," Charlie said, his voice strained.

"What happened?" I asked as I buckled the seatbelt and started the car. Nick and Tony looked at me quizzically.

"I showed up at her house around 2:45 this afternoon. Her mother had just driven up from Green Bay and was trying to break into the back door. I asked her what she was doing and she said she'd been worried about her daughter because she hadn't heard from her in more than two weeks. Mandy almost always checked in with her at least once a week because her mother is a diabetic and has heart problems. Anyway, there were no signs of life around the house so I used an old driver's license to get in the backdoor. The smell hit me like an avalanche. I told her to stay outside and then I called for backup. Haskell and Peterson were there within a few minutes and then we searched the place. Mandy was in the middle of the basement floor. The weird part is that she was stretched out prone with her hands folded over her stomach as though she had just laid down to take a nap, or else someone arranged her body. I mean it's a cement floor, for Pete's sake, no one's going to take a nap on a cold cement floor in the middle of winter. There's hardly any heat in the basement because they have all the ducts going directly into the main house. Still, her body was, well, let's not go there.

"I did a cursory check of the body and didn't see any signs of direct trauma like broken bones and her clothes didn't show any signs of bullet holes or stab wounds. Her mother said Mandy has always struggled with a drug addiction so it's possible she overdosed, but why the hell would someone put her in the basement?" Charlie wondered aloud.

"Because she died at a place where people didn't want to draw any unnecessary attention to themselves, like maybe Kyle Sullivan's apartment," I said, thinking back to my Aunt Gina's adamant statement Sunday evening that someone had died in that apartment recently. How would I ever explain that to Charlie?

"What makes you say that? You holdin' out on me?" he asked, irritation evident in his voice.

"No, let's just say we may have a bit of what you would call the woo-woo factor at work here. I promise to explain it later. Just play that hunch for now and see where it leads. Maybe someone in that apartment building saw her around. Lots of people in that neighborhood probably know Mandy if she frequents the local bars."

"Good point. I'll check back with you later."

I closed the phone, threw my head back against the seat and groaned.

"More dead bodies. Everywhere I turn it's just more dead bodies."

"Let me guess, Mandy Miller's dead," Nick said.

"Yup." I relayed the events of Charlie's afternoon.

"Damn." Nick slammed his fist into the armrest on the back door. "She might have been useful too."

"That was someone's daughter," I murmured. "Try to imagine how her mother feels right about now."

Tony brushed my hair from my face and smiled. "That's what so great about people who aren't cops. They can still feel. Me, if I thought about all the grieving people behind the bodies, I'd go insane. There's just too much pain."

I backed out of the sheriff's department lot and headed toward my apartment where I would have to face my own pain locked away in a cedar chest.

My hands shook as I opened the padded lid of the cedar chest I'd stashed in the back of the walk-in closet in my bedroom as soon as I'd moved into the apartment in May. The sweet woodsy smell drifting from its depths had always been pleasant, something I would linger over anytime I opened the chest, but I had no time for lingering now. While Tony sat on the edge of my bed and Nick paced in the hall, I lifted the aqua and turquoise quilt my paternal grandmother had presented me with on my tenth birthday, just a few months before my mother died. Beneath the quilt was the ceremonial flag that had been draped over Mitch's coffin during the funeral and then carefully folded by his comrades and placed in the triangular glass and wood case that would protect it from the effects of age, wear and light. It seemed so contradictory that a simple box not much bigger than a toaster could shield the very fabric that had shrouded another box that would shield from the elements a man who had been wearing a bullet-proof vest when he'd been killed by a shotgun blast. That flag would survive long after the world had forgotten the sound of Mitch Montgomery's laugh, the sparkle in his eyes, or the curl of his hair over his forehead.

"Robin?"

I lifted my face to look at Tony.

"Are you alright?" he asked softly.

"No. I don't want to do this. I want to go back to this time last year, when everything was fine. I hate my life now. I hate this apartment. I hated my crappy job at that crappy little newspaper. I hate that my life is full of death and misery. I hate that I can't sleep at night. I hate that I'm so lonely that I just want to dig a hole in front of his headstone and bury myself and never have to face another miserable day."

By the time I'd finished my tirade I was screaming and crying and clutching the flag's case so tightly that its edges cut into my fingers. Tony slid off the bed, grabbed a box of tissue from the nightstand and calmly sat down next to me on the floor, took the case out of my hands, wrapped me in his arms and let me cry, rocking me back and forth in a hypnotic rhythm.

After about five minutes, he whispered into my hair, "I'm sorry you have to go through this. You tried to run away from the pain but now it's running after you because it's locked inside you. You can't hide from memories, or love, or sorrow."

I pulled back, blew my nose and scowled at him. "Yeah, I know that."

"I would bet that when this is over, after whoever is behind all this is brought to justice, you will want to get out of this apartment, which really is pretty nice, you'll want to find a different job, make new friends and start living again," he said, brushing a strand of ash blonde hair from my face. "But, to get to that point, you have to focus on the task at hand. Now, I know a good cry helps everyone feel better so have another tissue."

I took the tissue with a weak smile and blew my nose. I did feel a little better after every outburst, like I was a boiler on the verge of an explosion until the steam of emotion was expelled. In the past, I'd been embarrassed by my unexpected breakdowns, but it had felt natural to sit with Tony and let him soak up some of that emotion. I gave him a peck on the cheek and said, "You're an awfully sweet guy for a bodyguard."

He began fingering the edges of the quilt and shrugged. "I've been through this before," he said and exhaled a deep breath. "My wife died of cancer three years ago. We were together four years so there was quite a lot of sorting through things that brought back memories."

"Tony, I'm so sorry," I said, set the case down and took his hand in mine. I gazed into his deep chocolate eyes, into his bared soul and saw my own grief reflected back at me. He really did understand. Somehow that made what I had to do a little easier.

Nick cleared his throat and tapped his watch.

"Right, we better get moving," I said and turned back to the chest. There at the bottom of the chest was the large shoebox that held Mitch's notebooks, among other things that his mother had packed and wanted me to have. I lifted it out and set it on the floor.

"What's in there?" Tony asked.

"All sorts of stuff. I haven't had the strength to open it since I put it in here— too afraid I'd start crying uncontrollably," I said, sliding a glance at Tony, who rubbed my shoulder.

"Go on, open it," he said, nodding at box, the lid secured with several strips of packing tape. I ripped them off and opened the box and moaned.

Inside was every card and letter I'd ever given Mitch, the travel journal he'd kept from our many driving excursions around the country and some knick-knack souvenirs including a small replica of the ill-fated Edmund Fitzgerald ore freighter that had sunk off the Upper Peninsula's Whitefish Point in November 1975. He'd bought it at a gift shop in Duluth, Minnesota, when we'd traveled the western shore of Lake Superior the fall before he died.

I skipped going through the cards and letters. That would have to wait a few more months. Underneath those items were six spiral-bound five-subject notebooks.

"Here they are. Let's hope they shed some light on this mess," I said and gingerly pulled them out and handed them to Nick.

He shuffled through them to look at the covers. "They begin when he started as a cop with Crescent and end two days before he was killed. Each of you grab a notepad and get comfortable. We need to go through each one of these page by page because we can't assume anything. There could very well be a link between his death and something that happened in his first year on the job," he said.

I placed the other items back in the chest, closed the lid and followed Nick and Tony into the kitchen where Nick piled the journals in the center of the table while I retrieved my reporter's notebook from my purse. It was a few minutes after five o'clock when we sat down and opened the first one, dated September 13, 1995, his first full day on the job after completing four years at Northeastern Illinois University and sixteen weeks at the police academy. I was amazed at how meticulously Mitch had recorded even the most mundane of events, from visiting an elderly woman who had just lost her husband and was concerned about strange noises around the house, to helping extract a golden retriever from between two boards in a fence after he got stuck while chasing a squirrel in his back yard. Most of the entries weren't more than a couple of neatly-written paragraphs, but some ran longer as he tried to digest tragedy and inhumanity. As the months turned into years, it became clear from his writing that Mitch truly loved law enforcement, especially those times when he felt he had made a difference in how a case progressed or how a resident perceived the police department. He also showed a knack for investigation, keeping notes on each and every case that did not have a clear, immediate path to resolution. In some instances, he questioned the decisions of superior officers but his training kicked in and he kept his comments to the confines of his journals.

From a reader's standpoint, the journals were surprisingly well-written. By the time we got to the sixth and final notebook, my long-held opinion of Mitch as a kind, caring person with the soul of an old poet was justified. On the surface, it would seem that law enforcement was a strange career for such a man, but Mitch saw the good that police could do if they could just connect with people on a personal level. He didn't go for the kind of commando tactics displayed on television. He knew how to negotiate in a hostile situation and avoid confrontation in most cases. So what got him killed? The last journal began about a year and a half before he died and included the usual entries up until December 7, 2005, when he was approached by a middle-aged man offering him a briefcase full of cash in exchange for some information. Mitch had told the guy to get lost and threatened to arrest him for attempting to bribe a police officer. The man continued to approach him both at work and off duty, always with the same offer, but never any threats. Finally, the man revealed himself to be a DEA agent who had indeed been trying to trick Mitch to see if he could be trusted. As I read the succeeding entries aloud, disbelief filled my voice, not to mention anger at Mitch for not revealing the elaborate scheme to me, the woman he was supposed to marry in a year and a half.

The DEA had uncovered a drug smuggling operation based in Crescent that had tentacles spreading out in every direction across the United States and into Canada and Mexico. The feds believed a cop, maybe more than one, within the Crescent Police Department was ensuring the operation worked without interference from law enforcement. The DEA wanted Mitch to find out who was dirty within the department. In his notes, Mitch never expressed any doubts about assisting in the investigation even though it meant going undercover to set up drug buys so he could get close to the source. Not even Chief Rex Harper was to know what he was doing. His only contact with the DEA was the man who'd first approached him, an agent named Matt Hanson. Mitch had confirmed his identity and felt confident this was a legitimate investigation.

After about a month of disguising himself with a fake beard and mustache and powder in his dark brown hair to make it appear gray and dingy, he finally made contact with a runner who gave his name as Joe Smith, but his fingerprints had matched up with a man named Edward Carlson, hardly an exotic moniker. Eddie, as he was called according to the FBI, had done time for robbery and assault at Alger Maximum Security Prison in Munising, Michigan, a small town located at the western edge of Pictured Rocks National Lakeshore on Lake Superior. Carlson was moving large quantities of marijuana from the U.P. into the Chicago area. Mitch started making calls to the prison and the Northern Michigan Drug Enforcement Squad that was now helping Detective Tom Vale investigate Kyle Sullivan's murder.

Mitch started doing little favors for Carlson to build trust and finally got to meet Carlson's boss at a faded nightclub in downtown Crescent.

The boss? None other than Steve Sampson. Mitch had made the mistake of sitting with his back to the door and was surprised when he heard Dave Whelan's voice behind him. After receiving a thick envelope from Sampson, Whelan had left the club, but not before scrutinizing Mitch. The DEA said Mitch was too close to getting solid evidence of wrongdoing on Whelan's part and too close to Sampson's boss to pull him off the case. He hadn't pushed the issue because Whelan never said a word about seeing Mitch so he didn't know for sure if his cover had been blown. We now knew the answer to that question.

"So that's why the DEA is so interested in this case," Tony said softly.

I slammed the book shut and stared at both of them in disgust. "Where the hell were the feds when he was killed? Why didn't they provide some protection?"

Nick got up from the table and resumed pacing. "It's not that easy. Mitch knew the risks but he believed in the cause. There's no point in second-guessing the DEA now. I would bet they were left high and dry without Mitch, though. Sampson's people probably closed ranks around him once Mitch was killed so the feds have nothing to work with."

Tony took the journal and scanned the last section. Finally, he asked, "Does anything he wrote about this Edward Carlson ring any bells with you?"

I shook my head. "There are probably hundreds of Carlsons in the U.P. Just because he served time in Alger Max doesn't mean he was even from the area. Besides, it's well known that prisons are great recruitment facilities for drug traffickers. I could spin any number of possibilities. He could have made contact with a crooked employee who set him up with the job of driving the drugs south. He could have made a deal with another inmate. It doesn't look like Mitch got too far with the prison or NOMIDES," I said, rereading the notes he'd made about his conversation with the drug squad's commander. The lieutenant had said the team was simply too overwhelmed to be of much help when it came to crime originating within the prison system and that Mitch would be better off working with the DEA. But the DEA had nothing on Carlson or Alger Max.

I waved my hand over the journals. "These only lead to more questions. Did this Carlson work for Karastova? Is Karastova even the one behind all this? How did Whelan become a crook?" I folded my arms on the table and put my head down.

"We're late," Nick said quietly.

"What?"

"We're late for dinner at your aunt's house. It's already six-forty. We were supposed to be there ten minutes ago."

"Good grief! I have to call her and let her know what's going on," I said, jumped out of the chair and ran to my bedroom. My snowmobile suit was stuffed at the end of the closet and smelled strongly of the lilac sachet Mrs. Easton had placed on the shelf above it to "freshen" things. I tore it from the hanger and rummaged in a cardboard box on the floor for a warm pair gloves and toque. Looking down at my feet I wondered if my sturdy but comfortable work shoes would be enough and decided they would have to be since I couldn't remember where my winter boots were hidden. I hadn't needed them yet since moving from Chicago. I raced back into the living room and grabbed my coat and purse.

"We still have to get you guys some warm clothes for tonight. All the stores downtown are closed but I think Dunham's is still open in the mall. C'mon, let's go," I yelled over my shoulder as I thudded down the stairs.

They grabbed the journals and followed me down the stairs. While I drove to the Delta Plaza mall on the corner of Third Avenue North and Lincoln Road, Tony called my aunt to let her know we would be an hour late.

Nick held up my heavy black snowmobile suit with purple piping and grunted with disgust. "You want me to wear something like this? I'll look like the Michelin man."

"Are you kidding? There are people who spend a thousand bucks on gear like that for snowmobiling so they can stay warm and look cool on the trails. Besides, this thing is about fifteen years old. Snowmobile gear doesn't look much like this anymore," I said. I hadn't worn it in years but it should still fit since I hadn't gained any weight, much to my frustration. "Anyway, I was thinking you two would fit in as Yoopers more if you had a pair of hunting bibs and a jacket. That's what a lot of guys who work outside wear."

Nick rolled his eyes. "Groovy."

Tony just laughed

It took the clerk at Dunham's Sporting Goods store just fifteen minutes to get them outfitted with bibs, coats, gloves and hats that would keep them warm and well-hidden if we had to stay out all night.

"Camouflage," Nick grunted as he looked down at the pile of clothes on the counter. "I haven't worn green camo since my days in the Army. Oh well, when in Rome, do as the Romans, right?"

"Don't worry, no one will see you and that's the point," Tony said and looked at his watch. "Hurry, it's almost seven-thirty!"

Chapter Fourteen

*A*unt Gina's house was full of wonderful smells that hit me as soon as I opened the front door.

"Curry!" Tony shouted with joy. "How did you know I love Indian food?"

She laughed as she came down the hallway from the kitchen and wrapped me in a bear hug while her two Yorkies and Belle attacked Tony's pant legs, sniffing furiously. Nick moved past them quickly to avoid getting dog hair on his black wool slacks.

"Anyone with taste buds loves Indian food. I learned to prepare a few dishes when I was in grad school and roomed with a beautiful girl from New Delhi who could entrance you with her culinary creations. But she wasted her talents and became a mathematician, made millions inventing some software and dodged the dot.com bust. I think she lives in a castle somewhere north of Edinburgh," Aunt Gina said with a wistful sigh and surveyed her humble but colorful abode.

Tony followed her eyes and took in the brilliant purple, royal blue and teal wall hangings, rugs and furniture with interest. "You have a unique sense of style that is soothing without being boring. I feel a sense of warmth and peace. My apartment is just basic white—sterile, cold and empty," he said.

Nick rolled his eyes and shook his head. "What? Now you're an interior decorator? Do you mind if we eat before you sew some doilies? I'm hungry."

Aunt Gina laughed again, a comforting sound like light rain on the roof at night, and took him by the hand and led him into the kitchen, done in soft greens. Over her shoulder, she replied to Tony, "That's because your apartment isn't home to you. When you feel at home, you'll make it personal by filling it with things that bring you peace."

Nick sat at the table and smiled up at her as she served a rice dish and deposited a spicy chicken breast onto his plate. "How do you know he's not just cold and empty?"

"Because he wouldn't be here if he were and neither would you. You guys care about the people who've proved themselves to you and you both have a lot of passion. Part of that is just your ethnic makeup, but it's also in your personalities. I can see it in your auras," she said.

"What color is his aura?" Tony asked as he pulled a carton of milk from refrigerator.

My aunt started to answer that question and then stopped and looked at me. "You tell me."

"I don't know anything about that stuff," I scoffed.

She winked and left the room for a moment and came back with a slim, well-used paperback titled Aura Reading for Beginners. "Here, read this, practice and we'll talk," she said as she handed me the book and sat down to eat. "Now, tell me what's new with the investigation."

The three of us filled her in on the information I'd learned from Heather, what we'd found in Mitch's journals, the death of Mandy Miller and our plans for this evening. Aunt Gina looked at me with concern.

"That must have been very hard for you going through Mitch's words. Are you alright?" she asked and reached for my hand.

"It was hard, but I'm okay. I just need to focus on getting this resolved first," I said.

"Well, be careful tonight. I must admit I'm surprised the police are letting you tag along. Isn't that rather verboten to have civilians and police from outside jurisdictions aid in investigations?" she asked.

Tony shrugged. "Not really. We're just there to observe tonight. Mainly, Nick and I are there to see if we recognize anyone from the Chicago area. Anything's possible. Besides, these cops are way understaffed if they're going up against what I think they are," he said and got up to clear the table.

"No, no, I can do that," Aunt Gina protested.

"Sorry, I don't eat and run. C'mon Nick, you can dry while I wash."

While they did the dishes, I asked my aunt, "Do you think I should try to get a hold of my dad and let him know what's happening?"

Aunt Gina shook her head. "Let him have his fun. He'll be back on Sunday and you can tell him all about it then. Besides, you don't want him to worry. He needs this time to develop his own life. Sophie's a welcome addition. I wouldn't be surprised if those two get hitched by the end of the summer. Would you be okay with that?"

I smiled. "I hadn't really thought about it, but sure, he deserves to be happy," I said and then gasped when I caught a glimpse of the clock on the wall over the stove. "Guys, we've only got fifteen minutes to meet Vale and Martens."

As Aunt Gina walked with us to the Outback wagon, she said, "You guys be careful. There's a winter storm moving into the area tonight. They're calling for well over a foot of snow before it's done."

"Great," Nick said with a groan. "That's all we need. Let's hope we can wrap this up before it hits. Thanks for dinner, Gina. You're an angel." He kissed her hand and then got in the back seat as Tony reached over and started the engine.

"I bet you say that to all the ladies," she called and turned to me. "Robin, are you coming back here tonight?"

I nodded. "If you don't mind?"

She smiled and hugged me tightly. "Of course not, it's great having roommates again. Besides, Victoria and Albert love having Belle around. Maybe they see her as an older sister."

"Thanks," I said as I got in the Outback and then hit the down button for the power window. "By the way, how is Kyle's father? You haven't said anything about him. Is the funeral scheduled?"

Aunt Gina wrapped her arms around her body and said, "He's doing okay. We've been in touch quite often these last several days. You'll get to meet him Saturday. That's when they've scheduled the funeral at St. Michael's in Marquette. Now get going before I freeze to death."

By the time we'd reached U.S. 2 and were heading east toward Ensign it was already five minutes to ten. "We're going to be late to meet them, too," I said. "What do you think we'll see tonight?"

From the back seat, Nick answered, "I wouldn't even begin to guess. Remember, this may have nothing to do with Kyle or Mitch or even anything criminal. It better, though, because we don't have time to waste, not with Sampson in jail. I wish it hadn't been necessary to arrest him. In time, he would have led us to his boss."

"I wonder if Sampson knew I was Mitch's fiancé?" I pondered aloud.

Tony rubbed his chin and said, "I don't think so. It's the same with Leeds. I don't think any of those guys knew there was a connection between the two of you before Mitch was killed. Afterwards, though, it's obvious someone knew who you were because someone told Leeds just before he was hit."

Nick asked, "How exactly did you end up back here?"

"My dad called to tell me the paper needed a reporter," I said. "I called my former editor and had the job within about ten minutes.

"I wonder why he would do that. You're way over-qualified at this point. From what you've said, that editor doesn't sound like a fool. He had to know you would get bored working here after six years at the Tribune so why did he agree to hire you back? I don't think I would have if I were him. I would have used my connections to get you another job at a larger newspaper," Nick said.

"What are you saying, that this was some sort of trap?" I asked, incredulous.

"I don't know, Robin. Something smells bad, though. Just think about it, okay?"

"Okay, but I think you're off base on this one. Bob wouldn't do something like that," I said.

"I'm not thinking about Bob," he mumbled.

I was about to protest when I noticed we were getting close to Heather's house. "There!" I shouted and pointed to the next house on the left. Vale and Martens were sitting in the front seat of a four-wheel drive Chevy pickup when we pulled into the driveway.

"I hope you dressed warm. There's a storm moving this way and the temperature is supposed to drop another ten degrees tonight and it's already below ten," Vale called as we all poured out of our vehicles. Nick, Tony and I quickly donned our winter gear and then I watched in amazement as Nick pulled an AR15 rifle outfitted with a night vision scope from a case in the back of the Outback and inserted a clip.

"Where did that come from?" I asked.

"Brought it up in the Mustang, just in case," he said and looked at Vale. "You mind?"

"I've no doubt you know how to use that thing as well or better than I do," Vale said.

"I spent four years as an Army Ranger. I know a little about weaponry," Nick said.

Vale looked at Tony. "You carrying?"

Tony patted his shoulder holster and nodded. "Forty-five. Doesn't fit too well with all this padding," he said, eliciting a laugh from Nick and Kevin.

I felt Aunt Gina's rose quartz pendant under my snowsuit and said a little prayer that there wouldn't be any shooting tonight and then followed the men around the house, now devoid of light and life, and toward the woods that bordered the property. There was no moon to aid our movement as thick clouds shrouded the sky. Martens, having found the small camper Heather had seen, led the way through the snow, now compacted to about six inches. To every fifth tree he had tied a series of florescent pink ribbons, the type used by foresters to mark trees for harvesting. It took us about twenty minutes of walking through a mix of jack pines and oak until we reached a spot that provided a bit of cover yet allowed a relatively unobstructed view of the trailer, which was exactly as Heather had described—old, rusted and abandoned. We swept an area about ten feet by ten feet square clear of snow, fallen leaves and twigs that could give away our position should someone inadvertently move at the wrong time. Using our hands, we then constructed a snow and earthen berm about eighteen inches high, just enough for concealment if we had company. When we were finished digging in the frozen dirt, we settled into position.

Vale pulled a thermos and five plastic cups out of a black daypack and poured each of us a cup of steaming coffee. "I made it strong. We'll need to stay alert, at least I will. It's been years since I've been on a stakeout," Vale whispered.

Tony laughed quietly. "They're such a part of my routine that I can't remember the last time I got eight hours of uninterrupted sleep. Sometimes I feel like a pervert for all the things I've seen that weren't illegal but definitely weren't intended for my viewing pleasure," he said.

Martens nodded. "Tell me about it. I've seen more in the last year in NOMIDES than my whole three years put together as a deputy before that. Some people are sick."

"Not sick, just adventurous," I volunteered. Everyone looked at me and snickered.

"I don't even want to know where that's coming from," Nick said and then nudged Vale. "How long are we going to stay here?"

Vale looked around and said, "Since the homeowner told Robin she heard most of the activity in the early hours of the morning, I think we should stick around until about three. If nothing happens by then, we'll call it a night."

Then he added, "Kevin, tell them what you saw when you went back there this afternoon."

The undercover detective described finding the trailer easily enough and noticing fresh tracks around the perimeter. "There's definitely been activity here recently. I got out of the truck and tried to look in the windows but they're all boarded up. I couldn't smell any chemicals, though, but that doesn't mean it's not a meth lab. It's sealed up pretty well and there was no license plate," he said.

"What about Shasta? Have you been able to make contact with her?" I asked.

Vale snorted. "Yeah, one of our deputies spotted her coming out of her mother's shop and stopped her. She started to get mouthy, I guess, but then decided it would be better to just come along quietly. The deputy brought her to my office at about five. We questioned her for an hour and got absolutely nowhere. She admitted to dating Kyle but said she hadn't seen him for several days before he was killed. She said she'd never seen him take drugs and that he didn't seem to have any enemies. She denied even knowing where his camp was in the Hiawatha National Forest or that he even had a camp. She claimed she didn't really know him all that well. As for Steve Sampson, she said he borrowed a hundred bucks from her last month and she went to his office today to collect but he claimed he was broke. She never wavered from her story. I'd love to give her a lie detector test but I doubt she would consent. She asked if she needed an attorney and I advised her that that was entirely up to her. She's pretty savvy, that one."

"Obviously she's lying. She was probably standing right there when Kyle's head was bashed in," I said. What made a person so cold? Was she some sort of sociopath? I couldn't see Sam raising such a self-centered person, but then again, drugs had a nasty way of altering personalities.

While Tony, Nick and Kevin surveyed the area with a night scope they passed between them, I tried to find a comfortable position. The night was eerily quiet, no sounds of birds or deer or squirrels moving through the forest. Only the distant rumble of an occasional truck passing on the highway to the south broke the stillness. Time seemed to drag and I began to wonder if this was going to be a massive waste of time. I was fantasizing about my big, warm, soft bed back in my apartment in Escanaba when, just after midnight, headlights appeared to the west on the road that ran about a hundred and fifty feet in front of our position.

"It's a pickup in four-wheel-drive mode," Martens whispered.

The truck, a two-tone Dodge Ram that looked to be about ten years old, rolled through the snow easily and finally came to a stop about forty feet east of the trailer. The lights went out and the engine quit just before two men got out of the truck, took a couple snow shovels from the back and began digging a path to the trailer.

"You recognize either of them?" I whispered.

Tony and Nick shook their heads in the negative, but Kevin said, "I'm not sure. I think I've seen both of them around but I don't know their names."

Vale took the scope from Kevin. "There's someone still inside the truck," he said and handed it to me.

The world turned a bright shade of green, like something out of a sixties-era science fiction movie. I was amazed at how clearly I could make out details despite the darkness. The light from the men's flashlights cast a wicked glow through the scope. I trained it on the cab of the truck and studied the lone occupant.

"That's Shasta," I whispered excitedly.

Martens grabbed the scope from me. "Yup, that's her all right. Hey, those guys are working on the camper's hitch. They must be getting ready to pull it out."

Vale cursed. "Damn it! We'll never be able to get back to the truck and follow them out of here. These logging roads go all over hell and back. They could come out anywhere. Kevin, once they start moving, try to get the license number off that truck."

Vale pulled out a small radio and turned it on low. "Delta Five to Delta Fifteen."

"Delta Fifteen."

"Location?"

"Corner of Ogontz Road and the highway."

"Keep your eyes peeled for a red and dark gray Dodge Ram truck pulling a beat-up travel trailer."

"10-4."

After a few minutes of installing a hitch, one guy took a license plate from the cab and disappeared around the back of the trailer. Then the other man got into the truck, started it up and put it in reverse, backing it up while the first man guided him to the hitch. On the second attempt, the truck made contact and the driver got out to connect the trailer's taillight wires.

"Kevin, go!" Vale whispered.

He began snaking through the trees to the west and was just ten feet off the road when the men got back into the truck and prepared to drive away. Vale cursed again.

"These guys are pros," Tony said. "They've probably hooked and unhooked trailers hundreds of times. It would take most people a helluva lot longer to do that."

"But where are they going and what's in that trailer? Damn it," Vale said through clenched teeth as the truck and camper disappeared into the night. Martens emerged from the woods with the night scope in hand and began sprinting after them. After a minute or two, Vale's radio crackled. "Delta Twenty to Delta Five."

"Delta Five. Go ahead Delta Twenty."

"All I could get was a partial plate number off the trailer, V251. I couldn't see the rest. But it was a Michigan plate. They passed the turnoff to go back to the highway so they must have another way out. I've lost 'em now," Martens said.

"Okay, get back here, Delta Twenty."

"10-4."

While we waited for Kevin to return, I asked if what we had seen was enough probable cause to pick up Shasta Burns for questioning.

"We didn't witness anything criminal except for trespassing. But we don't even know who those two guys with her are. They could be part owners of the land. We could always use the excuse that we have some more questions regarding Kyle Sullivan's death," Vale said and sighed. "Then again, will she be around tomorrow? Your friend said that camper has been there since at least this spring. Looks to me like they pulled it out for good. But why now? Did Sampson's arrest spook them?"

Nick nodded. "That would be my guess. Either way, that Shasta character knows a lot more than she's letting on. I'm willing to wager she's our key to solving this whole mystery."

"I think it's time I had another talk with Sam," I said reluctantly. As if the poor man hadn't been through enough, what with losing his wife in a car accident and adopting a drug-addicted, ungrateful brat. Now he might find he had a killer in the family.

Chapter Fifteen

*I*t was nearly three o'clock by the time Nick, Tony and I trudged back into my aunt's house, trying not to wake her. As usual, Belle met me at the door, excited to see me and undoubtedly feeling neglected by my recent lack of attention.

"I'll take the couch, guys. You can take the spare bedroom tonight. I just want to build a fire and zone out," I said as I hung my snowsuit on a hook by the back door.

Nick went into the bedroom and eyed the frilly rose-patterned comforter and white cotton sheets with eyelet trim. "Gee, do you think it's me?"

I playfully socked his arm. "I'm sure your manhood will survive."

"Alright, if you insist. I could use some sound sleep," he said and then looked at Tony. "You don't snore, do you?"

Tony laughed. "I don't think so, but I know there isn't room enough in that bed for the two of us without getting cozier than I'd like so I'll just camp out in the living room on the floor like I did last night."

"Okay, kiddies, don't stay up too late sharing ghost stories," Nick said.

I made up the couch while Tony built a fire and then paged through the last journal Mitch had written.

"Are we missing something?" I asked quietly.

"Yes, but what? Robin, think back to those last few weeks. Did Mitch ever give you even a tiny clue that something was different?" Tony asked.

I sat on the coach, pulled the comforter around me and tried to focus on the first few weeks of April. The signs of spring were everywhere as green grass, daffodils and tree buds replaced dirty snow. The earth smelled fresh, alive; the sun shone brighter, warmer; people moved with more grace, not so huddled against the cold winds that made Chicago winters famous. Mitch had been his usual upbeat self, but I did remember one dinner conversation about three days before his death when he'd seemed preoccupied. He'd said there was a lot going on at work and he was tired. He was looking forward to taking some time off and visiting my family in the U.P. Then he'd asked me if I'd ever known anyone who used drugs.

I'd known people I suspected of using drugs but I had never actually seen anything. He'd then asked whether the U.P. had much of a drug problem. I'd answered that, other than marijuana and prescription drugs, I didn't think so. He'd then changed the subject.

"Even if I'd known what he was working on, I couldn't have been much help, although I would have known Steve Sampson," I said to Tony.

"You can't blame yourself for any of this, Robin," he said. "Mitch made his choice to work with the DEA, and he made it for the right reasons. He just didn't realize how dangerous a game he was playing. And it is a game, with winners and losers, good guys and bad guys. The bad guys won that round. We have to make sure we take the match."

I reached out and brushed a lock of wavy black hair that had fallen across his brow. "I'm really glad I met you. I couldn't handle any of this by myself and, well, it's great to have someone to talk to who understands."

He took my hand in his and touched his soft lips to the palm. A shiver ran down my back, a delightful, warm, electric shiver. I looked into his eyes and felt myself fall. I landed on the floor next to him, our faces inches apart, breaths soft on each other's cheeks. The kiss was warm, gentle and slow, like the fire swelling in my core as my hands moved over his face and down around his shoulders and his arms snaked around my waist.

Suddenly someone was stumbling into the hall. I sprang back onto the couch and rubbed my mouth as Nick flicked on the light in the kitchen.

"Sorry, guys, but I'll never get to sleep without some warm milk."

Tony gritted his teeth and rolled his eyes while I suppressed a giggle.

I helped Nick find a saucepan and then crawled beneath the covers on the couch. "We're both exhausted so let's try and get some sleep," I said. "I'll talk to Sam Burns tomorrow and see if he can shed any light on what's going on with Shasta. Maybe she's made contact with her mother."

"Right. Good night, Robin," Tony said, sounding disappointed, and nestled into his makeshift bed on the floor.

My aunt was up at five forty-five but I hid under the covers another half hour and then shuffled to the shower and let water pour over me for several minutes before I came to life. I tried to think about Shasta Burns and how, or whether, she fit into Kyle and Mitch's deaths, but my mind kept drifting to the man sleeping on the floor of my aunt's living room. He had reawakened emotions and sensations that I thought were lost to me forever. Mitch had been "the one" and I'd always believed there could be only "one." Was Tony a bridge to a new life or just a warm memory in the making? I smiled as the hot water splashed against my skin. The memory of last night's kiss was already making me warm. Maybe he had the same questions and feelings, especially if there hadn't been anyone in his life since his wife's death. What else did we have in common besides grief and a love of the outdoors? I wanted to know more about Tony Granati, why he stayed in police work when it seemed so futile at times, why he still had faith in a process that had failed his family.

There was a knock at the bathroom door. "I'll be out in a minute," I yelled. The response was inaudible. I turned off the water, quickly toweled myself dry and donned a robe. Nick was in the kitchen making coffee when I stepped into the hallway. "It's all yours," I said.

"What, you don't spend half an hour on hair and makeup in the morning?"

Tossing my wet hair, I said, "With natural beauty such as this, it would be like throwing latex paint on the Mona Lisa," and went into the spare bedroom Nick had just vacated and shut the door so I could get dressed. I'd lived alone for a long time but I now marveled at how comfortable I felt at my aunt's house with the Granati men around. I hadn't realized just how lonely I was, how much I needed companionship. People had tried to fill that void—Mrs. Easton, Aunt Gina, my dad, even Charlie. But it hadn't worked. Still, when I thought about Charlie I knew I had a friend for life. He'd gone to extraordinary lengths to help me over the last several months.

After my aunt left for work, Nick, Tony and I gathered at the kitchen table to strategize. Out of curiosity, I flicked on the radio and tuned it to Steve's former station, but there was no sign that anything was out of the ordinary. The DJ never mentioned the fact that she was filling in for the station manager who'd been arrested on murder charges the day before. As the chatter gave way to rock music, I perused the pile of back issues of the *Daily Press* my aunt left on the table. A recently hired young reporter had covered the Kyle Sullivan murder investigation but the articles revealed nothing I didn't already know. I tossed the papers back in a pile, turned off the radio and sat down to inhale the fumes from the steaming cup of coffee before me.

"So, what do we do now?" Tony asked, yawning and stretching his arms above his head.

I drank some coffee and said, "I'm going to stop by the *Daily Press* to turn in my key and try to track down Shasta. Hopefully Sam Burns is a little more forthcoming this time."

Nick glanced at me and then at Tony and then back at me. "You given any thought to what you're going to do for a job when this is all over?"

Groaning, I rubbed my eyes and said, "None at all. I don't think I want to be a reporter anymore, but I still want to write, maybe teach, but I don't have the credentials. Mitch's insurance policy would certainly cover a graduate writing program," I said and took another sip of coffee.

"Aren't UW-Superior and UM-Duluth next-door neighbors?" Nick asked.

Tony grinned sheepishly.

"Not very subtle, am I?" Nick said with a playful wink at both of us.

"Before you go sending out invitations to her bridal shower, would you like to solve this case?" Tony asked and lightly kicked his cousin under the table.

"Naturally. I think the first thing to do is check in with Detective Vale and that officer in Gladstone. If there is a hearing, they'll probably need me to testify. I'm kind of surprised no one's tried calling me. There're no messages on my cell phone. I wonder if that little puke decided to waive extradition," Nick said.

"Maybe he's scared," I suggested. "If the ringleader really is in the U.P., how hard would it be to pay some schmuck already in jail to shank him?"

With an approving nod, Nick chucked me under the chin. "Good thinking, Blondie," he said. "Either way, I want to get a better handle on the entire drug picture in this region and maybe even get some background on this Edward Carlson who worked with Mitch. How far is Alger Max from here?"

"It's a little east of Munising so I'm guessing maybe a seventy-minute drive. Remember, there's a winter storm coming. Munising is right on Lake Superior and if that storm's coming out of the north, it will get nasty there real fast. The demarcation line for the snowbelt that runs across the U.P. begins around Trenary about twenty miles north of here. Everything north of there gets hammered with snow whenever something blows in off the big lake," I said.

"Hey, we get a little snow in Chicago once in a while too, you know," Tony said.

I let that pass. Chicago wasn't the U.P. but they would learn that soon enough. We left my aunt's house in Rapid River a little before nine and stopped at Escanaba Public Safety to update Charlie on last night's activities before we went to see Vale. Everyone was buzzing about Steve Sampson when we walked into the lobby. One of the dispatchers said Charlie wanted to talk to me and led us down a long hallway to his office where he was studying some photos on his desk. He looked up, revealing dark purple circles under his eyes.

"What's going on?" I asked.

"Close the door and sit down," he ordered. When we were seated in cushioned straight back chairs across from his desk he dropped a bomb. "Sampson's dead."

"What! How can that be? There are cameras everywhere in that jail," Nick cried and looked at me, incredulous. How had I known? Something in my gut had given me a warning too late.

Charlie heaved a sigh and threw his hands up in the air. "A fight broke out about three cells down from him. It took every deputy on duty to break it up and by the time they did a bed check Steve had hung himself. At least it looks like he hung himself."

"What do you mean?"

"He's got some weird bruising on his neck that isn't consistent with the blanket he used. I don't know, maybe it's nothing. There's no way anyone could have gotten into his cell without the key," Charlie said.

"Can't you just look at the security camera tape and see what happened?" I asked.

Charlie shook his head and gave me a disgusted smile. "That little brawl took out the camera in their cell and managed to knock out the entire system," he said and then shook a finger at me. "I know what you're thinking. It sounds too neat and tidy, like it was planned. Unfortunately, no one in the entire jail is talking and state law prevents us from beating it out of them."

"What time did all this happen?"

Before he could answer there was tap on the door.

"Yeah?"

The same dispatcher opened the door and said, "Vale is here to see you."

"Send him in."

The dispatcher nodded to someone in the hall and Det. Tom Vale appeared.

He shut the door and leaned against it, exhausted.

"Well, here we are again, one big happy bunch of stooges."

Charlie just shook his head and turned back to me. "You asked what time Sampson died. I'll let Vale finish the story."

Vale nodded and said, "The brawl started at about 3:30 this morning. It took about ten minutes to get everybody apart and calmed down. One guy, the one who was thrown against the camera system, was taken to the hospital for a few broken ribs and some internal bleeding. It got pretty ugly." He toyed with the edge of the belt on his trench coat for a bit before continuing. "Robin, for your own safety, I want you to step back from this case. I was wrong in asking for your help. I can't believe I allowed myself to endanger a civilian. I apologize."

I leaned back in the chair and shook my head. "No, don't apologize. Remember, for me, this is personal, not just another case. Steve Sampson is just the tip of the iceberg. That iceberg may have brought down my fiancé."

Vale looked at me as though I were a ghost and whispered, "It was an iceberg that brought down the Titanic. No one's invincible."

Charlie cleared his throat. "That's not all I have to report. It turns out you were right about that Mandy Miller dying in Kyle's apartment. We tracked down her latest boyfriend and he figured he'd better talk. Apparently they were having a big bash two weeks ago Friday, probably a day or two before Kyle was murdered. They were doing everything from pot to coke. When he went to leave at about two in the morning, he found Mandy passed out in the bathroom. He didn't think much of it and got our friend Shasta to help him get Mandy into his truck. Once he got her home, he realized she was dead. He freaked, took her down to the basement thinking no one would smell her for a while and left the house for good. I'm telling you this guy is a creep with the IQ of a houseplant. He was coming off another three-day drunk from when we found him last night loitering near the party store."

"Once again, it all leads back to Shasta. Vale, you're going to be sorry you didn't hold her yesterday," I said.

Vale held his head in his hands and groaned. "Tell me about it, but there wasn't even enough evidence to get a warrant. Now, we've got it, but she's probably long gone, spooked by our clumsiness."

"You had no way of knowing about this Mandy Miller. Hell, I never even heard of her until yesterday," I said and fell silent with everyone else, lost in a swirling pool of frustration, exhaustion and confusion. "Shasta's just a kid, maybe twenty-one or twenty-two. I can't believe she's the ringleader."

"No, too young and impulsive," Charlie said. "There's a reason chiefs of police aren't hired right out of college. You need time to learn the shit they don't teach you in a classroom. Same thing goes with criminal operations. You gotta make a name for yourself."

"I guess I should have seen that coming," Vale said.

"Don't beat yourself up over this. It doesn't sound like there was anything those deputies could do anyway. This was just too well-planned if you ask me," Charlie replied. "So what do we do now?"

I told him my plan to try and find Shasta. Vale started to object when Tony said, "Look, I know you're not crazy about involving us further, but you aren't going to get within a mile of that girl without us. She still doesn't know a thing about me. Maybe we can use that to our advantage."

Vale reluctantly acquiesced and the three of us left for the *Daily Press*. Where would it end, I wondered, and how many more people would die before this was over? Suddenly I wished that Mitch had been just an average cop who went with the flow and did what he was told, but then again, I probably wouldn't have fallen in love with a man like that.

Nick and Tony stayed in the car watching fluffy flakes begin to collect on the windshield. Inside the morning hustle of the newspaper, Bob Hunter saw I was distressed and called me into his office.

"Robin, I've worked at this paper for nearly thirty years and have never seen more violent crime than I have in the last seven months since you've blown back into town. I'm beginning to wonder if you're a jinx," he said and leaned back in his squeaky old chair that had probably spent the last thirty years supporting him.

"I know you're joking, but you may not be too far off base," I said. His eyebrows jerked upward. "Bob, how come you hired me back? It took just a ten-minute phone call in May for you to offer me the job. Why?"

Startled, Bob straightened in his chair and folded his hands on the desk. "Actually, I knew you were going to call. Sam told me about what had happened to your fiancé and thought you might want to come home for a while. He said that since we had an opening anyway, it would be worth it to wait for you if you wanted to come back," he said and then stopped and scratched his silver and white beard, as though considering his next words carefully.

"Robin, you value honesty and so do I. The truth is, I didn't think it was wise. I'm not surprised you quit again. You're too good for this place. At the Tribune, you proved you could handle the big time. You thrived down there. This was a stepping stone, that's all it was meant to be, but I was overruled when I pointed that out to Sam. I respect him and didn't see any real harm in letting you come back to the nest, if only for a little while," he said.

"But, Bob, why did you encourage me take the news editor position before I left if you think I'd be better off somewhere else?" I said, genuinely confused.

With a sigh, Bob shrugged. "Sam wants me to try and hang on to you. Look, Carol is fifty-five and wants to retire in five years. Sam's thinking about the future of this newspaper. I can't say I blame him. Good talent is hard to come by, especially at a small outfit like this. Please don't be mad at me or Sam. You're the one who called about the job," Bob said.

"I'm not mad at all, but how did Sam know about Mitch?" I asked. Apparently the grapevine stretched all the way from Chicago to Escanaba.

"I'm sure he heard it on the street. Your father probably said something to him. They're both members of the country club," Bob said. That was true. I could see my dad thinking Sam would want to know I had just lost my fiancé. Nick was probably just paranoid. I couldn't picture the meek and mild Sam Burns as a mastermind criminal.

"You're probably right. Anyway, where is Sam? I haven't seen him around today and I'd like to talk to him."

"He has a press association meeting to attend downstate next week and was going to take a little time off to prepare for some presentation," Bob said and then added with a shake of his head. "I think this whole thing with Shasta is finally getting to him. The whole town is talking about her. I feel bad for the guy."

"Do you think he's at home now?" I asked.

Bob thought for a few seconds and frowned. "I doubt it. He and Janet do have a place on March Lake off Highway 13. Sometimes he likes to spend time up there when he's prepping for these things."

"Isn't that several miles north of Boone Lake where that Sullivan kid died?" I asked.

"Yeah, I think so. I've never been to the cottage. He doesn't seem to entertain much there," Bob said.

"Bob, I want you to know I'm grateful for everything you've done for me since I first interned here. You've been the best mentor a young reporter could ask for and you've been beyond patient with me. I'm really sorry to leave you in the lurch like this," I said as tears welled in my eyes. "I—I just want you to know I have some very fond memories of this place and wish you all the best in retirement. It was you who taught me to stretch myself, not to get too comfortable. That's what I'm doing."

Bob blinked several times and cleared his throat. "Well, kiddo, you mean a lot to me too. You're a brave one, and smart too. Go make us proud," he said and gave me one of his famous bear hugs. "Take care of yourself."

"You too, Bob," I said and started to leave. I turned back and asked one last favor. "Do you have Sam's cell phone number?"

He wrote it down and then chased me out of his office. I left my key with Amy, the news clerk, cleaned out the few odds and ends I'd stashed in and around my desk and gave everyone a goodbye hug. I had no idea what lay ahead, but I felt in my gut I was making the right decision and was moving toward something better—if I lived through the next few days.

Back in the car, I told Nick and Tony what Bob had said about my return to the newspaper. Something bothered me about Sam asking Bob Hunter to hire me if I just happened to call looking for a job. Maybe Nick was onto something but the thought of Sam Burns doing anything outside the law, even letting the speedometer slide past sixty on the highway, was hard to swallow. Still, I wanted to hear his explanation straight from his own lips so my first stop after leaving the paper was at Janet's wine shop six blocks west of the newspaper on the twelve hundred block of Ludington Street. Hopefully she could tell me the whereabouts of her husband or, better yet, her errant daughter.

While I had been cleaning out my desk and saying goodbye to the *Daily Press*, Tony had contacted the warden at Alger Maximum Security Prison. The man agreed to see us but didn't think he'd be much help.

"Why should he be any different than anyone else in this case?" I said cynically as I put the car in gear and turned from North Sixth Street onto Ludington.

Janet had aptly named the store Bacchanalian Delights, evoking just the right mix of high-brow snobbery and low-brow debauchery that the local population took to immediately and made the business a success. Set in the middle of the block on the south side, the shop occupied the first floor of one of many century-old buildings lining Ludington, aka "downtown." Cedar shingles set below large windows and Old English-style lettering gave the store a decidedly Old World feel that did not blend at all with the rest of the shops, which were trying for Victorian charm. Then again, "blending" had never been a concern of Janet Burns, the proud owner of one of Escanaba's few late model Mercedes sedans and wearer of a full-length mink coat that made me want to cry for all the little minks that had been sacrificed just so some lady could flaunt her wealth. The more I thought about it, the more I could understand how Shasta had seen herself as coming from money when one considered her mother and ignored her father, a man who wore JC Penney Oxford shirts and drove a pickup.

I told the Granatis to stay in the car again while I darted across the street to track down Sam and Shasta. The salesclerk, a middle-aged woman whom I recognized as the wife of the local urologist, was helping a young couple select the proper wine for a dinner they were hosting Friday evening. Not seeing Janet lurking in the back, I waited impatiently, perusing the shelves of wine, arranged by country of origin, type and vintage. Janet had amassed a spectacular collection with prices ranging from the affordable to the unimaginable in a working-class town. Still, the store had been going for more than fifteen years so who was I to quibble with success? After the couple had finally selected two bottles of French merlot (they were serving steak) and were safely out of the store, I approached the clerk, introduced myself and asked for Janet.

"Oh my, I thought you would have heard. She's down at Public Safety this very minute." She then leaned forward and whispered as though letting me in on a state secret, "Shasta, it seems, has disappeared,"

"Disappeared? When?"

"Janet said she's been missing since Sunday, after the police questioned her about that young man's death on Boone Lake. Poor thing has had a rough time of it, you know, with the drugs and all," she said, folding her hands on the counter and shaking her head. "I just don't understand young people these days. Why do they need artificial substances to sustain themselves?"

I had to force myself not to laugh at this hypocrisy from a purveyor of spirits used to alter the mind ever since humans had discovered fermentation. Instead, I inquired if she knew where I could find Sam.

"Oh, he never comes here. I think it's wonderful that he's so supportive of Janet. Most men would be constantly butting their nose in, making sure the little woman was running the business properly and not squandering the profits, but not Sam. He knows he's got a smart one," she said.

"You said that Janet went to the police. Didn't Sam go with her?"

"Well, I wouldn't know about that. She doesn't talk about him," she admitted and then leaned across the counter and whispered. "If you ask me, there's trouble in that marriage, maybe that's why I never see him. But that's not our business now, is it?"

"No, not at all," I said, shaking my head. I thanked her for her time and left.

When I told Nick and Tony about Janet reporting Shasta missing, Nick sat in silence and tapped his gloved fingers on the armrest while Tony said, "Missing? What a crock! This is definitely part of someone's plan. I say we head for that prison and see if we can learn something useful about this Edward Carlson. I'm gettin' real tired of chasing after this little brat."

We all agreed that was the best course of action so I drove toward the highway, now patterned with circles of light snow swirling across the asphalt. The sky to the north was thick with clouds. During the drive to the prison Nick filled me in on a phone call he'd made to some "connections in Chicago" while I was in the wine shop. Dave Whelan was nowhere to be found. He hadn't reported to work since Friday.

"You think he might be the one who shot Leeds?" Tony asked.

Nick nodded. "I do. My uncle is running a check through the airlines to see if Whelan was on a plane south but, thanks to 9/11, it's harder than ever to get information out of them," he said. "Also, a classmate of Mitch's and mine who now works for the FBI finally came through for me with some information. He said the bureau has long considered Dmitri Karastova a person of interest in the drug trade since the market on illegal weapons grew soft with the fall of communism. Apparently he drew the line at supplying weapons to terrorists. He confirmed the old man is in declining health and rarely leaves his house in Crescent, which leads me to believe one of the kids has taken over the business—either the college professor or the missing daughter."

"I could have my aunt try to contact the professor and feel him out. She's great at concocting scenarios. What's the son's name?"

Nick screwed up his face in thought and then said, "Good question. I don't recall, but she should be able to pull up the Northwestern University website and do a search for his last name."

I dialed her office number, and, after explaining the situation, she enthusiastically agreed to make the call to Dr. Karastova. I could almost hear her mind shift into gear as she planned her approach.

"You said his father's parents were Russian immigrants? I could say I'm doing an article about how Russians handled religion in the new country and ask if he could put me in touch with his father. I also have a former graduate student who's now teaching in their social sciences department. She must know him. I'll call her too and then let you know as soon as I hear something," Aunt Gina said, adding with a giggle, "This is exciting. I feel like Miss Marple."

I laughed, said goodbye and closed the phone. "She's on the trail. She'll call as soon as she knows something."

"Great," Nick said and then peered through the windshield at the leaden sky and the tree-lined highway broken by the occasional ancient wood-frame house. "Depressing. Why would anyone want to live way out here? There's nothin' here."

"That's why people do live here—they don't want any neighbors," Tony said. "It's quite convenient for people who don't want to be found, like drug traffickers."

"Good point," Nick said. "However, my specialty is inconveniencing people."

I had to admit he was good at that.

Chapter Sixteen

$\mathcal{A}$lger Maximum Security Prison is located in the woods east of Munising, a picturesque town of less than four thousand residents that lines the Lake Superior shore for a couple of miles. Commonly known as the snowmobile capital of Michigan, it is also home to a small paper mill and the Pictured Rocks National Lakeshore, a park popular with hikers, campers and boaters who skirt the shore studying the layered rock formations that tower over jewel-toned Lake Superior. The prison, a modern facility less than two decades old, houses men convicted of the most serious felonies—murder, rape, attempted murder, extortion. Since Michigan does not have the death penalty, anyone convicted of first-degree murder is automatically sentenced to life in prison without possibility of parole. Alger is one of three maximum security prisons in the U.P., providing the area with needed jobs and the state with remote places to put its most undesirable residents. Alger Max is located in the Industrial Park off M-28 on 78 acres. It consists of ten buildings surrounded by double fences topped with razor-ribbon wire and five gun towers. Since Tony had contacted the warden ahead of time the guards were prepared for our arrival. Under leaden skies, we made our way into the administration building where we were required to show identification and leave our wallets, purse and cell phones with a guard. Another guard took us to Warden William Russo's office, overlooking the compound. Russo, a tall, solid man with short gray hair and brown eyes, stood and gave us each a firm, quick handshake and invited us to take a seat in the standard issue government chairs in front of his desk. In the center of his blotter was a half-inch thick file. He opened the file and looked over the facing page as though refreshing his memory.

"Mr. Granati, as I said on the phone, Ed Carlson doesn't stick out in my mind at all. Sometimes they do, you know, sometimes for good reasons, sometimes for the wrong reasons. From his file, Ed just seemed like a normal prisoner. He did five years for armed robbery; the original sentence was eight but he got off for good behavior. He worked in the laundry, minded his own business most of the time, got into a few fist fights but nothing out of the ordinary. Tension runs close to the surface with these men, especially the ones who will get out someday," Russo explained.

"I would think it would be the other way around, that the lifers would be the troublemakers," I said.

Russo smiled coldly. "It depends on the kind of trouble. Some of the lifers won't hesitate to kill someone who gets in their way because, hey, what's another murder when you're already in until you die. In general though, most lifers reach a point of acceptance, then adjustment and, finally, comfort with their situation. It's the ones who have some hope of getting out of here some day, the ones who have calendars in their cells to mark off each long, boring, miserable day, that have to be extra careful. They know that if they make one too many mistakes in here, it'll delay getting back out there," Russo said and hooked his thumb toward the prison's gates.

"What about the drug trade?" Nick asked.

"It happens, and I'm sure it happens a lot," Russo said, throwing up his hands. "We try to keep a lid on it, but you have to remember that most of these guys are from urban areas where drugs are a part of everyday life. Even if they're not in here for drug-related offenses, they've probably tried them at some point, or sold them, or killed somebody who was muscling in on the gang's territory. This is a rough place. I don't have any prisoners studying poetry or ornithology. These guys live by a dog-eat-dog code."

He looked down at the file on his desk and then back at Tony. "On the phone you asked me earlier if there was any way to know who befriended Ed Carlson while he was here. The guards do take note of that stuff in case it becomes important down the road. I spoke to a few who worked in Carlson's building when he was here, but I'm afraid there isn't much to tell you in this case. As I said, Ed was a normal prisoner. He didn't have any real enemies and he didn't have a lot of friends. He hung around with these three other white guys from more rural parts of the state. One of them had a conviction for making and selling meth, one for murdering his girlfriend in a fit of rage and another for armed robbery. As far as I can tell, none of them knew each other before they came here and none of them kept in touch once they were released, which both Ed and Jesse Levin have been, released that is. Levin was the meth seller."

"Where were Ed and Jesse from?" I asked.

Russo consulted the file and said, "Ed was born in Elmhurst, Ill. He was arrested for armed robbery in Kalamazoo, robbed a convenience store at gunpoint and might have gotten away with it if his buddy's getaway car hadn't broken down on the highway. I'll have to make a call on Jesse." He picked up the phone, dialed three numbers and asked, "Will you please bring me Jesse Levin's file? Thanks."

Less than a minute later an efficient-looking woman with a haircut similar to Russo's delivered a slim manila folder to him and made her exit without a sound. He flipped open the file and reviewed its contents for a few minutes.

"It looks like Levin is originally from Escanaba, but he was arrested near Gaylord. Carlson was released in May 2004 and Levin got out in February 2005," Russo said, comparing notes from each file as he spoke. "There's something in here about Carlson getting cited for reckless driving north of Milwaukee in May 2006, but Levin's record has been spotless since his release. That doesn't mean that he's been a Boy Scout, just that no one's caught him at anything."

"That's rather cynical," I said.

Russo looked at me over the tops of his steel-framed eyeglasses. "Ms. Hamilton, I've been in law enforcement for thirty-five years. I may sound cynical to you, but I call it being realistic. Few men who have served time in a maximum security facility ever truly turn their lives around. It's the cruel irony of incarceration. All too often they simply learn how to be better criminals."

"I'm sorry. Perhaps I'm being naïve," I said and shot a glance at Tony as he tried to hide a smirk.

Russo's smile reached his eyes for the first time. "My job is to make sure you have the luxury of being naïve by not having to deal with these characters."

"Actually, it's the murder of her fiancé, a cop in Crescent, that brings us here," Nick said.

Russo's eyes widened. "I'm sorry. Please accept my condolences."

"Thank you," I said, holding my chin firm.

"I wish I could be of more help to you guys. About all I can give you is the last address I have for Jesse Levin and the name of his probation officer in Escanaba." He wrote down the information and handed it to Tony.

"Do you have a photo of these men?" I asked.

"Of course," Russo said, turning each file so that they faced me. Each folder had a three-by-five color photograph attached to the opening flap. Ed Carlson was unfamiliar, but we recognized Jesse Levin immediately.

"It's the guy who drove the pickup last night," Tony said.

"Yeah, I'm sure of it, just imagine him with a black toque," I replied.

Nick leaned over and peered at the photo. "You're right, that's definitely him. Mr. Russo, can we get a color copy of those photos? A paper copy will be fine."

"Sure, one moment," Russo said and turned to his computer and began maneuvering the mouse, clicking through a series of screens. The printer to his right whirred to life and spit out a full-size color rendition of Jesse Levin and then Edward Carlson, neither looking like someone with whom I'd want to be alone, but they were one more link to Shasta Burns.

Snow was falling more heavily by the time we drove through the prison gates. "Here it comes," I said. When we got to the highway, I turned right.

"Where are we going?" Tony asked.

"Down Highway 13 to see if Sam Burns is at his camp. I really want to talk to him," I said, adding, "Nick, do you think Ed Carlson had ties to this Karastova guy and when he met Jesse Levin, who was already involved in the drug trade, decided to bring him on board?"

"It sure looks that way, doesn't it? Try calling Detective Vale and tell him what we learned," Nick said.

Vale was in his office and accepted my call. The first words out of his mouth were: "Shasta Burns' mother has reported her missing."

"I know. I stopped by the wine shop a few hours ago and the clerk there told me Janet had gone to Public Safety to report her missing. Did you talk to her?"

"Yeah, Charlie Baker called me and I went over there. I told her I saw Shasta last night in the hope that maybe she could shed some light on her daughter's activities but she was clueless. She even apologized for her rude behavior the other day when our deputies went to her house looking for her daughter. She said she knew Shasta had a drug problem in the past but that she'd gone through a treatment program during the summer and seemed to be doing well. She said Kyle Sullivan had been a good influence on her daughter and she was horrified that he'd been murdered.

"We also got some details on the little hunks of skin under his fingernails. The DNA didn't match his so it's likely from the killer. We're working with the state police crime lab to see if we can find a match with the FBI's DNA database," he said.

"That's great! Maybe they'll find a match with Steve Sampson," I said.

"Yeah, well, that may take some time. Who knows when Sampson's autopsy will be completed," Vale said, dejected.

"Don't sound so depressed. I have some news too," I said. "Tony, Nick and I just saw the warden at Alger Max and discovered that one of the guys who hung around with Ed Carlson, the guy my fiancé made contact with in Crescent and led him to Steve, is from Escanaba and was the one driving the pickup last night. His name is Jesse Levin."

I gave Vale the information about Levin and he said he would check it out, excitement building in his voice.

"This may be the break we've been looking for," he said and hung up.

I tried to call Sam's cell phone but we were out of range from a tower so I stashed it back in my purse and concentrated on the scenery. The leafless trees were now shrouded in a thin blanket of snow and the road was beginning to blend into the shadows as the flakes grew in size and fell harder.

"Be careful. It's probably getting slippery," Nick cautioned, eyeing the weather with trepidation.

"Yes, Mother," I snapped and let off the gas.

I slowed at the sign for March Lake and turned onto a gravel road that forked around the water to the north and south. I stopped and pondered which way to turn.

"Now what, Blondie?" Nick quipped from the backseat.

I bit my lower lip and shrugged. "I don't know, I guess we just drive around the whole thing and see if I recognize anything that might indicate it belongs to Sam."

I turned the Outback to the south and followed the road as it wound past a few cabins and around the long, narrow lake, now even grayer than the sky. During a normal winter the lake would be frozen, but the warm, rainy December had kept the center of the lake open. We were on the far west side of the lake when I spotted a log archway over a wide, long gravel driveway and the name Burns Getaway carved into the arch. We pulled into what could only be described as a compound, complete with a main house that looked to be about three thousand square feet and constructed of light-stained logs that matched the archway, a guest house about the size of the home where I grew up, a standard two-car garage and a much larger tan steel building with huge double doors that slid open laterally at each end so a vehicle could drive straight through.

"They must park an RV in there," Tony said, pointing at the larger building.

I parked in front of the main house and stared at the scale of everything.

"I had no idea they had this much money. This doesn't even look like something Sam would enjoy. He always talks about going fishing in his aluminum boat. I've seen a picture of that boat and it's not much more than a dingy with an outboard motor. This is, I don't know, too much," I said and then remembered Janet's Mercedes and mink. "I guess this is Janet's getaway. She seems to like to do things on a grand scale."

Nick looked at me curiously and said, "Robin, who is Janet Burns?"

I told him the story Sam had related to me Monday morning. Nick rubbed his chin and scowled.

"I don't like this. I don't like this one bit," he mumbled.

"Well, I don't either. I'm going to see if anyone's home," I said and got out of the car.

"Robin!" they yelled simultaneously.

I ignored them because I already knew where Nick's mind was traveling and there was no way I was going to believe that Sam was a drug dealer and Janet certainly didn't need the money considering how well her wine shop was doing. I pounded on one of the double doors painted pine green and yelled, "Sam, it's Robin. If you're in there, please come to the door."

No answer. A deck about fifteen feet wide wrapped around the back and sides of the house and opened onto a much larger multi-level veranda on the lakeside. As I walked around the house I peered into the windows but most had the curtains drawn or opened onto elaborately-furnished rooms obviously devoid of life. The snow was now falling so hard that the other side of the lake was lost in the storm. Disappointed, I made my way back to the Outback. My hand was on the door handle when I decided to take a look at the garages. The smaller one had a window that was too high for me so I motioned for Nick and Tony to get out and give me a boost.

"Robin, what are you doing?" Tony asked, nervously looking around.

"I want to see if anyone's here. Give me a boost," I said.

He wrapped his arms around my thighs and hoisted me up so I could peer into the dark garage. It was empty.

"Okay, down," I said and plowed through the fresh snow to the larger windowless structure. I tried the front doors but they were locked, as were the back doors. Nick tried the regular entry door on the side facing the main house. It was also locked, but not tightly as it gave when he forced his weight against it. He waggled his eyebrows at me when it opened and then stepped inside.

"Someone didn't close this very tightly," he said.

I scanned the property and shivered. Something didn't feel right. Tony felt it too.

"Nick, maybe this isn't such a good idea. I suddenly get the feeling we're being watched," Tony said, looking over his shoulder again at the dark house.

I looked around and saw nothing but couldn't shake my unease.

"We're in too deep to turn back now," Nick said. "Come in here."

Tony and I stepped into the building and I shut the door behind me. Nick had flicked on the overhead lights. In the center of the vast room sat a late-model, dual-wheeled Chevrolet one-ton pickup. Hooked to it was a long black enclosed snowmobile trailer with a bright green Arctic Cat logo emblazoned on the side. The trailer could probably hold six sleds and plenty of tools. I estimated the truck, trailer and sleds inside would be worth more than a hundred grand.

Tony whistled. "Holy cow! This is quite a set-up."

"Robin, check this out," Nick said from the rear of the trailer. When I reached his side, he pointed at the trailer's license plate.

"Illinois. So what? Maybe it's friends of theirs. Maybe they heard about the coming storm and came up to ride this weekend. That's not so unusual. Lots of people from Illinois ride snowmobiles in the U.P.," I said.

He walked around to the front of the truck and felt the hood and then looked underneath the engine. "Robin, this truck hasn't been moved in at least a day or two." He pulled on each of the truck's doors but they were locked. On the passenger side he glanced at the Illinois registration sticker in the lower right-hand corner and tapped it.

"Crescent, Illinois."

My stomach fell to my knees. "Oh, no," I whispered.

"Oh, yes. Let's get out of here," Tony said, grabbed my arm and motioned to Nick to follow. After shutting the light off and slamming the door behind him, he pushed me into the driver seat of the Outback. We peeled out of the driveway, wheels spinning on the fresh snow, riding in silence until we reached the highway and headed south to U.S. 2.

"I want to know more about this Janet Burns," Nick finally said from his place in the back seat. His face tightened as his jaw muscles clenched. "I think I know who she is, but for your sake, let's hope I'm wrong."

"Janet is not Dmitri Karastova's daughter," I said.

Tony and Nick both looked at me like I was naïve.

"That's crazy," I protested. "Sam would never marry someone like that. For heaven's sake, his first wife was an elementary school teacher."

Nick continued to look grim and remained silent.

"Okay, okay, let's assume she is the daughter of this guy. So what? We have absolutely no proof that she's done anything illegal. How do we tie her into Mitch's murder, or Kyle's?" I asked.

I had to slow down as a tow truck labored to pull a car out of the ditch on the north side of the highway at the foot of what was locally known as Whitefish Hill about a mile east of Rapid River.

"We may not make much more progress with the way this storm is picking up steam," Tony said as large flakes swirled in front of the headlights. Winter had arrived in full force but its timing could not have been worse. I couldn't help feeling that something was about to happen, that someone behind the scenes was orchestrating a major move and we were getting in the way.

The ringing of my cell phone caused me to jump. Tony dug it out of my purse and answered it while I pulled into a gas station in Rapid River, then he handed the phone to me. It was Aunt Gina.

"Mission accomplished," she said. "Well, sort of."

"What did you find out?"

"After listening patiently to my tale of inquiry, Dr. Bernard Karastova wasted no words in telling me that he hadn't spoken to his father in thirty-two years. He said his father was not the kind of person a serious scholar would want to interview and, besides, he had heard that the man was in poor health. I then asked if he could be of much help to me, just to make it sound legit, and he said he hadn't kept in touch with that side of the family. He apologized and said a curt goodbye."

"Actually, that tells us quite a lot—if he was being honest," I said.

"I believe him. I talked to that former graduate student I mentioned. Susan said Dr. Karastova is a highly-respected scholar of Russian history, particularly as it relates to World War II military endeavors. He's spent a good chunk of the last fifteen years in Russia since the Iron Curtain fell, doing research and writing books. She said he even married a Russian woman, also a college professor except her specialty is physics," Aunt Gina said. She sounded pleased with herself. So was I.

"You did a great job. That helps us narrow things down a bit."

"Any other assignments, Sarge?"

I laughed. "No, not right now. You better get home. The roads are getting bad fast. Take care of Belle."

"What are you guys doing?" she asked.

"We need to find Shasta Burns and a few other characters that might have a line on who killed Kyle and Mitch."

She gasped. "So the two murders really are related?"

"Not directly, but the same person may have ordered both killings. I have to go. I'll call you as soon as I can," I said and closed the phone.

Nick was smug when I told him about Aunt Gina's detective work. "That just leaves the daughter," he said.

"We still don't know that Janet is any relation to this guy," Tony pointed out. "Without that, we've got nothing."

There was only one thing to do, what every girl does when she needs help, call my dad. I drove to Aunt Gina's house and found the itinerary for his trip with Sophie. The two of them were scheduled to be at a chalet in the Aquitaine region of southwestern France. It was late in the evening and the proprietor was not happy to have to disturb one of her guests, but she obeyed when I told her it was urgent.

It took about five minutes for her to get Hank Hamilton on the phone but when his voice finally crackled in my ear I felt a sense of relief.

"Dad, I need to ask you a question," I said, suddenly feeling foolish at bothering him on the first real vacation he'd taken in twenty-five years.

"Robin? What's the matter? Are you alright?" he asked.

"I'm okay, sort of. Nick Granati's here—you remember me telling you about the Chicago cop who was working behind the scenes trying to dig up some information about Mitch's death? Anyway, he and his cousin Tony have been helping me follow some leads. It's a long story. Oh, by the way, one of Aunt Gina's students was murdered sometime around New Year's and I quit my job at the *Daily Press*," I rambled, my mind unable to focus on one topic.

"Good grief! One thing at a time, Robin. Is your aunt alright? Who killed Mitch? And why on earth did you quit your job?"

I laughed. "You're as bad as I am. Aunt Gina is fine. We don't know for sure what happened with Mitch, but there's a chance that his death and the student's are related. That's kind of why I called. Dad, when you found out Mitch was killed, who in Escanaba did you talk to about it?"

He was silent for a moment and I could picture him squinting his sharp green eyes, the way he always did when he tried to remember something from long ago. "Well, I left for Chicago right after I got your phone call early that morning. I slipped a note in the Olsens' front door telling them that I had to leave for a few days and asked if they could collect the paper and the mail and keep an eye on the place. I think I called them three days later to tell them I'd be staying for a couple of weeks because your fiancé had been murdered. They were very sympathetic, shocked actually. I don't remember telling anyone else. I just stuck by you, remember?"

"Yes, I remember and you'll never know how grateful I am that you were there, but what I'm trying to figure out is who told Sam Burns about what happened," I said.

"Honey, I haven't talked to Sam Burns since you left the *Daily Press*. I don't think I've even seen him more than once or twice. He doesn't play golf at the Escanaba County Club anymore, not since he had a falling out with the management some years back, and you know I don't go in for those swanky fund-raisers that he always attends," he said. My dad was too down-to-earth to put on a tuxedo. He had even threatened to show up at my wedding in a golf shirt and walking shorts.

"So when you saw the ad for the reporter position at the *Daily Press* you just told me about it but didn't have any conversation with anyone from the paper?"

"Of course not. You certainly didn't need my help to get a job at that little outfit after doing so well at the Tribune. I just figured you might want to come home for a while. I don't think the Olsens talked to Sam. They don't even subscribe to the paper. I give them mine when I'm done with it. Robin, what is this all about?" he asked in frustration.

"I honestly don't know. Something weird is going on with Sam and his wife and their daughter Shasta. The daughter's missing and Nick suspects that Janet might be related to some old big-time arms dealer in the Chicago area. I know it sounds crazy, but Nick thinks Janet might be the one who ordered the hit on Mitch," I said, finally putting into words the crux of Nick's theory. It sounded crazy the minute the sentence left my mouth.

"Honey, I don't know anything about Sam or Janet other than that she runs a heck of a wine shop. Sophie loves going in there and finding new wines to try with her recipes," he said and then sighed. "I'm afraid I'm not much help."

"Actually, you've been very helpful because at least now I know what to ask Sam, if I ever see him again. He seems to have disappeared too," I said.

"Sounds serious. Don't get too carried away. Let your friend Nick and—what's his name? Tony?—and the rest of the cops do the digging this time. Please? Now, what's this about you quitting your job? Are you finally going to do something with that insurance money? You should write a book, you know that? Just look at all the trouble you seem to find that you could write about."

"Great, I'll be the next Agatha Christie. Dad, just forget I called, enjoy the rest of your vacation and say hello to Sophie for me. How was the cruise?"

"It was wonderful. The food was fabulous, the ports of call were full of fascinating people and color and the weather was sunny and warm every day," he said. "Now we're visiting museums, historic sites, everything. It's beautiful here and there are no crowds since it's off-season; you'd love it!"

I had never heard him sound so happy. I told him I loved him and that I would see him when he got home that weekend.

Next I called Vale again and asked him if he'd talked to Sam Burns.

"No, Janet said he was out of town at a conference but that he would be coming back tomorrow to help with the search. Why?"

"That's odd. Bob Hunter told me the conference wasn't until next week and that Sam was taking some time off to prepare for a presentation he was going to make. I'd really like to talk to him about, well, it doesn't matter right now," I said. "Just keep me posted, okay?"

"Yup, hey, I told the lab to put a rush on completing the DNA testing on those skin samples found under Kyle's fingernails, but it could take awhile. I went to that address for Jesse Levin but the landlord said he moved out about two weeks ago. Naturally, he did not notify his probation officer so he is now officially in violation of the terms of his probation and a felony warrant is being sought as we speak, which means when we find him we can arrest him and bring him in for questioning," Vale explained and then paused, as though he wanted to tell me something more.

"Tom?"

He sighed into the phone and said, "I can't find Sean. He moved out of his dump of a trailer east of Rapid River around the same time that Jesse Levin bailed out of his apartment. Sean and Jesse are friends. I'm afraid my son is right in the middle of all of this."

"I'm sorry, Tom," I said, searching for something appropriate to say. There wasn't anything that wouldn't sound trite. "Listen, maybe it would be best if you stepped back from this investigation. Can you call in the state police?"

He swallowed hard. "I already have," he said and hung up on me.

Chapter Seventeen

Nick's cell phone rang while I was telling him and Tony about Vale's fears about his son.

"It's Charlie," he said to me. "What? When did that happen? Yes, I know what they were looking for—Mitch's journals."

He clicked the off button on his phone and turned to me. "A neighbor reported that your apartment's been broken into. She was walking her dog in the alley and noticed the back door swinging in the wind. She went to close it and then saw that your door at the top of the stairs was open so she ran home and called the police. Charlie says the place is an absolute mess."

Now they'd violated my personal space, as if killing Mitch wasn't enough. I said a little thank you to the powers that be that Belle was safely with my aunt. But how safe was she? I frantically dialed her office number.

"Aunt Gina, I don't have time to explain but do you have someone nearby you could stay with for a couple of days, and take Belle and the Yorkies with you?"

She sputtered, "Well, yes, I suppose but do you really think we might be in danger there? I mean, we're in the middle of a blizzard."

"I don't know. Charlie just called. My apartment's been ransacked. I don't want to take any chances," I said.

"Alright. I have a friend from my spiritual group who would probably take us in for a few days. Here's his name, address and number." I wrote down the information. I didn't recognize the name but the house was located on the north side of the highway on Main Street in Rapid River with plenty of other houses nearby.

"Give me a call as soon you get there," I said.

We drove to my apartment where two gray patrol cars were still parked in the alley. We bounded up the stairs and found Charlie and two other officers in the living room talking quietly. As soon as he saw me Charlie turned to me and said, "I feel like I'm trapped in some overdone eighties television detective series. Why does this stuff always seem to happen to you?"

I couldn't answer. All I could do was look around what had once been my little sanctuary from the big bad world and gape in horror. Every single piece of furniture had been flipped over and torn apart. Drawers were scattered around, their contents strewn everywhere. I somehow made it into the bedroom where a similar scene awaited. The mattress and box spring had been flung across the room and the dresser drawers were on the floor with my clothes thrown with vigor unmatched by a tornado. Nick pulled down a bra that hung from one of the blades of the ceiling fan and handed it to me.

"They were thorough, I must say that for them," he said with a wry smile.

I flung the garment across the room and stomped toward the kitchen.

"You don't want to go in there," Charlie called after me.

He was right. There was dishes and glasses smashed on the counter and the refrigerator's contents, what little there was, splattered across the floor.

"Looks like they didn't find what they were looking for," Charlie said, placing a hand on my shoulder. "You want to update me on what's happened since this morning? The three of you have obviously kicked someone in the shins and they're pissed."

"They were looking for Mitch's journals, but I still don't know for sure who was doing the looking," I said, clenching and unclenching my fists.

"Let's start at the beginning again and don't leave anything out," Charlie said, clearing the mess off of one of the kitchen chairs and taking a seat.

I looked at Tony and waved a hand at him. "You tell him. I want to get this place cleaned up. Are you done taking photos?" I asked a uniformed officer with a camera. He nodded and told me to go ahead. While Nick and Tony filled Charlie in on what seemed to be transpiring I tried to restore some order to my material world. The first thing I did was search for the contents of my cedar chest, mainly the flag that had draped Mitch's coffin and the shoebox of cards and letters. I found the case, undamaged, under a pile of crumpled blankets. The cards and letters were scattered in the corner of the room, as though each one had been perused and then discarded for lack of information. Tears stung my throat as I returned them to the shoebox and put them back in the chest. My anger rose with each second. How dare they, I wanted to scream. Not only had they killed someone I loved with all my soul and with whom I was planning on building a life, but they had violated precious, private memories of him by reading the words he'd meant only for me. When I found who was behind all this, they were going to pay dearly, very, very dearly.

My aunt called at five to me tell me she and the dogs had reached her friend's house safely. She wondered when she would be able to go home but I didn't have an answer.

Between Nick, Charlie, Tony and me, it took three hours to get the apartment back in some sort of reasonable order. Nick and Charlie hauled the ruined sofa and chair into the backyard to dispose of later. That left just the rocking chair and four oak kitchen chairs on which to sit. I still hadn't calmed down when I sank into the rocking chair in utter exhaustion while Nick ordered a large pizza and breadsticks and Charlie went back to the department to file his report and return the patrol car before coming back to my place.

Tony knelt at my feet and wrapped his hands around mine. "This has been one hell of a year so far, hasn't it?"

I nodded and started to cry. He pulled me on to the floor and held me until I was done. Embarrassed I pulled back and said, "Honestly, I don't usually cry this much. I'm normally a very strong woman."

Tony smiled and brushed his lips across the tip of my nose. "I think you are either the strongest, or craziest, woman I have ever met. I knew it from the moment I saw you when you landed in a strange city ready for anything. You've lived through so much already and yet you haven't lost the ability to reach out to people, even people you don't know very well. That's a beautiful quality."

I squeezed his hand, got up and scoured the room for some tissue. During the melee, the box had landed behind one of the long drapes hanging over the large window overlooking Ludington Park. The box was nearly empty. Sitting back down in the rocking chair, I said, "I just want this to be over. Then I'll find a new sense of normal, a new comfort zone that doesn't involve feeling like I'm losing my grip on the world."

Tony nodded. "I know what you mean. I think we're close to the end of this though."

"Do you think the local police can handle a criminal investigation of this size?"

From the kitchen, Nick interjected, "No, they can't."

"So what do you suggest?" I asked, rising from the chair again to straighten some animal knick-knacks scattered on the entertainment center.

Tony stood and said, "I don't think Uncle Rudy can help us this time. This is too far out of his element. I think we're on our own."

Nick snapped his fingers. "Speaking of him, he called my cell when Charlie and I were taking the sofa out back. Whelan didn't take a commercial flight to Miami, rather he flew in on a private jet Friday morning. The jet was registered to an LLC out of Chicago. No info on the company yet, but he's working on it."

"No wonder these people get away with so much. They never use their real names for anything," I grumbled as I followed them into the kitchen to get ready for the arrival of the pizza. "Nobody answered my question. What do we do now? Raid the Burns compound and see who comes out? Maybe Shasta, Sean, Dave, Janet, Edward, Jesse and the rest of the gang will come out with their hands up and beg for mercy."

Nick and Tony finally cracked smiles after a very long day.

Dinner arrived, with Charlie about three minutes behind it, bearing a half-gallon of milk. ("No booze in case in we have to move," he'd said.) The four of us sat down at the table to eat and mull over what to do next.

"Seriously, should we approach this Janet Burns?" Tony asked. "We kicked one hell of a hornet's nest and they're swarming all over trying to defend their territory. They're inevitably going to wear themselves out but they may take a lot of other people with them."

"If Janet is involved, which we haven't confirmed, how do we prove it?" I asked, glancing out the kitchen window and falling snow.

Charlie shrugged his wide shoulders, swallowed a mouthful of pepperoni and mushroom pizza and replied, "I don't know much about Sam or Janet. I don't associate with the high muckity-mucks in town and I don't drink much wine so I've never had a reason to talk with them about anything other than Shasta, who's been a thorn in their side since high school. Sam was really heart-broken by her behavior but her mother seemed more embarrassed than anything, like Shasta had exposed the family to unwanted attention. Nick, I'm intrigued by your theory that Janet may be the daughter of this Dmitri Karastova. I mean, the woman drives a Mercedes and wears a mink coat. You can't tell me that business earns that much money, and I know publishers do well, but this ain't the New York Times."

"Nick, isn't there some way we could track down Dmitri's daughter? Someone down in Crescent must know something," I said.

Nick balled up his napkin and threw it on the table. "I've tried everything I can think of to find out what happened to her but everyone seems to have lost track of her about twenty years ago."

"That's around the same time that Sam married Janet. Do you think that could mean something? Hey, what about their marriage license? I know Janet was married before, but wouldn't her maiden name be on that certificate anyway?" I asked.

The trio looked at each other in surprise. "I don't know. I've never been married," Nick said and then rose from the table. "Let me make a few phone calls. It's late but I might be able to get someone to help us." He pulled his cell phone from his jacket, which hung in the hall closet, and went into the living room to make his calls.

"Tell me again what you saw in the big garage at Burns' camp," Charlie said.

"There was a late-model pick-up with dual rear wheels and a huge, enclosed snowmobile trailer, like the ones professional race teams use. It was hooked to the truck via a fifth wheel. Both the truck and the trailer had Illinois plates and the truck had a Crescent registration sticker," I said.

"C'mon, Robin, that's just too much of a coincidence. Nick's right. Janet has to be Karastova's daughter. I'll bet she's the ringleader of this whole operation. I'd sure love to get a look inside that trailer. I wouldn't be a bit surprised if they're using it to smuggle drugs," Charlie said.

"But where are they smuggling to and from? The U.P. wouldn't produce enough of marijuana crop to fill that trailer in a year," Tony replied.

Charlie combed his thick mustache and concentrated. "Didn't you say Mitch wrote that the DEA suspected someone down there of smuggling drugs from Chicago to Canada or vice versa? We're only three hours from Sault Ste. Marie, Canada. Once they get across that International Bridge, they could head east to Toronto or Quebec City or anywhere. I'll bet those border guards are so used to seeing snowmobile trailers in the winter that they wouldn't think too much about it," he said.

I shook my head. "I don't buy it. Since 9/11, they've been doing random searches of every type of vehicle going over that bridge, even at the Soo.

Sooner or later they would stop that truck and trailer and search it."

Charlie grunted and went back to thinking. Suddenly I got an idea. "Charlie, have you done much snowmobiling?"

He shook his head. "I went once or twice in high school but I don't like being cold."

"Well, I have. My best friend Michaela and I used to go out all the time in high school and college. I loved driving on those trails. I even raced a few people. Boy, were they shocked when I pulled off my helmet and they saw I was a girl," I said with a chuckle. "Anyway, I used to help her two older brothers work on them. There's all kinds of places you could hide things on those machines."

"Really?" Charlie asked, his eyebrows raised.

"Could Vale get a search warrant for that trailer?"

"On what grounds? We have no probable cause at this point," Charlie said and then stood up and waved his hands at me. "Oh no, I know what's going through that little blonde brain of yours. No way am I going to risk my career by breaking and entering and doing an illegal search."

"You don't have to risk anything. Just stand in the woods while I go in there. Look, there wasn't anyone around when Nick, Tony and I stopped by this afternoon. If it's still deserted, I can take a quick peek and see if our suspicions have merit. If not, we forget about it. But if I find something, then we can tell Vale and he can make up some excuse about Shasta and get a proper warrant. C'mon," I said and got up to tell Nick my plan.

He was standing in the living room with the lights out watching the street below and talking into his cell phone.

"Humph. I see. Okay, keep me informed," he said and folded the phone with a slap.

"Nick, we have a plan."

"No, no. There is no we in this. You have the plan, and a lousy one at that," Charlie said.

Nick held up his hand and said, "Quiet. We have one complication and one interesting development. Stay away from the window."

"What's wrong?" I asked, feeling shards of fear prick at my spine.

"We're being watched. That pickup we saw last night east of Rapid River is now sitting over in that park." Nick pointed to the east, near the tennis courts in Ludington Park. I moved to look over his shoulder and saw the outline of the truck through the blowing snow. "Now for the development. Your publisher has just been detained by the Crescent Police Department for allegedly creating at disturbance at our friend Dmitri Karastova's house."

Tony whistled. "I'd say that's proof enough for me that Janet is his daughter. Now what? That still proves nothing with regard to Kyle Sullivan or Mitch."

Never taking his eyes off the truck, Nick said, "Tell me about this plan." I did.

"You're not seriously considering this?" Charlie howled. "We're in the middle of a blizzard. We'll be driving in whiteout conditions."

Nick rubbed his chin and grinned malevolently. "This blizzard could play right into our hands. It's very difficult to tow a trailer when the weather's this bad. I wouldn't be a bit surprised if the International Bridge is closed due to high winds. Charlie, you take care of that truck out there," he said, jerking his head toward the park. "Robin, get into your cold weather gear. A whiteout means it's just as hard for other people to see you as it is for you to see them. Let's move."

A patrol car just happened to drive through Ludington Park about ten minutes later and just happened to pull up and block the path of the mysterious pickup while the four of us exited the house and piled into the Outback. Charlie asked me how much experience I had driving in blizzards lately. I nodded. "Probably not as much as you, here take the keys."

Charlie let the wagon inch out of its parking spot behind Mrs. Easton's rambling old Victorian house, now lost in a shifting wall of white. The snow in the alley was six inches deep down the middle and well over a foot where the powder had drifted and swirled around buildings but the Outback was just high enough to pull itself through. Streetlights loomed overhead, providing more of an optical illusion than helpful illumination.

"I don't know about this, Robin. It's a good sixty miles to the Burns camp and this storm is showing no signs of letting up before we get there," Charlie said, his hands resting on the steering wheel, allowing the vehicle to wander until it found traction.

"I know. Listen, if you really don't want to do this, I understand. This is my fight. I don't want to endanger you," I said from the back seat, my voice sounding calmer than I felt.

Charlie grunted and shook his head. "No, this isn't just your fight. Don't forget Kyle Sullivan, Mandy Miller and all the other people who've been impacted by drugs in this community. I hate to sound sanctimonious but there has to be a way to stem the supply of that crap. If this insane little trip leads to that, well, count me in."

From where he sat hunched against the rear passenger side door, Tony reached over and silently enveloped my right hand in his left and squeezed. A soothing yet electric warmth spread from my fingers to my toes. When this was all over, what would become of us, I wondered. There was a connection between us that was moving beyond friendship, but would it be right to give the remains of my battered heart to this man? I pondered this as Charlie guided the Outback onto the highway and out of Escanaba toward Gladstone, Rapid River and beyond. These last few days I had seen what kind of man Tony really was beyond his handsome exterior—loyal, devoted, intelligent, humble and caring. Those qualities were becoming harder and harder to find in the few single men still available around my age. But he carried a lot of emotional baggage, as did I. Would he even want to risk his heart the way he had risked his life so many times?

Charlie periodically grunted as he squinted through the snow, trying to keep to our side of the pavement but not too far to the right. Eventually we passed Gladstone, the town appearing as nothing more than a blur of faint light visible only when the wind died down for a second or two. When we reached Rapid River, the four-lane highway merged into two lanes, making travel that much more treacherous as the drivers of oncoming vehicles struggled to find the road as well. We all breathed a sigh of relief when the headlights flashed on the brown and white sign indicating that Federal Forest Highway 13 was a mile ahead. A blinking yellow light marked the point where 13 came down from the north at its starting point on M-28 and ended about 36 miles later here at U.S. 2. Charlie slowed and made the turn onto 13, which had seen little traffic all afternoon and not a hint of a plow since it had begun snowing. I glanced at the clock on the dashboard. It was nearly half past nine. It had taken us an hour and a half to just get this far. Perhaps we should have let someone know where we were going, I thought. I pulled out my cell phone and dialed Tom Vale's cell number. The connection was poor when he answered on the third ring but I could still make out what he was saying.

"Robin, is that you? I'm glad you called. I've got some news. That camper those two guys and Shasta retrieved last night is now just a pile of smoldering rubble. A property owner west of Round Lake found it late this afternoon when he was leaving his cottage. Someone had just set it on fire and abandoned it. He called the fire department but the thing was a total loss by the time they got there," Vale said through the static. Round Lake was on the western edge of the national forest, just a few miles from the Sullivan camp where Kyle had been murdered and maybe ten miles as the crow flies from the Burns retreat.

"Janet must have ordered it destroyed," I said through the static. "Tom, I'm about to lose you but I wanted you to know that Charlie Baker, Nick, Tony and I are headed to the Burns property. Don't ask why. I just wanted someone to know where we were if, well, you know. Tom? Are you there?" I looked at the phone but the connection was gone and I had no way of knowing how much he had heard or understood.

"It looks like we're on our own if something goes wrong," I said.

"Having second thoughts?" Nick asked, uttering his first words since we'd left the house.

"No, if someone's there, fine. We turn around and come back or head for a motel in Munising, which would be a lot closer than Escanaba. If no one is around, I'll take the risk and break into the garage. You guys just stand outside as lookouts. You're law enforcement officers; I know what you're risking just being here with me. I'll take the heat if this backfires," I said.

"Robin, we're with you. You heard Charlie, and I'm not going to let you go in there on your own. You're my responsibility," Tony said, still holding my hand.

I released his hand, unzipped my snowsuit, reached into the inside chest pocket and pulled out the .38 revolver I'd purchased in December and kept hidden under my bed after taking the classes and obtaining a concealed weapons permit. It was a small, hammerless pistol with five shots that wouldn't pack much of a wallop but might be enough to buy some time if any shooting started. Tony took the pistol from me, checked the loads and handed it back.

"Hollow points. Good choice. Do you think you could use that if you had to?" he asked.

I fingered the cold steel barrel and shrugged. "I don't know. The person who murdered Mitch didn't seem to have any trouble with killing."

"It's one thing to kill someone in cold blood. It's very different for the average person to take a life. Some cops never recover after they've had to kill someone in the line of duty, no matter how justified their actions," Nick said.

I looked at him and shook my head. "You of all people should understand,

Nick. This isn't cold blood and I'm not the average person. Janet Burns may have been the one who ordered that hit on someone I loved dearly, someone who was just doing his job and got in the way of dope pushers."

"What will revenge accomplish? It won't bring Mitch back, but it will haunt you for the rest of your life," he said.

"Haunt me? It can't be any worse than the memories that haunt me now," I said.

Nick sighed and turned his eyes back to the road, what little was visible through the windshield. "I can't argue with that. You're not a fool. You'll know in your heart what the right action will be when the time comes."

Charlie finally spoke. "I'm the one who wanted you to get that gun and get your permit to carry it because I was tired of seeing you put yourself in situations where you could easily get killed. Now I'm the one behind the wheel driving right into what may very well be a trap. Well, I guess that's what they call destiny. Get ready; I do believe the turnoff to March Lake is just ahead."

Chapter Eighteen

*I*s there another cottage maybe a quarter of a mile away where we can park this thing?" Charlie asked as he nosed the Outback through the trees that lined the March Lake road. "I'd like to mask our approach as much as possible, just in case someone is there."

Tony shifted in his seat. "I remember seeing a few cottages along here this afternoon. They looked like they were closed up for the winter. Hopefully we won't get stuck," he said as he released his seat belt and edged forward between the front bucket seats. "I don't see any tracks but, with this wind, they'd be blown away or filled within a half hour. I also don't see any lights around the lake. Then again, I can't even see the lake."

We seemed to be traveling through an alternate universe, our vehicle providing the only light and sound, everything else being obscured by snow and wind. I marveled at how snow could bring such delight to skiers, sledders and snowmobilers but also shield the specter of death, looming in the gusts of wind and clouds of white, ready to snatch the weary traveler who happened to be caught on foot or in an ill-destined vehicle.

March Lake was long and narrow at its southern tip where a single clapboard-sided cabin occupied its shore. I spotted the mailbox as we slid past and tapped Charlie on the arm. "Stop the car. Back up. We can pull in there. That place was shuttered when we went by earlier this afternoon so I know no one is there now."

Charlie skillfully backed into the driveway, parking the wagon about six feet from the road. He shut off the engine and we sat in silence for a few moments. Finally Charlie said, "Okay, what's the plan?"

I looked at Nick. "You three are the experts on tactical maneuvers. You guys saw the layout. What do you suggest?"

Nick rubbed his chin and thought for a moment. "I've been going over the layout of the property in my mind and think it might be best if we split up. Unfortunately, we have no effective way to communicate with each other. The cell phones won't work and bird calls sure as hell won't be heard over this wind. We'll have to look around first and then meet somewhere to give the all clear and then go from there," he said and had Tony hand him the duffle bag he'd thrown in the back of the wagon the night before. He pulled out a notebook and pen while Charlie focused a small flashlight on the paper while Nick drew a map of the Burns property.

"This is the guest house. Charlie, you take that. I'll take the main house. Robin, I want you to check out the big garage we were in today and wait on the far side away from the house. Tony, take the small one. Visibility is good enough right now that we should be able to signal each other with our arms. If you see something, wave your arms in the air and we'll all circle around to the road and meet back at the wagon. If we don't see any sign of anyone we'll crouch and touch the ground. Robin, if you hear any of us get into trouble, run back here, get the car and bring it to the edge of the driveway. Remember, we'll have weapons, but we are trespassing so be careful. This ain't no Dirty Harry movie. If we see any sign of life there, we meet Robin and get the hell out of here. Got it?"

We nodded.

"Charlie, what do you carry and how many rounds do you have?" Nick asked.

"Smith and Wesson .40 with eight rounds in the clip and I have two spare clips."

"Okay, Tony and I each have forty-fives with eight-round clips and one spare each. Right?"

Tony nodded and patted the lump under his left armpit.

"Good. I've also got an AR-15 rifle, but with that 20-inch barrel it's not concealable so I'll leave that in the wagon. Robin, you keep that pea-shooter in your pocket unless you absolutely have to pull it," Nick ordered. "Let's go."

We got out of the wagon, each of us pulling on a ski mask. "We look like we're getting ready to rob a bank," I said.

Charlie laughed. "I remember when someone robbed a bank in a blizzard about twenty years ago and got away on a snowmobile. I think it made the national news."

Nick pulled out four small LED flashlights and handed one to each of us. "Use these only if necessary. If we get separated, Tony will flash his twice in quick sequence and Charlie will do four short ones. I'll do two long ones like this," he said and demonstrated. "Robin, you just keep flashing until one of us gets to you."

Looking at me Charlie said, "So what do we do if no one is around? I'm assuming you have a plan for that as well."

"I do, although I'll have to admit it's not a very good one. It seems that I've become adept at breaking into and out of buildings over the last year so I might as well put that talent to use here," I said and, with a sheepish grin, pulled my old Tribune Blue Cross Blue Shield insurance card out of the pocket of my snowsuit and waved it at them. The card was thick, sturdy plastic, perfect for a little illegal entry.

Nick patted me on the back and said, "I see we city folk taught you well." Then he surveyed the area and added, "Should we take the road or the shoreline? The snow will be about as deep either way."

"I vote for the shoreline," Tony volunteered. "That way if someone comes along the road, we won't be so exposed. I'm not crazy about leaving the car so close to the road, but it will be much easier to get out of here this way."

"I agree. Let's get going. It's already pushing eleven o'clock," I said.

With Nick in the lead we made our way around the small cottage, shuttered tightly for the winter, trudging through snow nearly a foot deep in places. If not for the sound of lapping of the water against the ice-edged shore, it would have been impossible to find our way in the dark. Visibility was now less than ten feet as the wind whipped across the open lake, stirring up clouds of thick, heavy snow. I began to wonder if we should have brought a long piece of rope to tie around each other's waist. As though he were reading my mind, Tony reached back to take my hand and then I reached back for Charlie's. We moved without a word, conversation being a waste of time and energy over the roar of the storm. Later, it would occur to me that anyone watching us would be right to think we were crazy, driven by an insane passion that blinded us to the very real danger we faced in challenging Mother Nature's fiercest wrath.

Nick stopped so suddenly that Tony plowed into him. He started to say something when Nick held up his hand for silence and then pointed. I followed his gaze to the northwest of our position and saw the outline of the Burns house looming in front of us. No lights were visible through the snow. We huddled together one final time to go over plans A and B and then separated as Nick headed for the main house. Tony let go of my hand and moved toward the small garage close to the house. Charlie and I split when we reached the guest house and I continued toward the large steel garage. There was no sign of life as I approached the side door. I saw no evidence of tire tracks or footprints but the wind and snow were so intense as to quickly cover up any sign of human or vehicle traffic. I could barely see the main house but I'd made a mental picture of the layout of the property when we had been here earlier and sensed more than saw my way to the far side of the metal structure to wait for the others.

After what seemed like hours Tony signaled the all-clear, quickly followed by Nick and Charlie and then the trio scurried to my side.

"This is crazy!" Charlie said. "We're going to freeze to death. The temperature's dropping fast. The wind chill must be below zero now."

I couldn't feel the cold. Adrenaline was keeping my inner furnace well-fired and ready to move. "Nobody saw anything?" I asked.

Nick shook his head. "Nada. Charlie, wait in the woods by the road and give me a signal if you see anyone coming. Do the four short ones again. Tony, you take the west side of the garage and keep an eye on the road too. I'll stake out the front corner of this building here so I can see the house while you work on that trailer," he said, pointing a finger at me. "If I see or hear anything, I'll bang on the door. If you hear that, get the hell out of there. Don't worry about relocking anything or tidying up."

I nodded and then walked around the front of the garage to the side door Nick had pushed open earlier that afternoon. I tried to do the same, but naturally he had closed it tight behind him so I went to work with my insurance card, sliding it back and forth as I heaved my weight against the door. I'd done this more than a few times to get into apartments or offices when I'd forgotten my keys. It was a trick my dad had taught me in high school when he realized I had inherited my late mother's propensity toward absentmindedness. It took three agonizing minutes but I finally hit the magic spot where the card blocked the tumbler and the door pushed inward and I was plunged into blackness.

I shut the door behind me, careful to unlock it from the inside. I didn't dare turn on a light, but Nick's little LED flashlight provided more than enough illumination. There was a padlock securing the trailer doors but any well-stocked garage had a good pair of bolt cutters. I trained the light on the shelves that lined the west side of the garage. The wind howled like a hungry wolf and rattled the metal panels where they had loosened from the studs, causing me to shiver even though I felt no chill. I finally spotted an especially large, heavy set of bolt cutters hanging from a hook on one of the studs. Hefting them down, I tried to cut through the padlock but simply wasn't strong enough. I finally gave up and went outside to find Nick.

He was crouched on the ground at the edge of the garage, his head turning periodically to survey the area.

"Nick!" He turned to face me.

"Did you find anything?" he asked.

"I can't get the damn padlock off. I don't have the strength," I said.

"Alright. You stay here and keep watch. I'll go through the trailer."

"No! Just get the padlock off and come back."

He disappeared into the garage, but was back in less than twenty seconds.

"It's off. Get to work, Nancy Drew."

I darted inside and shut the door behind me. Nick had left the broken lock in place. If it came down to it, I could tell one more little white lie that I had been the one to break the lock. I put the bolt cutters back on the wall and then pulled the lock off the trailer and swung the doors open.

I'd been in many snowmobile trailers and expected to be overpowered by the smell of burnt oil and gasoline common when two-stroke engines were run in a confined space. Instead, there was just a faint whiff of gasoline, odd since all six sleds inside the trailer were older model Arctic Cat 600 ZRs that definitely had two-strokes, unlike many of the newer models that had small, clean, fuel-efficient four-stroke engines. I played the light over each of the sleds. They were in perfect condition, as though never ridden. Even the most careful snowmobiler would inflict some wear and tear on the skis and tracks by having to cross roads and get into gas stations. These sleds were at least four years old but didn't have a scratch on them. I released the straps for the cowling around the engine on one of the sleds and pulled it back. It was a standard two-stroke engine but, again, it showed no signs of ever having been run. These sleds were used for something besides recreation. After replacing the cowling, I lifted the Velcro flap over the tiny trunk in back but it was empty. I then unscrewed the fuel cap. At first it looked like a plain old ordinary tank filled to the brim with gasoline. Then I shook the sled slightly and noticed the gas didn't go down very far even though the tank should have held about 12 gallons. There was something inside the tank. I quickly checked the other five sleds and saw their tanks were filled with the same substance. I left the trailer in search of a screwdriver with a long head and found one on a work bench. Removing the cap again from one of the sleds at the rear of the trailer, I plunged it through the gas and into something that shifted like plastic. Ripping and digging, the material gave way and a white powdery substance floated to the surface. It was likely either heroin or cocaine, each sled probably carrying a dozen or more kilograms of the drug, making this trailer worth a million dollars or more.

"Oh Sam, I hope you have nothing to do with this," I murmured as the gasoline turned cloudier as more of the drug leached out of its packaging. It finally dawned on me that I'd been in there long enough and needed to get back to the trio outside, who were probably half-frozen by now. I shut doors to the trailer, pocketed the padlock and shined the light around the garage for one last look. A series of helmets lined the counter near the door where I'd entered. I picked up a feminine-looking helmet with pink and black zig-zag stripes. Shasta's? It seemed her style.

I heard an unidentifiable noise outside. With the helmet still in hand, I poked my head out the door but was stunned to see no sign of Nick. A finger of fear traced down my spine as I shut the door behind me. Where was he? Why hadn't he banged on the door like he said he would if Tony or Charlie signaled him or if he'd seen or heard something himself? There was movement behind the garage. Nick or Tony must have been investigating something and was back there. I rounded the corner and froze. It wasn't either of them.

A figure in a snowmobile suit was pulling the cover off one of a pair of sleds I'd failed to notice earlier parked near the tree line at the edge of the property. The person hopped on, turned the key and fired up the sled. I darted back around the corner of the garage and waited. What the hell was going on? Where were Tony, Nick and Charlie and who was this guy? Suddenly shots rang out from the guest house, a bullet crashing into the metal wall at a point just above my head. I hit the ground and belly-crawled toward the snowmobile as it raced toward a break in the trees parallel to the driveway. I was torn. Should I follow the mysterious rider or stay here and try to find the guys? Over the roar of the wind, I heard footsteps thudding through the snow behind me. Nick was at the other end of the garage.

"That's Janet. She got Charlie. Go after her!" he screamed, his .45 in hand.

"What about those guns?" I yelled.

"I'll take care of it. Go!"

I pulled on the helmet, ran for the second sled and pulled off the cover as more shots came from the guest house. My prayers were answered when

I saw the key was in the ignition. The sled, a Polaris 800, more powerful than anything I'd ever ridden, roared to life with one turn of the key. I had no idea where Janet was going and she already had at least a minute on me so I would have to follow her tracks as best I could. The gas gauge needle was hovering near the full mark. No problem there. I hit the throttle and headed for the break in the trees where Janet had disappeared.

I could barely make out her tracks but she was probably headed for a north-south trail that linked up with an old railroad grade that was the main east-west trail that could take you anywhere in the U.P. The narrow stretch of trail I was on now ran for about a mile before it fed into that larger, wider trail. When I reached it, I stopped for a moment to see where Janet's tracks led. The wind was fiercer than ever, making it nearly impossible to see any definition in the snow. Nosing the sled onto the trail, I saw a faint groove heading north and hit the throttle again. Michaela, her brothers and I had been over these trails at least a hundred times between high school and college. But did Janet know them just as well? The needle on the speedometer hit fifty, sixty and then seventy—much too fast for these conditions but I wouldn't slow down until I saw a tell-tale little red light in front of me that indicated Janet was near. Trees whipped by me at an alarming rate but I knew the trail was straight for a good three miles until it rounded a sharp corner and then crossed a county road. I pushed the sled to eighty, well below its top speed. My fingers were growing numb, but I hardly noticed as I hunched over the handlebars and searched for that red taillight. The odometer marked off each tenth of a mile. I slowed as the sled approached the sharp corner. Suddenly the red light glowed ahead, well off the trail about forty feet into the woods straight ahead. She must have missed the corner. I nosed my machine to the side, turned off the engine and pulled my .38 out of my snowsuit. With the flashlight in my left hand and revolver in my right, I threaded through the trees on the east side of the trail.

Soldiers and cops talk about tunnel vision that occurs when one is in a life-and-death situation. The rest of the world disappears—all sound except for the beating of your heart in your ears, all sight except for what's directly in front of you and all intuition as your brain focuses on a narrow field of awareness. It's a natural human reaction to danger, fight-or-flight, but it will get you killed if not controlled. Feeling myself starting to slip, I stood behind a massive oak tree, removed the helmet and took several deep breaths. The wind had briefly let up, but the snow was falling in thick, heavy squalls. I waited for a sound that was unnatural but heard nothing except my own breathing. She had to be out there somewhere. If Janet had missed the curve, it was possible that she was dead, having slammed into a tree. I began moving again, slowly, hunched over to make a smaller target should she be simply waiting for me to get in range of a bullet. When I was about ten feet from the trail and about fifty feet from her sled, I saw that it had come to rest against a tree, its red fiberglass cowling shattered in front. The taillight was still functioning, meaning the battery was still operating even though the engine had quit. Janet must be nearby. Suddenly a twig snapped. I dived behind a tree and readied my pistol. The darkness had us trapped. I began to belly-crawl through the snow, across the trail and back into the woods and then stopped and waited for her to make another sound. It came in the form of her voice.

"Who is that? I know someone's out there. Robin? It's you, isn't it?"

I said nothing, just waited.

"I knew you were going to be trouble. It had to be my luck that that damn cop was connected to you." She tried to laugh at the irony but the sound was garbled, as though she was choking on something. She probably had some broken ribs and maybe a punctured lung.

"Well, you won. I'm hurt pretty bad." She coughed again and said weakly, "There's blood. Please help me."

As the wind picked up again, I felt torn. She was responsible for murdering Mitch and maybe others but could I just let her lay there and die? I began crawling forward.

Her helmet was lying at the bottom of a towering white pine near the sleeve of her snowmobile jacket. To improve their visibility, sled riders often wore brightly-colored gear and Janet's jacket served that purpose beautifully. What if this was another trap? One of us, maybe even both of us, would not make it out of these woods alive. I could have run the other way, but then Janet might make a clean getaway and disappear into a life of leisure and luxury in some tropical country that didn't have an extradition treaty with the United States, probably following Shasta.

My stomach flipped as a vehicle approached on the road a couple of hundred feet from us. It slowed near the trailhead and then came to a stop. Two doors opened and slammed shut. Were they here to help me or Janet?

I glanced around for a place to hide and then belly-crawled back across the trail, exposing myself to Janet. She was waiting. The blast from her pistol echoed through the forest, lonely and desolate. I continued scrabbling with my face plowing through the powder, just as I'd seen Belle do every time we went for a walk in the snow.

"Robin!"

It was Tony.

"Tony, she's armed and injured. She's about fifty feet to the west of the trail and about fifteen feet from the wreckage of that sled," I yelled. "How's Charlie?"

"I'm here," he shouted, sounding triumphant.

Another blast erupted from Janet's location.

"That was Janet!" I yelled.

"Janet Karastova Burns," Nick voiced thundered above the howl of the storm. "I'm placing you under arrest for assault with a deadly weapon."

"Why don't you just go back to Chicago?"

"What makes you think I'm from Chicago?" Nick asked.

"If you think you're going to get some tear-filled confession from me, you are sadly mistaken," Janet said with a laugh.

"You have the right to remain silent." Blam! Janet fired in Nick's general direction but hit a tree a good ten feet to his left.

"Anything you say can and will be used against you in a court of law." Blam!

As Nick continued to move in, I doubled back to the south and west until I had a clear view of Janet. I had no idea where Charlie and Tony were so I didn't dare take a shot.

"You have the right to an attorney. If you cannot afford one, the court will provide you with one." Blam!

By the time Nick had finished the Miranda Warning, Janet had fired a full clip and was reloading when I spotted Nick through the trees. The AR-15 was leveled in Janet's direction, his posture relaxed but alert.

"Mrs. Burns, do you really want to do this?"

Her answer was more gunfire. Nick dived behind a tree.

"Nick, I've got a clean shot," I yelled. Janet turned and looked in the direction of my voice.

"Then shoot me! You don't have the guts, little Miss Reporter," she sneered and fired. The bullet hit the front of the tree about four inches above my head, showering me with shards of pulp and bark.

Suddenly Tony appeared through the snow behind her.

"Drop the gun," he ordered.

She turned on him but he fired first, placing three rounds in her center of mass.

Before I realized it, I was up and running to her. Before she gasped her last breath, she managed to smile at me and say, "I'm free." Then she was gone.

Chapter Nineteen

*C*harlie kept scratching at the stitches on his head as Father Mahesh Purandi presided over the Mass of Christian Burial for Kyle Sullivan. I nudged Tony in the ribs and nodded at him to get Charlie's attention and gave him a stern look, which he returned and continued scratching.

St. Michael's Catholic Church in Marquette was standing room only as family, friends and acquaintances gathered to say goodbye to a young man I didn't know but with whom I felt a strange kinship. Aunt Gina, Charlie, Nick, Tony and I sat in the second row behind Kyle Sullivan's father and two sisters. His mother and her new husband were in the opposite pew. Periodically I would reach out and squeeze my aunt's hand as she dabbed her eyes and sniffled quietly. The Sullivans all sat straight and tall, somehow finding the strength to not cry out as their youngest son was eulogized by their oldest son, William Jr.

When the service was over and Kyle's body had been wheeled to the back of the church, the Sullivans followed and waited in the vestibule as several hundred people filed past and offered their condolences. The five of us remained seated until the sanctuary was empty and then we would make our way to Dr. Sullivan's house for a traditional Irish wake celebrating Kyle's brief life. The family had learned the whole truth behind Kyle's death only this morning and it had been a bitter pill, but his murderer, Jesse Levin, was now secured in the Alger County jail, recovering from a bullet wound to his shoulder courtesy of Nick and awaiting his preliminary hearing.

After the church had emptied, Aunt Gina stood, turned to face the four of us and said, "Alright you guys, tell me what happened. You've been so tied up with interviews that I haven't had a chance to get the full scoop, and I'm obviously not going to get all the juicy details from the *Daily Press*." She winked at me and waited for one of us to start talking.

I told her about my plan to get into the Burns garage and how it would have gone off without a hitch if we hadn't walked into the trap set by Janet and three of her network of dealers, runners and enforcers, estimated around one hundred. According to Levin, Janet had driven by her camp when Nick, Tony and I were parked in her driveway—she recognized the Outback because she'd been having me watched almost since the day I'd moved back to Escanaba in late May. She guessed that we were up to something and made plans to have a team in place should we return that night. Jesse and his partner from the Chicago area, a guy named Dirk Gleason, were to drive the truck and sleds to Canada the next morning while Edward Carlson acted as Janet's bodyguard.

Not being one to sit out a good fight, Janet had insisted on taking care of us personally so she'd hid outside and waited until we got into position. She'd targeted Charlie and, thinking it was Nick, snuck up on him and bashed him in the head with a branch, except Charlie's head turned out to be a lot harder than anyone ever realized. He'd received a nasty bump and a two-inch long gash, but wasn't even knocked unconscious. He'd played dead to get her to make a mistake, which she did by trying to run when she came around the back of the garage and saw footsteps all around. She rightly guessed that I was inside discovering her secret stash of dope to be smuggled out of the country. The three guys were watching all this from the guest house and started firing as soon as Janet was safely out of harm's way. Charlie had stumbled back to the Outback and driven to the Burns place to help Nick and Tony, who were pinned down behind the garage. Once Nick had the rifle in hand, he was able to pick off the trio, who couldn't match his skill with weapons. It was over in a matter of minutes when Jesse surrendered; Gleason having been shot in the neck and Carlson sustaining a fatal head wound. Charlie had arrested Jesse and handcuffed him to the porch railing and then accompanied Nick and Tony in the direction they thought was most logical for Janet and me to travel. As soon as they hit Highway 13 they were able to call for help from troopers from the state police post at Munising and the Alger County Sheriff's Department, who picked up Jesse and secured the drugs, which turned out to be cocaine.

Jesse proved there was no honor among thieves as he immediately started confessing to his role in the Karastova operation. It turned out that Kyle was just in the wrong place at the wrong time with the wrong crowd. Jesse, yet another victim of Shasta's charms, claimed he been consumed with jealousy after Kyle began dating the girl in the fall and had tried to get her away from her bad crowd. Little did Kyle realize that Shasta's mother was the leader of one of the largest drug smuggling operations in the Upper Midwest. The actual sequence of events leading up to Kyle's brutal beating was still in doubt since Jesse was telling only his side of the tale. The other party in this love triangle, Shasta, with Sean Vale as her chaperone, was safely out of the country, on her way to who-knows-where. What was known was that Kyle had begun taking uppers and downers in an effort to balance his workload at the hardware store and his studies at Bay College. It was likely that the drugs were Shasta's idea of a way to lure yet another person as a regular customer.

An investigation was under way at the Delta County Correctional Facility to determine who was behind Sampson's death, which seemed less and less like a suicide. Speculation was that Janet, perhaps through Shasta or even Sean, had paid someone to create a disturbance distracting the guards but it didn't explain how Steve had died with bruises on his neck inconsistent with hanging.

The NOMIDES detectives were still trying to decipher the code in the address book found in Kyle's apartment. About twenty people listed had been questioned but it would take weeks to sort out all of the information being collected.

Jesse had no knowledge of Joey Leeds but did know Dave Whelan and admitted to working with him and Edward Carlson to connect in Crescent with traffickers bringing drugs up from Mexico. The Crescent police had tried to question Janet's father (he'd denied the assistance of his usual army of attorneys) but Dmitri Karastova was clearly showing all the signs of dementia and spent most of the time arguing that he'd only had one son and that boy had died as an infant. Sam Burns was still in police custody in Illinois, denying all knowledge of his wife's activities until the previous week when he, thinking his wife might be interested, told her about me heading to Miami to find the man who'd killed Mitch. She'd reacted with palpable fear and then he'd overheard a telephone conversation where she asked the person to "track down Robin and put a stop to this. Kill Leeds if you have to, but take care of it." He put two and two together and figured out that Janet had been up to no good for some time. He told Bob Hunter to order me to come back to work in the hope that I would drop the investigation and not get hurt. If he was telling the truth, my heart went out to him. The poor man had lost his first wife in a tragic accident and now his second wife had turned out to be nothing but a greedy, opportunistic career criminal. Sam did admit that it was Janet who'd encouraged him to hire me back at the *Daily Press*. He was planning on contacting my father to get my phone number the day I called Bob Hunter about the job last May. Again, I'd fallen right into Janet Karastova's trap.

Dirk Gleason, now facing multiple terms in the federal penitentiary, was recuperating at Marquette General Hospital and talking faster than the police could take notes. A friend of Janet's since college, he confessed that their snowmobile operation had allowed them to smuggle millions of dollars worth of heroin, cocaine and methamphetamine across the border into Canada for more than a decade, right under the noses of customs officials.

"Does this mean it's over, for you, I mean?" Aunt Gina asked, eyeing me with trepidation.

Was it? I took a deep breath. "Yes, it's over. There are still some unanswered questions but I have to put my anger behind me and get on with my life. That's what Mitch would want."

Tony put his arm around my shoulders and said with hope in his eyes, "Maybe I can help with that."

"Maybe," I said with a sly smile.

As we walked outside and down the stairs to the parking lot, blinking against the bright sunshine on snow, Aunt Gina looked from Nick to Tony and then to Charlie and said, "I still don't understand how you all aren't in jail right along with the rest of them. After all, you were co-conspirators in a felony."

Nick placed a gloved hand over her lips and whispered, "Shh. That's our little secret," and then winked.

Sunday morning dawned cold and sunny, a perfect winter day in the Upper Peninsula. Nick and Tony had left for Chicago after the Sullivan wake so Belle and I had the apartment to ourselves. I curled up on the couch, a blanket over my legs and Belle next to me, and tried to concentrate on a Sue Grafton novel but my mind refused to cooperate, or was it my heart, I wondered.

"Damn it, Belle, I miss him," I said. She raised her head, blinked her big brown eyes at me and yawned. Okay, so she had been unimpressed with Tony, but he'd sure made an impression on me. We'd had little time to talk before he'd left but we vowed to stay in touch via phone and e-mail and he agreed to help me move, if that was what I decided to do. The previous night, I'd spoken to Mitch's parents for more than an hour, telling them about Janet and Dave Whelan's part as a mole for her inside the Crescent Police Department, helping to guard a warehouse where drugs were stored for distribution across North America. Whelan had yet to resurface after disappearing to Miami, possibly to kill Joey Leeds before the hitman shared too much information, but the department had put him on leave without pay pending a full investigation. The Montgomerys were grateful for what we had done, but it still wouldn't bring back Mitch and it was time to stop wallowing in grief.

Mitch's dad made that clear when he said, "Robin, we're moving south in a week, to a little town just outside of Pensacola, Florida. Now that Peggy and I are retired, it seems only right that we should enjoy a little sun and fun. Besides, as you know, our daughter and her husband live in Orlando, and we just learned they're expecting our first grandchild."

"Phil, for God's sake, get to the point," Peggy Montgomery interjected from her end of the phone line.

"Right, well, anyway, we've been talking and we're worried about you. It's been almost a year. You're still so young. We want you to know you have our blessing to, well, find someone new. Mitch loved you so much. He wouldn't want to see you so angry and sad."

"I would give everything I have to see him with me now," I choked.

"I know, sweetie, but use the life insurance money he left you. Do something wonderful with your life. Write a book. Mitch always said you were a great writer."

I wondered what should I do, now that I didn't have a job or any commitments? I had enough money to get me through the next five years quite comfortably without having to leave the apartment if I decided to stay. I'd barely slept the night before as my mind played over my options. What about Tony? He was preparing to move to Superior, Wisconsin, to start his new job in a few weeks. I imagined my life at another large newspaper in a new city where I had no friends, in an industry that was dying a slow, painful death. Then I tried to picture myself as writer extraordinaire, spending my days creating grand works of fiction, giving lectures and signing books for eager fans. Neither scenario felt right. Now that I had the time and the means, what did I really want to do with my life? I had been through enough stress and strife to last three lifetimes but I had learned so much about myself and human nature, especially grief. Then, like a ray of sun through the clouds after a bad winter's storm, the answer shone.

Later that afternoon, after exchanging tales of our adventures over dinner with Aunt Gina, my dad and the elegant and talented Sophie, I announced my plans.

My dad put down his forkful of barbecue roasted salmon and stared at me. Sophie clapped her hands and Aunt Gina jumped up from her chair and threw her arms around me.

"A grief counselor! That's sounds wonderful! Oh, Robin, this is a new beginning for you," she cried.

"Is that enough money to go to graduate school?" my dad asked.

"Yes, Dad, I already checked out the master's program at the university in Duluth, Minnesota, and several other schools. It will be more than enough to complete the degree at any of them," I said.

"But what about your journalism career? You're such a good writer," Sophie said.

My aunt shook her head and retorted, "You can still put your writing gifts to work by creating books about handling grief, books targeted at women your age. Besides, UMD is, what, maybe twenty minutes from UW-Superior where a certain handsome young man will soon be working? I approve."

My dad raised an eyebrow at her and then asked, "Nick?"

"No, his name's Tony. You didn't get to meet him because he and Nick had to go back to Chicago before your flight landed," I said, adding with a knowing smile, "I' think you'll like him though. His aunt is almost as much fun as mine."

My dad reached for my hand and said, "Honey, I'm sure I'll like him." He then looked at my aunt, who flashed her most devilish smile, and added with a snarl, "We'll see about the aunt."

Epilogue

April 20, 2007 :~ Forest Park, Illinois

As she had done the day before leaving Chicago eleven months earlier, Belle lay next to Mitch's grave, her long snout resting on her front paws, her large brown eyes shifting from me kneeling at her side back to the headstone. Unlike that day in May, though, we finally had closure. In its own bizarre way, some justice had been served and a very painful chapter in my life was closed.

Tears streamed down my face as I zipped my jacket against the chill of a spring storm receding to the northeast. I took a deep breath and began to speak from my heart words that may not have been heard but maybe sensed on some cosmic level.

"You really were my first true love," I whispered as my throat clenched. "I will never forget you. You taught me so much, even after you were gone."

Unable to speak further, I scratched Belle's ear vigorously with one hand and applied a tissue to my face with the other hand. I swallowed hard and tried again. "I know the one thing you wouldn't want is for me to stop living life to the fullest. If anything, your death means I have to embrace life for both of us. That's what I'm going to do. I'll always love you."

I arranged the white roses in the brass holder in front of his headstone, picked up the end of Belle's leash, brushed the dirt and grass from the knees of my jeans and started walking toward Tony, standing against the passenger side door of my station wagon.

"You okay?" he asked.

I nodded. "Yes. It still hurts, but not as much. It's a different kind of hurt, more sadness than rage. Does that sound weird?"

Tony swept a strand of hair out of my eyes and kissed my forehead. "No, it makes perfect sense."

Five minutes later we were back on the freeway heading north toward a new apartment in Duluth, Minnesota, where in a few months I'd be starting the graduate program in social work. As I drove, the sun peeked from behind a cloud. It seemed appropriate.

BAR POPULAR